Arvid Nilson

The TIMBER TREES of New South Wales

Arvid Nilson

The TIMBER TREES of New South Wales

ISBN/EAN: 9783741121944

Manufactured in Europe, USA, Canada, Australia, Japa

Cover: Foto ©Andreas Hilbeck / pixelio.de

Manufactured and distributed by brebook publishing software
(www.brebook.com)

Arvid Nilson

The TIMBER TREES of New South Wales

THE TIMBER TREES

OF

NEW SOUTH WALES:

BY

A·RVID NILSON.

PRINTED FOR THE FOREST CONSERVANCY BRANCH,
DEPARTMENT OF MINES.

SYDNEY: THOMAS RICHARDS, GOVERNMENT PRINTER.

1884.

Department of Mines,
Sydney, 1st September, 1884.

THIS work having become the property of the Government, is printed by direction of the Minister for Mines, as a useful and convenient book of reference for the Officers of the Forest Conservancy Branch and others.

It is intended to supplement the information from time to time.

HARRIE WOOD,
Under Secretary for Mines.

PREFACE.

IN submitting this little work for the consideration of the Honorable the Minister for Mines, I lay claim to no originality, except as regards the general arrangement of the matter. I have made free use of everything that has been published on the subject, including the incomparable *Flora Australiensis* by Bentham and Von Mueller, and the meritorious writings of the Reverend Dr. Woolls, of Parramatta, and Charles Moore, Esq., F.L.S., of the Sydney Botanic Gardens, besides valuable Manuscript Notes on the timbers of the Murrumbidgee and Lachlan Districts kindly lent me by Mr. John Duff, Inspector of Forests. May it prove the humble forerunner of a work more worthy of the magnificent forests of this Colony.

ARVID NILSON.

Surveyor General's Office,
Sydney, 15 *July,* 1884.

CONTENTS.

TIMBER TREES OF NEW SOUTH WALES.

1. Structure and General Characteristics of Timber.— Timber is the material of trees belonging almost exclusively to that class of the vegetable kingdom in which the stem grows by the formation of successive layers of wood all over its external surface, and is therefore said by botanists to be *exogenous*.

The exceptions are, trees of the palm family, and tree-like grasses, such as the bamboo, which belong to the *endogenous* class; so called because, although the stem grows partly by the formation of layers of new wood on its outer surface, the fibres of that new wood do nevertheless cross and penetrate amongst those previously formed in such a manner as to be mixed with them in one part of their course, and internal to them at another.

The stems of endogenous trees, though light and tough, are too flexible and slender to furnish materials suitable for important works of carpentry. They will therefore not be further mentioned, except incidentally, as affecting the general appearance of a certain kind of forest.

The stem of an exogenous tree is covered with bark, which grows by the formation of successive layers on its inner surface, at the same time that the wood grows by the formation of successive layers on its outer surface. This double operation takes place in the narrow space between the previously-formed wood and bark, during the circulation of the sap. The sap ascends from the roots to the leaves through vessels contained in the outer layers of the wood; at the surface of the leaves it acquires carbon from the atmosphere, and becomes denser, thicker, and more complex in its composition; it then descends from the leaves to the roots through vessels contained chiefly in the innermost layers of the bark. It is believed that the formation of new wood and bark takes place either wholly or principally from the descending sap.

The circulation of the sap is either wholly or partially suspended during a portion of each year (in tropical climates during the dry season, and in temperate and polar climates during the winter); and hence the wood and bark are usually formed in distinct layers, at the rate of one layer in each year; but this rule is not universal. Each such layer consists of parts differing in density and colour to an extent which varies in different kinds of trees.

A

The tissues of which both wood and bark consist are distinguished into two kinds—*cellular tissue*, consisting of clusters of minute cells; and *vascular tissue*, or *woody fibre*, consisting of bundles of slender tubes; the latter being distinguished from the former by its fibrous appearance. The difference, however, between those two kinds of tissue, although very distinct both to the eye and to the touch, is really one of degree rather than of kind; for the fibres or tubes of vascular tissue are simply very much elongated cells, tapering to points at the ends, and "breaking joint" with each other.

The tenacity of wood when strained ,, along the grain" depends on the tenacity of the walls of those tubes or fibres; the tenacity of wood when strained "across the grain" depends on the adhesion of the sides of the tubes and cells to each other. Examples of the difference of strength in those different directions will be given afterwards.

When a woody stem is cut across, the cellular and vascular tissue are seen to be arranged in the following manner :—

In the centre of the stem is the *pith*, composed of cellular tissue, enclosed in the medullary sheath, which consists of vascular tissue of a particular kind. From the pith there extend, radiating outwards to the bark, thin partitions of cellular tissue, called *medullary rays*; between those, additional medullary rays extend inwards from the bark to a greater or less distance, but without penetrating to the pith.

When the medullary rays are large and distinct, as in the European oak or the native white beech (*Gmelina Leichhardtii*) and red ironbark (*Eucalyptus siderophloia*), they are called "*silver grain.*"

Between the medullary rays lie bundles of vascular tissue, forming the woody fibre, arranged in nearly concentric rings or layers round the pith. These rings are traversed radially by the medullary rays. The boundary between two successive rings is marked more or less distinctly by a greater degree of porosity, and by a difference of hardness and colour.

The annual rings are usually thicker at that side of the tree which has had most air and sunshine, so that the pith is not exactly in the centre.

The wood of the entire stem may be distinguished into two parts —the outer and younger portion, called "sap-wood," or *alburnum*, being softer, weaker, and less compact, and sometimes lighter in colour, than the inner and older portion, called "heart-wood," or *duramen*. The heart-wood is alone to be employed in those works of carpentry in which strength and durability are required. The boundary between the sap-wood and the heart-wood is in general distinctly marked, as if the change from the former to the latter occurred in the course of a single year.

The structure of a *branch* is similar to that of the trunk from which it springs, except as regards the difference in the number of annual rings, corresponding to the difference of age. A branch becomes partially embedded in those layers of the trunk which are formed after the time of its first sprouting, causing a perforation in those layers, accompanied by distortion of their fibres, and constituting what is called a *knot*.

2. Geographical Distribution and Mode of Occurrence of New South Wales Timber Trees—Brush Forests—Open Forests—Scrub Forests.

—Considered with reference to their distribution, general character, and mode of growth, the timber trees of New South Wales form naturally three distinct kinds of forest, which may de designated as (1) *Brush Forests;* (2) *Open Forests;* and (3) *Scrub Forests.*

The first, or the *Brush Forests,* are characterized by an extraordinary luxuriance and denseness of growth, great diversity of species, and an almost tropical aspect—most of the trees being of lofty stature and magnificent proportions, with an abundant undergrowth of tree and other ferns, and clothed or adorned above with an almost infinite variety of beautiful mosses, orchids, and other epiphytes, climbers, twiners, and creepers, and intermixed here and there with stately palms, some of which attain a height of 130 feet, while many of the tree-ferns exceed 50 feet in height. The most prevalent kinds of trees are those belonging to the natural families of *Sapindaceæ, Proteaceæ, Meliaceæ, Myrtaceæ, Rutaceæ, Euphorbiaceæ, Urticeæ,* and *Saxifrageæ.* Less common, but still numerous, are representatives of *Leguminosæ, Laurineæ, Sterculiaceæ, Pittosporeæ, Monimiaceæ, Tiliaceæ, Sapotaceæ, Apocyneæ,* and *Myrsineæ. Coniferæ, Rhamneæ, Jasmineæ, Ebenaceæ, Araliaceæ,* and *Celastrineæ* are represented by several species each, whilst *Anacardiaceæ, Anonaceæ, Styracaceæ, Olacineæ, Malvaceæ, Capparideæ, Santalaceæ,* and *Verbenaceæ,* furnish at least two species each, and about another dozen orders at least one species each. With rare exceptions, this kind of forest is only met with east of the Great Dividing Range, on mountain slopes or terraces, where the soil consists of decomposed trap and other rocks, in sheltered fertile valleys and ravines, or on rich alluvial flats along the courses of rivers and creeks. During the heats of summer the atmosphere in these forests is generally surcharged with moisture and the temperature always more equable than upon adjacent lands with poorer soil and a vegetation either more open or stunted. Bush fires seldom or never occur in these forests, which are frequently difficult to penetrate or explore, owing to inequalities of surface, the presence of rocks or gorges, and the dense and tangled nature of the vegetation. Yet nothing could be more charming and delightful to the

beholder, especially where a glade or open vista occurs enabling
him to take a comprehensive view of the scenery. Shrubs are
rare, and the stems of the trees are seldom cylindrical, but
generally of irregular growth, or forming massive angular pro-
jections, wings, and buttresses, sometimes of fantastic shape, which,
together with the mighty branches and the beautiful, dense, usually
dark green and glossy foliage, and the world of *lianes* and epiphytes
clasping and embracing them, are exceedingly picturesque—the
peculiar, quivering, green, and almost sunless light, which, even
on the brightest day, pervades these recesses, contributing in no
small degree to intensify the impression of strangeness, mystery,
and delight. But although the scenes are charmed, the difficulties
of exploring these forests and ascertaining the true character of
the trees are very serious, and, with the exception of the "Red
Cedar," the "Pine," the "Rosewood," the "Ash," the "Beech,"
the "Tulipwood," and the "Silky Oak," the most experienced
sawyers have frequently no names for the great majority beyond
the general designation of "brush-trees," and are unable to give
any reliable information regarding the qualities of their timber.
Even the practised botanist sometimes finds himself at a loss in
these regions ; for the foliage of the trees is so far overhead and
so intermingled with that of neighbouring trees and climbers, the
trunk so hidden by epiphytes, and the light so uncertain or
imperfect, that in most cases a tree has to be cut down before its
identity can be determined. Even then it often becomes necessary
to cut down several of the neighbouring trees, which have their
branches intertwined with it or tied together by the "bush-ropes,"
before the tree will fall and bring the foliage, &c., within the
reach of the explorer. No two brush forests are exactly alike,
fresh species of trees meeting the traveller as he advances from
one brush to another, whilst others disappear. The most marked
difference in this respect is, perhaps, the absence in the brushes of
the southern districts of such trees as the *Araucaria*, the *Flindersia*,
the *Castanospermum*, the *Mallotus*, the *Owenia*, and the *Tarrietia*,
which are so very prevalent and give almost a distinctive feature
to the brushes of the northern districts. Besides the species
already mentioned, the "White Maple," the dark and the light
"Yellowwood," the "Marblewood," the "Coachwood," the "Beefwood," the "Black Apple," the "Red Ash," the "Sycamore," the
"Native Tamarind," the "Sassafras," the "Native Laurel," the
"Maiden's Blush," the "Negrohead Beech," the "Colonial Deal,"
the "Damson," the "Corkwood," the "Marara," the "Lignum-
Vitæ," the "Blueberry Ash," the "Mock Orange," the "Native
Ebony," the "White Sallow," the "Native Mulberry," the
"Turmeric," the "Brush Cherry," the "Teak," the "Native
Pear," the "Brush Bloodwood," the "Giant Nettle," huge
enormous figs, various kinds of "Hickory" and "Myrtle," with

numerous gigantic Eucalypti, Pandaneæ, &c., are but a few of the vast number of beautiful and useful trees which are common and have their home and flourish in most of our brush forests.

As a general rule, the timber produced by the trees of the brush forests is finely grained, often ornamental in texture, and mostly sound at heart, strong, and durable. Even when the trees are of enormous size, and not sound at the butt, they are nearly always solid at no great distance from the root, and differ from those growing in the open forests in being easily worked, and in splitting or clearing freely in planes radiating from the centre.

The second, or the *Open Forests*, are met with in all parts of the Colony except portions of the Monaro, Murrumbidgee, and the Lachlan Districts, where immense " downs " or treeless saltbush plains are common. They are composed of trees belonging almost exclusively to the natural order of *Myrtaceæ*, or species of the genera *Eucalyptus, Melaleuca, Callistemon, Angophora, Syncarpia,* and *Tristania*, yielding timber which is known by the general name of "hardwood." This class of trees is characterized by a more or less naked and lofty stem, with the bark sometimes deeply furrowed or wrinkled and persistent, sometimes smooth and deciduous, or hanging in long strips from the branches ; a comparatively small head of persistent, dry, dull-coloured foliage; the branches generally few, sometimes haggard-looking, gnarled, or blown into odd shapes, with the scanty leaves arranged *vertically*, instead of horizontally, and affording the traveller neither shade nor shelter. Most of these trees are found on well-grassed "ridges," and grow to a greater size and produce better timber on soil rather poor than otherwise, the more fertile lands frequently producing trees of comparatively small dimensions, thinly scattered over their surface. The rich alluvial flats on the margins of rivers and creeks are exceptions to this rule, being almost always heavily timbered, especially with "apple-trees and "flooded gums." Some species of Eucalyptus, like the "Blue gum" and "Blackbutt," are of rapid growth, while others, like the "Ironbark" and the "Box," are of exceedingly slow growth. The "Colonial Pine" (*Araucaria*) and the various kinds of "Oak" (*Casuarina*) sometimes grow among the trees of the open forests, as well as some species of *Acacia*, especially the "Myall" and the green and black "Wattle," which in many instances take entire possession of vast plains, constituting open forests by themselves. There is much perplexity and confusion in regard to the common names of the various species of *Eucalyptus*, the same name being frequently applied many times over to different species in different localities, but it is hoped that the nomenclature adopted in this essay will be found as reliable as any hitherto published. The species of *Eucalyptus* of most frequent occurrence are those known as " Box," " Bastard Box," " Yellow

Box," "Stringybark," " Ironbark," "Blackbutt," "Woollybutt," "Blue Gum," "Red Gum," "Flooded Gum," "White Gum," "Spotted Gum," "Grey Gum," "Yellow Gum," "Drooping Gum," "Mountain Ash," "Hickory," "Leather-jacket," "Mahogany," "Messmate," "Peppermint," "Tallowwood," "Bloodwood," &c. The species of *Angophora* are known as "Apple-trees," those of *Callistemon* and *Melaleuca* as "Tea-trees," while the species of *Syncarpia* are known as "Turpentine-trees," and those of *Tristania* as "White Box," "Brush Box," "Bastard Box," "Hickory," "Swamp Mahogany" or "Water Gum."

Perhaps one of the most remarkable and interesting denizens of the open forests is the "Flooded Gum " of the interior (*Eucalyptus rostrata*), also known as "Red Gum," "White Gum," or "Yarrah," a tree affecting the banks of rivers, and often attaining a height of over 100 feet. This tree appears to have been a great favourite of Sir Thomas Mitchell's, who records his opinion of it in the following words :—" Its huge gnarled trunk, wild romantic-formed branches, often twisting in coils, shining white or light red bark, and dark masses of foliage, with consequent streaks of shadow below, frequently produced effects fully equal to the wildest forest scenery of Ruysdael or Waterloo. Often as I hurried along did I take my last look with reluctance of scenes forming the most captivating studies. Its shining bark and lofty height inform the traveller of a distant probability of water, or, at least, the bed of a river or lake ; and, being visible over all other trees, it usually marks the course of rivers so well that in travelling along the Darling and Lachlan I could with ease trace the general course of the river, without approaching its banks, until I wished to encamp."

The third, or the *Scrub Forests*, are also common in all parts of the Colony on dry and arid, strong, or sandy land, consisting generally of low, short-stemmed, stunted trees, which, with the exception of some kinds of Cypress Pine and Wattles, rarely produce serviceable timber. The great majority of the trees belong to the natural orders of *Leguminosœ*, *Coniferœ*, *Proteaceœ*, and *Myrtaceœ*, the remainder being made up of representatives of such orders as the *Verbenaceœ*, *Santalacea*, *Capparideœ*, *Epacrideœ*, *Sapindaceœ*, *Polygonaceœ*, *Pittosporeœ*, *Apocyneœ*, and *Phytolaccaceœ*, while the undergrowth is of an exceedingly varied character, and includes most of the under-shrubs and bush-flowers of the Colony. The botanical characters and affinities of many species found in the scrub forests of the interior are still only imperfectly ascertained, and great confusion or uncertainty prevails regarding their local or common names. The most widely-distributed and best-known species are those met with under the names of "Pine" or "Cypress Pine," "Honeysuckle," "Myall," "Boree," "Silver Wattle," "Currawang," "Yarren," "Berrigan," "Quandong," "Kurrajong," "Dogwood," "Swamp Oak," "She Oak,"

"He Oak," "Bull Oak," "Belah," "Emu Bush," "Hop Bush," "Needle Bush," "Sifting Bush," "Currant Bush," "Cotton Bush," and "Native Cherry"; less frequent, or less known, generally, are "Budtha," "Coolibah," "Goborro," "Bimbil," "Warrior Bush," "Mustard Bush," "Umbrella Bush," "Mogil-Mogil," "Sandalwood," *Bursaria*," "Byrnum," "Cuba," "Mulga," "Wilga," "Gidgee," and "Modderumbung." In some parts of Riverina "Mallee Scrubs" are formed by three different species of Eucalyptus (*E. dumosa, E. incrassata*, and *E. oleosa*), and also by a species of *Myoporum* ("Black Mallee"), while arborescent species of *Muhlenbeckia, Polygonum*, and *Viminaria* form impenetrable "scrubs" in other parts of the interior, and *Avicennia officinalis* constitutes the well-known "Mangrove" scrubs of the coast districts. The Pine scrubs of Riverina and other parts of the Colony are formed by species of *Frenela*, which are sometimes also found associated with Eucalyptus in the "Mallee Scrubs." Bush fires are of frequent occurrence in most of the scrub forests, and probably preclude many of the trees from attaining the dimensions which they might otherwise attain. At each burning most of these trees are killed to the ground, to be reproduced from the collar. Notwithstanding the great number of beautiful flowering herbs and shrubs which inhabit the scrub forests, the impression produced on a traveller by these forests is one of barrenness and desolation. In the daytime the heat is usually oppressive, and shade is unknown; and the whole of the vegetation being evergreen, there appears to be neither summer nor winter, neither spring nor autumn. Most of the flowers are without perfume, and even the forms of animal life met with are unknown in other parts of the world, and generally grotesque in form and manners.

3. **Classification of New South Wales Timber Trees.— Pine Woods—Leaf Woods.**—For purposes of carpentry, trees may be classed according to the mechanical structure of the wood. It has already been stated that the botanical classes of Endogens and Exogens correspond to essential differences of mechanical structure.

In further dividing the class of Exogenous trees, or timber trees proper, according to the structure of the wood, a division into two classes at once suggests itself, which exactly corresponds with a botanical division, viz :—

PINEWOOD, comprising all timber trees belonging to the natural order of *Coniferæ*; and LEAFWOOD, comprising all other timber trees, including the *Casuarineæ*, or Colonial Oaks.

Beyond this primary division, the place of a tree in the botanical system has little or no connection with the structure of its timber.

Pinewood, or coniferous timber, in most cases contains turpentine. It is distinguished by straightness in the fibre and regularity in the figure of the trees; qualities favourable to its use in carpentry, especially where long pieces are required to bear either a direct pull or a transverse load, or for purposes of planking. At the same time, the lateral adhesion of the fibres is small; so that it is much more easily shorn and split along the grain, or torn asunder across the grain, than leafwood; and is, therefore, less fitted to resist thrust or shearing stress, or any kind of stress that does not act along the fibres. Even the toughest kinds of pinewood are easily wrought. A peculiar characteristic of pinewood (but one which requires the microscope to make it visible) is that of having the vascular tissue "*punctated*"; that is to say, there are small lenticular hollows in the sides of the tubular fibres. This structure is probably connected with the smallness of the lateral adhesion of those fibres to each other.

In leafwood, or non-coniferous timber, there is no turpentine. The degree of distinctness with which the structure is seen, whether as regards medullary rays or annual rings, depends on the degree of difference of texture of different parts of the wood. Such difference tends to produce unequal shrinking in drying; and consequently those kinds of timber in which the medullary rays and the annual rings are distinctly marked are more liable to warp than those in which the texture is more uniform. At the same time, the former kinds of timber are, on the whole, the more flexible, and in many cases are very tough and strong, which qualities make them suitable for structures that have to bear shocks.

4. **Examples of Pinewood.**—The following are examples of timber of this class :—

I. "MORETON BAY WHITE PINE."—This is the produce of the *Araucaria Cunninghamii*, which occurs only in the northern coast districts, its southern limit being the Bellinger River; it is soft, easily wrought, and used for ships' spars, planks, flooring-boards, and joiners' and cabinet-makers' work generally, but not very durable when exposed.

II. "RED OR BLACK PINE."—This is a valuable timber, the produce of the *Frenela Endlicheri*, found near Berrima, on the Liverpool Plains, and on the Lachlan and Darling Rivers. It is of a dark colour, strong, and very durable; largely used for telegraph posts, ornamental fittings, and cabinet-making, taking a fine polish.

III. "PORT MACQUARIE PINE."—This is the produce of the *Frenela Macleayana*, a small-sized tree, found near Port Macquarie, and generally cut up into weatherboards, deals, battens, and other small scantlings.

IV. "RICHMOND WHITE PINE."—This is produced by the *Frenela robusta, var. microcarpa,* and is a very useful timber for many purposes, the root-stock furnishing excellent veneers for cabinet-making.

V. "WHITE CYPRESS PINE" of the interior.—This timber is the produce of the *Frenela robusta var. verrucosa,* strong, durable, and used for telegraph posts, planks, weatherboards, rafters, battens, &c., but inferior to the Red or Black Pine.

VI. "ILLAWARRA MOUNTAIN PINE."—The produce of the *Frenela rhomboidea.* Timber very similar to the two last kinds.

VII. "BLUE MOUNTAIN PINE." — Produced by the *Frenela Muelleri,* a small tree, found on the Blue Mountains. This timber is soft and easily worked, but somewhat deficient in strength and durability, and not much used.

VIII. "COLONIAL DEAL."—This beautiful and valuable timber is the produce of two species of *Podocarpus (P. elata,* and *P. spinulosa),* one of which attains a height of 120 feet, and a diameter of 2 to 3 feet. It is free from knots, soft but close-grained, easily wrought, and largely employed for planks, flooring-boards, joinery and cabinet-making.

5. Examples of Leafwood.— Hardwoods.—The class of timber known as "hardwoods" is the produce of trees growing generally in the open forests, and belonging to the natural order of *Myrtaceæ,* or species of *Eucalyptus, Angophora, Melaleuca, Callistemon, Syncarpia,* and *Tristania*—a most remarkable and important class of trees, possessing many characteristics in common. When at their full maturity, these trees are rarely sound at heart, and even when sound the heartwood has often to be rejected on account of its extreme brittleness. They are also distinguished from the trees of other quarters of the globe by being more easily split in concentric layers than in planes radiating from the pith, and a frequent blemish in their timber is the occurrence of cylindrical clefts of that kind, filled with gum, and known as "gum-veins." Another peculiarity of this class of trees is, that although most of them make excellent fuel and are valuable as such on account of the quantity of heat or steam they are capable of generating, the majority are slow to kindle, and a few will scarcely burn at all. When free from the defects of "gum-veins," heart and star shakes, their timber generally opens out red, yellowish, whitish or straw-coloured, hard, heavy, strong, and rigid, the texture always close, the grain sometimes plain and straight with minute pores filled with a hard white brittle secretion, but more generally twisted and inlocked, rarely finely figured, and always more or less difficult to work. Some of the kinds are said to be almost indestructible in any situation, impervious alike to the "white ant" and the *Teredo navalis,* and, with all their defects, probably unequalled in the world for railway sleepers, piles for

bridges, wharves and jetties, fencing, or any kind of heavy carpentry, as well as in ship-building for beams, keelsons, sternposts, engine-beams, and other works below the line of flotation, where great strength is required and a heavy material not objectionable. The "Ironbark" stands in the first class on Lloyds' list of ship-building timbers, and, together with several other kinds, is already extensively used by European ship-builders, although there is reason to believe that the specimens sent Home and tested at the various International Exhibitions, as well as by Lloyds' Committee and in Her Majesty's Dockyards, had mostly been cut at an improper time of the year, and were very imperfectly seasoned—two points of the utmost importance in connection with timber, yet universally disregarded by sawyers and lumber-men in this Colony.

I. EUCALYPTUS.—Besides the "Ironbark," already referred to, of which there are several varieties, such as the "Red or Large-leaved," the "White or Narrow-leaved," the "Silver-leaved," and the "Red-flowering," the most valuable and best-known species of *Eucalyptus* are those called "Box," "Bastard Box," "Yellow Box," "Blue Gum," "Tallowwood," "Flooded Gum," "Grey Gum," "Red Gum," "Slaty Gum," "Spotted Gum," "Drooping Gum," "White Gum," "Yellow Gum," "Blackbutt," "Woolly-butt," "Stringybark," "Red or Forest Mahogany," "Swamp Mahogany," "Messmate," "Lignum-Vitæ," "Hickory," "Leather-jacket," "Peppermint," &c.

II. ANGOPHORA.—There are four species of this genus, all known as "Apple-trees," and producing more or less excellent timber, largely employed by wheelwrights for naves, but otherwise generally used only for slabs and rough constructions, being very subject to the defect of "gum-veins."

III. MELALEUCA.—This genus furnishes several species of large-growing timber trees, known as "Common Tea-tree," "Prickly-leaved Tea-tree," "Broad-leaved Tea-tree," "Narrow-leaved Tea-tree," "White Watergum," &c. The timber of these trees is singularly hard and close-grained, exceedingly durable underground, even in wet situations (except salt or brackish water), and largely used for fencing-posts, &c., but subject to "gum-veins," and apt to rend if carelessly seasoned.

IV. CALLISTEMON.—The species of this genus are also known as "Tea-trees," and furnish timber which is scarcely to be distinguished from that of *Melaleuca*, and employed for the same purposes.

V. SYNCARPIA.—There are two species of this genus, both of which are called "Turpentine-trees." Their timber is exceedingly heavy, hard, and close-grained, and much in request for piles for wharves, jetties, and bridges, as it is said that the *Teredo* or water-worm will not touch it. The chief defect of this timber, which is almost fire-proof, is its liability to rend in drying, especially if cut at the improper season of the year.

VI. TRISTANIA.—The four species of this genus are indiscriminately known as "White Box," "Brush Box," "Bastard Box," "Watergum," "Swamp Mahogany" or "Hickory." They produce most excellent timber for many purposes, but especially for boat and ship building, cogs of wheels in machinery, &c. Ribs of vessels made of this timber have been found perfectly sound at the end of thirty years' service.

6. Examples of Leaf-Wood continued.—Softwoods.—

The trees of this class, although often exceedingly hard and close-grained, are called by the general name of "softwoods" or "brush-woods," in contradistinction to the "hardwoods" of the open forests, and are, as a rule, only found in the "brush forests," or between the sea-board and the Great Dividing Range. The exceptions are the *Casuarinas* and *Acacias*, which are mostly or often found in open forests; and a few trees like the "Sandal-wood," the "Quondong," and the "Honeysuckles," which belong properly to the scrub forests. Of course the species of *Araucaria*, *Frenela*, and *Podocarpus* are "softwoods" also, but they are not leaf-woods, and have been already considered separately as pine-woods. The trees now to be considered belong to such natural orders as *Meliaceæ, Proteaceæ, Tiliaceæ, Saxifrageæ, Leguminosæ, Laurineæ, Pittosporeæ, Jasmineæ, Verbenaceæ, Rutaceæ, Sapin-daceæ, Monimiaceæ, Sapotaceæ, Santalaceæ, Olacineæ*, &c., and may be subdivided into three sub-classes, viz., (1) *Cabinet and Fancy Woods*, (2) *Coach-building Woods*, and (3) *Stave-Woods*.

I. CABINET AND FANCY WOODS.—The "Red Cedar" must be placed at the head of this class, not, perhaps, because it is the most beautiful, but because it is the most generally useful and valuable. The *Cedrela Toona* is indeed a noble tree, attaining a height of 150 feet, with a diameter sometimes of 10 feet, and yielding upwards of 30,000 superficial feet of saleable timber per tree. This timber is similar to mahogany in appearance, easily worked, very durable, and suitable for almost any purpose to which wood can be applied, but especially for internal fittings and cabinet-making, patterns, &c. About thirty years ago this tree was common and abundant in all the brush forests, but the great demand for its timber, and the want of legislation to regulate its felling, have caused it to become completely extirpated in many localities, so that it can now be obtained only from the northern rivers, such as the Bellinger, the Richmond, and the Tweed; and unless the Legislature take steps to prevent it, the day cannot be far distant when it will no longer be found anywhere in the Colony. The great majority of the other trees belonging to this class, though yielding timber of great beauty, strength, and durability, often exquisitely figured, veined, or marked, fragrant, taking a fine polish, and equal, if not superior, to many kinds now largely imported, are unfortunately very little known, and seldom used. The following may be quoted as worthy of the serious consideration of our local manufacturers of furniture, carvers, turners, instrument-makers, wood-engravers, &c. :—" Rosewood" *(Dysoxylon Fraseranum)*; "Tulip-wood" *(Harpullia pendula)*; " Dark Yellowwood" *(Rhus rhodanthema)*; " Light Yellow.wood" *(Flindersia Oxleyana)*; " White Maple" *(Villaresia Moorei)*; "Beefwood" *(Stenocarpus salignus)*; " Native Pear" *(Xylomelum pyriforme)*; "Turmeric" *(Zieria Smithii)*; " White Sycamore" *(Cryptocarya obovata)*; " Native Laurel" *(Cryptocarya glaucescens)*; " Native Tamarind" *(Diploglottis Cunninghamii)*; "Teakwood" *(Endiandra glauca)*; "Pencil Cedar" *(Dysoxylon Muelleri)*; " Maiden's Blush" *(Echinocarpus australis)*; "White Beech" *(Gmelina Leichhardtii)*; "Negrohead Beech" *(Fagus Moorei)*; "Sandalwood" *(Eremophila Mitchelli)*; "Native Chestnut" *(Castanospermum australe)*; "Native Plum" *(Achras australis)*; "Quondong" *(Fusanus acuminatus)*; " Corkwood" *(Duboisia myoporoides)*; "Lightwood" *(Ceratopetalum apetalum)*; "Nut-tree" *(Macadamia ternifolia)*; "Myall" *(Acacia pendula)*; "Bastard Myall" *(Acacia Cunninghamii* and *A. glaucescens)*; "Blackwood" *(Acacia melanoxylon* and *A. penninervis)*; "Spearwood" *(Acacia doratoxylon* and *A. homalophylla)*; "Marblewood" *(Olea paniculata)*; "Native Olive" *(Notelæa ovata)*; "Honeysuckle" *(Banksia integrifolia* and *B. serrata)*; "Forest Oak" *(Casuarina torulosa)*; "Brush Cherry" *(Trochocarpa laurina)*; "Mock Orange" *(Pittosporum undulatum)*; "Native Ebony" *(Diospyros hebecarpa)*; "Myrtle" *(Myrtus Beckleri)*; "Blueberry Ash" *(Elæocarpus holopetalus)*; "Lignum-Vitæ" *(Vitex lignum-vitæ)*; "Marara" *(Weinmannia rubifolia)*; "Union Nut" *(Bosistoa sapindiformis)*; "Native Mulberry" *(Hedycarya angustifolia)*; "Jemmy Donnelly" *(Euroschinus falcatus)*, &c. Full particulars of each kind will be given further on, but in the meantime it may be stated here that the great majority of them can be obtained either at Illawarra or on the northern rivers.

II. COACH-BUILDING WOODS.—The most celebrated timbers for coach-building purposes are those of the "Coachwood" *(Ceratopetalum apetalum)*; the "Red Ash" *(Alphitonia excelsa)*; the "Lightwood" *(Schizomeria ovata)*; the "Acacia" or "White Sallow" *(Eucryphia Moorei)*; the "Black Myrtle" *(Cargillia pentamera)*; the "White Myrtle" *(Myrtus acmenioides)*; with species of *Tristania, Eugenia,* and *Acacia* under the name of "Hickory"; the "Apple-tree" *(Angophora)*; and species of *Eucalyptus* under the names of "Cumberland Blue Gum," "Clarence Flooded Gum,"

"Spotted Gum," "Bastard Box," "Mountain Ash," &c. These, as well as those in the following class, will also be fully desribed hereafter.

III. STAVE-WOODS.—The following timbers are all excellent for coopers' work:—" Silky Oak" *(Grevillea robusta)*; "Beefwood" *(Stenocarpus salignus)*; "Ash" or "Cugerie" *(Flindersia australis)*; "Red Ash" *(Alphitonia excelsa)*; "Native Plum" *(Achras australis)*; "Swamp Oak" *(Casuarina stricta)*; "Colonial Chestnut" *(Castanospermum australe)*; "Flindosa" *(Flindersia australis)*; "Corkwoood" or "Lightwood" *(Schizomeria ovata)*; "Stave-wood" *(Tarrietia argyrodendron)*; "Green Wattle" *(Acacia decurrens)*; "Silver Wattle" *(Acacia dealbata)*; "Yiel-Yiel" *(Stenocarpus sinuatus)*; *Sterculia fœtida*; *Orites excelsa*; &c.

7. Appearance of Good Timber.—There are certain appearances which are characteristic of strong and durable timber, to what class soever it belongs.

In the same species of timber, that specimen will in general be the strongest and the most durable which has grown the slowest, as shown by the narrowness of the annual rings.

The cellular tissue as seen in the medullary rays (when visible) should be hard and compact.

The vascular or fibrous tissue should adhere firmly together, and should show no wooliness at a freshly-cut surface, nor should it clog the teeth of the saw with loose fibres.

If the wood is coloured, darkness of colour is in general a sign of strength and durability.

The freshly-cut surface of the wood should be firm and shining, and should have somewhat of a translucent appearance. A dull, chalky appearance is a sign of bad timber.

In wood of a given species, the heavier specimens are in general the stronger and the more lasting.

Among resinous woods, those which have least resin in their pores, and amongst non-resinous woods, those which have least sap or gum in them, are in general the strongest and most lasting.

It is stated by some authors that in pine-wood, that which has most sap-wood, and in leaf-wood, that which has least, is the most durable; but the universality of this law is doubtful.

Timber should be free from such blemishes as clefts, or cracks radiating from the centre; "cup-shakes," or cracks which partially separates one annual layer from another; "upsets," where the fibres have been crippled by compression; "rind-galls," or wounds in a layer of the wood, which have been covered and concealed by the growth of subsequent layers over them; and hollows or spongy places, in the centre or elsewhere, indicating the commencement of decay.

8. Influence of Soil and Climate on Trees.—Most timber trees are capable of flourishing in a great variety of soils. The best soil for all of them is one which, without being too dry and porous, allows water to escape freely, such as gravel mixed with sandy loam.

The most injurious soil to trees is that of swampy ground containing stagnant water; it never fails to make the timber weak and perishable.

As to the influence of climate, two general laws seem to prevail: that the strongest timber is yielded, amongst *different species* of trees, by those produced in tropical climates; and amongst trees of *the same species*, by those grown in cold climates. The first law is exemplified in such woods as teak, ironwood, ebony, and lignum-vitæ, surpassing in strength all those of temperate climates; the second in the red pine of Norway, as compared with colonial pines, in the oak of Britain, as compared with that of Italy, and even in the ironbark of this Colony, as compared with that of Queensland.

9. Age of Timber and Season for Felling.—There is a certain age of maturity at which each tree attains its greatest strength and durability. If cut down before that age, the tree, besides being smaller, contains a greater proportion of sap-wood, and even the heart-wood is less strong and lasting; if allowed to grow much beyond that age, the centre of the tree begins either to become brittle or to soften, and a decay commences by slow degrees, which finally renders the heart hollow. The age of maturity is therefore the best age for felling the tree to produce timber. It is known that some species of *Eucalyptus*, like the "Ironbark" and the "Box," grow very slowly, while others, like the "Blue Gum" and the "Blackbutt," grow sometimes very rapidly, but beyond this the age at which Australian timber trees attain their maturity is a question which as yet appears to have received little or no attention.

The best season for felling timber is that during which the sap is not circulating—that is to say, the winter, or in tropical climates, the dry seasons; for the sap tends to decompose, and so to cause decay of the timber. The best authorities recommend, also, as a means of hardening the sap-wood, that the bark of trees which are to be felled should be stripped off in the preceding spring.

Immediately after timber has been felled, it should be *squared*, by sawing off four "slabs" from the log, in order to give the air access to the wood and hasten its drying. If the log is large enough, it may be sawn into quarters.

10. Seasoning of Timber, Natural and Artificial.—Seasoning timber consists in expelling, as far as possible, the moisture which is contained in its pores.

Natural Seasoning is performed simply by exposing the timber freely to the air in a dry place, sheltered, if possible, from sunshine and high winds. The seasoning-yard should be paved and well drained, and the timber supported on cast-iron bearers, and piled so as to admit of the free circulation of air over all the surfaces of the pieces.

Natural Seasoning to fit timber for carpenters' work usually occupies about two years; for joiners' work, about four years; but much longer periods are sometimes employed.

To steep timber in water for a fortnight after felling it extracts part of the sap, and makes the drying process more rapid.

The best method of *Artificial Seasoning* consists in exposing the timber in a chamber or oven to a current of hot air. In Mr. Davison's process the current of air is impelled by a fan at the rate of about 100 feet per second; and the fan, air-passages, and chamber are so proportioned that one-third of the volume of air in the chamber is blown through it per minute. The best temperature for the hot air varies with the kind and dimensions of the timber; thus, for leaf-woods in general, in logs or large pieces, the temperature should be from 90° to 100° Fahr.; for pine-woods, in thick pieces, about 120°, and for thin boards of pine-wood, from 180° to 200°; while for cedar, in boards 1 inch thick, a temperature of from 280° to 300° might be employed. In this way, pieces of timber of 1, 2, 3, 4, 6, and 8 inches in thickness require, respectively, one, two, three, four, seven, and ten weeks to become dry, the current of hot air being kept up for *twelve hours per day* only.

The drying of timber by hot air from a furnace has also been practised successfully, in a brick chamber, through which a current is produced by the draught of a chimney. The equable distribution of the hot air amongst the pieces of timber is ensured by introducing the hot air close to the roof of the chamber, and drawing it off through holes in the floor with an underground flue. The hot air on entering, being more rare than that already in the chamber, which is partially cooled, spreads into a thin stratum close under the roof, and gradually descends amongst the pieces of wood to the floor. The air is introduced at the temperature of 240° Fahr. The expenditure of fuel in this method has been found in England to be at the rate of 1 lb. of coke for every 3 lbs. of moisture evaporated.

Many experiments have been made on the loss of weight and shrinkage of dimensions undergone by timber in seasoning, the results of which are so variable, however, that it is impossible to condense them into any general statement.

11. Durability and Decay of Timber.—All kinds of timber are most lasting when kept constantly dry, and at the same time freely ventilated.

Timber kept constantly wet is softened and weakened ; but it does not necessarily decay.   Various kinds of timber, some of which have been already mentioned, such as the " Tea-trees," the " Turpentine-trees," and the " White Box," possess great durability in this condition.

The situation which is least favourable to the duration of timber is that of alternate wetness and dryness, or of a slight degree of moisture, especially if accompanied by heat and confined air.   For pieces of carpentry, therefore, which are to be exposed to these causes of decay, the most durable kinds of timber only should be employed, and proper precautions should be taken for their preservation.

Slaked lime hastens the decay of timber, which should therefore, in buildings, be protected against contact with the mortar.

Timber exposed to confined air alone, without the presence of any considerable quantity of moisture, decays by " *dry rot*," which is accompanied by the growth of a fungus, and finally converts the wood into a fine powder.

The durability of " Ironbark " in ship-building has been estimated by Lloyds' Committee to be equal to that of the best descriptions of " Teak," " British Oak," " Mora," " Greenheart," and " Saul," or twelve years, and that of " Blue Gum " and " Stringy-bark " at nine years ; but these estimates are probably much too low.

12. Preservation of Timber.—Amongst the most efficient means of preserving timber are good seasoning and the free circulation of air.

Protection against moisture is afforded by oil-paint, provided that the timber is perfectly dry when first painted, and that the paint is renewed from time to time.   A coating of pitch or tar may be used for the same purpose.

Protection against the " dry rot " may be obtained by saturating the timber with solutions of particular metallic salts.   For this purpose, Chapman employed copperas (*sulphate of iron*) ; Mr. Kyan, corrosive sublimate (*bichloride of mercury*) ; Sir William Burnett, *chloride of zinc.*   All these salts preserve the timber so long as they remain in its pores ; but it would seem that they are gradually removed by the long-continued action of water.

Dr. Boucherie employed a solution of *sulphate of copper* in about one hundred times its weight of water.   The solution, being contained in a tank about 30 or 40 feet above the level of the log, whence it was forced by the pressure of the column of fluid above it through the tubes of the vascular tissue, driving out the sap before it at the other end of the log, until the tubes were cleared of sap and filled with the solution instead.

Timber is protected not only against wet rot and dry rot, but against white ants and sea-worms, by Mr. Bethell's process of saturation with the liquid called "*creosote*," which is a kind of pitch oil. This is effected first by exhausting the air and moisture from the pores of the timber in an air-tight vessel, in which a partial vacuum is kept up for a few hours, and then forcing the creosote into these pores by a pressure of about 150lbs. on the square inch, kept up for some days. The timber absorbs from a *ninth* to a *twelfth* of its weight of the oil in this process.

13. Strength of Timber—Amongst different specimens of timber of the same species, those which are most dense in the dry state are in general also the strongest.

The following are some general remarks as to the different ways in which the strength of timber is exerted :—

I. The TENACITY *along the grain*, depending, as it does, on the tenacity of the fibres of the vascular tissue, is on the whole greatest in those kinds and pieces of wood in which those fibres are straightest and most distinctly marked. It is not materially affected by temporary wetness of the timber, but is diminished by long-continued saturation with water, and by steaming and boiling.

The *tenacity across the grain*, depending chiefly on the lateral adhesion of the fibres, is always considerably less than the tenacity along the grain, and is diminished by wetness and increased by dryness. Very few exact and reliable experiments have been made upon it. Its smallness in pine-wood as compared with leaf-wood forms a marked distinction between those two classes of timber, the proportion which it bears to the tenacity along the grain having been found to be, by some experiments, from one-twentieth to one-tenth *in pine-wood*, and in *leaf-wood* from one-sixth to one-fourth and upwards.

II. The RESISTANCE TO SHEARING, by sliding of the fibres on each other, is the same, or nearly the same, as the tenacity across the grain.

III. The RESISTANCE TO CRUSHING along the grain, depending, as it does, on the resistance of the fibres to being crippled or "upset," and split asunder, is greatest when their lateral adhesion is greatest, and has been found by Mr. Hodgkinson to be nearly twice as great for dry timber as for the same timber in the green state. In most kinds of timber, when dry, it ranges from one-half to two-thirds of the tenacity.

Experiments have been made on the crushing of timber across the grain, which takes place by a sort of shearing ; but they have not led to any precise result, except that the timber is both more compressible and weaker against a transverse than against a longitudinal pressure ; and, consequently, that intense transverse compression of pieces of timber ought to be avoided.

B

IV. The MODULUS OF RUPTURE of timber, which expresses its resistance to cross-breaking, is usually somewhat less than its tenacity, but seldom much less.

V. The FACTOR OF SAFETY, in various actual structures of carpentry, ranges from 4 to 14, and is on an average about 10.

14. Table showing the Proof Transverse Strength, Modulus of Rupture, and Weight per Cubic Foot, of New South Wales Timbers, computed from the Results of Experiments by Colonel E. W. Ward and others* :—

	Proof Strength.	Modulus of Rupture.	Weight of a cubic foot in pounds.
1. Red-flowering Ironbark (*Eucalyptus leucoxylon*)	401	9,144	73
2. White Ironbark (*Eucalyptus crebra*)	364	8,568	69
3. Box (*Eucalyptus hemiphloia*)	350	8,064	73
4. Green Wattle (*Acacia decurrens*)	317	6,966	45
5. Red Ironbark (*Eucalyptus siderophloia*)	313	6,858	72
6. Grey Gum (*Eucalyptus saligna*)	308	7,560	62
7. Forest Oak (*Casuarina torulosa*)	301	6,930	69
8. Bloodwood (*Eucalyptus eximia*)	294	6,930	53
9. Grey Gum (*Eucalyptus tereticornis*)	285	6,300	71
10. Flooded Gum (*Eucalyptus rostrata*)	276	6,174	59
11. Oak (*Casuarina stricta*)	273	6,048	53
12. Turpentine Tree (*Syncarpia laurifolia*)	266	5,976	56
13. Stringybark (*Eucalyptus capitellata*)	266	5,958	55
14. Bastard Box (*Eucalyptus bicolor*)	262	5,724	69
15. Yellow Box (*Eucalyptus melliodora*)	259	5,796	66
16. Flindosa (*Flindersia australis*)	255	5,922	58
17. Pencil Cedar (*Dysoxylon Muelleri*)	245	5,724	49
18. Blackbutt (*Eucalyptus pilularis*)	245	5,544	56
19. White Gum (*Eucalyptus albens*)	238	5,040	62
20. Red Mahogany (*Eucalyptus resinifera*)	238	6,300	70
21. Mountain Ash (*Eucalyptus virgata*)	231	5,418	60
22. Woollybutt (*Eucalyptus longifolia*)	231	5,292	67
23. Marblewood (*Olea paniculata*)	231	5,220	63
24. Messmate (*Eucalyptus amygdalina*)	224	4,842	68
25. Light Yellow wood (*Flindersia Oxleyana*)	217	5,346	50
26. Tea-tree (*Melaleuca styphelioides*)	217	4,842	66
27. Apple-tree (*Angophora subvelutina*)	215	4,446	56
28. White Box (*Tristania conferta*)	210	4,788	61
29. Spotted Gum (*Eucalyptus hæmastoma*)	196	5,418	67
30. Swamp Oak (*Casuarina suberosa*)	196	4,662	52
31. White Gum (*Eucalyptus stellulata*)	156	4,536	54
32. Moreton Bay Pine (*Araucaria Cunninghamii*)	196	4,212	48
33. Native Myrtle (*Backhousia myrtifolia*)	192	4,338	52
34. Brush Cherry (*Eugenia myrtifolia*)	191	4,788	46
35. Peppermint (*Eucalyptus piperita*)	187	3,780	56

* The timber in every case is supposed to be *dry*. Green timber is much weaker, having sometimes only half the strength of dry timber, especially against crushing.

	Proof Strength.	Modulus of Rupture.	Weight of a cubic foot in pounds.
36. Hickory (*Myrtus acmenioides*)	182	4,914	42
37. White Cypress Pine (*Frenela robusta, v. verrucosa*)	182	3,870	40
38. Colonial Deal (*Podocarpus elata*)	178	3,960	36
39. Richmond Pine (*Frenela robusta, v. microcarpa*	174	3,870	39
40. Sassafras (*Doryphora sassafras*)	171	3,834	35
41. Dark Yellow wood (*Rhus rhodanthema*)......	168	3,654	49
42. Coachwood (*Ceratopetalum apetalum*)	168	3,744	38
43. Tea-tree (*Callistemon salignus*)	168	3,528	44
44. Red Cedar (*Cedrela Toona*)	140	3,296	28
45. Silky Oak (*Grevillea robusta*)	...	3,276	35
46. Beech (*Gmelina Leichhardtii*)	140	2,898	38
47. White Cedar (*Melia composita*)	...	2,700	32

The *proof transverse strength* is the weight in pounds avoirdupois which a bar of the ·timber 1 inch square, supported at two points 1 foot apart and loaded in the middle, is capable of sustaining without having its fibre and elasticity destroyed or impaired in any way. The *modulus of rupture* is eighteen times the load required to break the bar.

The results obtained by Col. Ward are no doubt in most cases much below the actual strength of the timber, as the specimens experimented on by him had been felled indiscriminately and were imperfectly seasoned. Recent experiments made in England by Mr. Thomas Laslett and others have shown the opinion here expressed to be correct in many instances.

15. Alphabetical List of New South Wales Timber Trees, with their Natural Orders, Common Names, Chief Characteristics, Habitats, and Uses.

I. ABROPHYLLUM.

(Natural Order SAXIFRAGEÆ.)

1. A. ORNANS.—A small handsome tree, with the young shoots and inflorescence pubescent; leaves alternate, elliptical or ovate-lanceolate, acuminate, 6 to 9 inches long with a few mucronate teeth in the upper part, narrowed into a petiole, glabrous or sprinkled with a few hairs on the principal veins underneath; flowers yellowish, rather small, in irregularly dichotomous panicles, terminal or in the upper axils; fruit a berry, ovoid, 3 to 4 lines long. Habitat, brush forests, Mount Tomah, Blue Mountains, Richmond River.

Qualities of *timber* unknown.

II. ACACIA.

(Natural Order LEGUMINOSÆ.   Sub-order *Mimoseœ.*)

2. A. ARMATA.—*Kangaroo Island Acacia.*—A small bushy tree, attaining 10 feet or more, with the branches angular-striate, hirsute-pubescent or rarely glabrous; leaves reduced to phyllodia, semi-ovate, oblong or incurved-lanceolate, undulate, obtuse or with a short oblique point, with a mid-rib and pinnate veins, from 4 lines to 1 inch long, the stipules straight and spinescent; flowers pentamerous, numerous, in pedunculate globular heads; pod straight or curved, $1\frac{1}{2}$ to 2 inches long, and 2 to 3 lines broad, softly villous, rarely glabrous or hispid. Habitat, scrub forests, Blue Mountains, New England, and in the interior.

Timber light and tough, but seldom used.

3. A. BINERVATA.—*Black Wattle; Hickory; Lightwood.*—A beautiful small tree, attaining 40 feet in height, and a diameter of 18 inches, with glabrous, slightly angular branchlets, soon becoming terete; leaves reduced to phyllodia, falcate, oblong or lanceolate, 3 to 4 inches long, with two or three longitudinal nerves, and pinnately veined; flowers at first on peduncles in an axillary raceme, which after flowering often grows into a leafy branch, with the peduncles at the base, each bearing a globular head of about 20 flowers; pod long, flat, and thin, about $\frac{1}{8}$ inch broad. Habitat, open forests, Port Jackson to Blue Mountains, Nepean, Hastings, and Clarence Rivers, southward to Illawarra and the Clyde.

Timber dark, close-grained, light and tough; used for axe-helves and bullock-yokes.

4. A. COMPLANATA.—A small glabrous tree, with the branchlets flattened and bordered by 2 or 3 acute angles or wings; leaves reduced to phyllodia, oval or oblong, obtuse, 2 or 3 inches long, $\frac{1}{2}$ to 1 inch broad, coriaceous, with longitudinal nerves and fine veins; flowers mostly pentamerous, numerous, in globular heads pedunculate in axillary clusters of 6 to 8 or more, or by the abortion of the upper phyllodia forming an irregular terminal raceme; pod curved, acuminate, very flat, 3 to 4 lines broad. Habitat, scrub forests, Clarence River.

Timber light, close-grained, and tough, but seldom used.

5. A. CUNNINGHAMII.—*Bastard Myall.*—A moderately large tree, glabrous or hoary-pubescent, the branchlets acutely triangular; leaves reduced to phyllodia, falcate, oblong or lanceolate, 5 to 6 inches long, 1 to $1\frac{1}{2}$ inch broad, or larger on barren shoots; flowers in spikes $1\frac{1}{2}$ to 3 inches long, often distinct or distant; pod long, linear, twisted, 1 to 2 lines broad. Habitat, scrub forests, Hunter, Hastings, Clarence, and Richmond Rivers, southwards to Illawarra.

Timber close-grained, hard, and dark; suitable for cabinet-making.

6. A. DEALBATA.—*Silver Wattle* ; *Sallow.*—An ornamental tree, attaining sometimes 80 feet in height, and a diameter of 36 inches ; leaves bipinnate, pinnæ 10 to 20 pairs, leaflets 30 to 40 pairs, linear, crowded, 2 to 3 lines long; flowers in small heads in axillary racemes paniculate at the ends of branches ; pod 3 to 4 inches long and about ½ inch broad, glaucous. Habitat, scrubs and open forests, Illawarra, Cumberland, Blue Mountains, also banks of rivers in the interior.

Timber handsome, light, strong, and tough; used for staves, axe-handles, and bullock-yokes. The bark is used for tanning.

7. A. DECURRENS.—*Green Wattle.*—An elegant tree, attaining a height of 40 feet and a diameter of 15 inches, glabrous or more or less tomentose-pubescent ; leaves bipinnate, pinnæ 8 to 15 pairs, sometimes more, rarely only 5 or 6, leaflets very numerous, linear, from 2 to 5 lines long ; flower heads small, globular in axillary racemes, the upper ones forming a terminal panicle, the flowers very numerous ; pod 3 to 4 inches long, ¼ inch or more broad. Habitat, scrub and open forests of the coast districts, Blue Mountains and New England.

Timber light, tough, and strong, used for staves, but liable to be bored by insects. The bark is very valuable, and extensively used for tanning.

Var. mollis.—Foliage softly tomentose-pubescent, the indumentum on the young shoots assuming a beautiful golden-yellow tinge; leaflets 2 to 3 lines long, obtuse. Habitat, northern districts.

Var. normalis.—Glabrous, or the young shoots slightly tomentose-pubescent ; leaflets 3 to 4 lines long, narrow. Habitat, chiefly about Port Jackson.

Var. pauciglandulosa.—Pubescent, sometimes almost hirsute, with a golden-yellow tinge on the young shoots ; leaflets small, often under 2 lines. Habitat, Hastings and Clarence Rivers and New England.

8. A. DISCOLOR.—A small tree, with the branchlets terete or angular, glabrous or pubescent ; leaves bipinnate, pinnæ 2 to 6 pairs, leaflets 10 to 15 pairs, oblong, obtuse, or acute, 3 to 4 lines long, firm, one-nerved, glabrous, pale underneath ; flowers pentamerous, rather large, in heads of 6 to 15 in axillary racemes, the upper ones forming a terminal panicle ; pod 1 to 3 inches long, 5 to 6 lines broad. Habitat, scrub forests, Port Jackson to the Blue Mountains, and Macleay River.

Timber light, firm, and tough, but seldom used.

Var. angustifolia.—Branches nearly terete ; leaflets linear, oblong, slightly falcate, numerous. Habitat, Port Jackson.

9. A. DORATOXYLON.—*Spearwood* ; *Currawang.*—A small tree, glabrous, with an ashy hue, the branchlets at first angular, but soon terete ; leaves reduced to phyllodia, elongated, falcate, acuminate,

often with oblique or recurved points, 4 to 8 inches long, 2 to 4 lines broad, narrowed towards the base, with numerous fine parallel veins, the central one rather prominent; flowers mostly pentamerous, in dense pedunculate spikes, solitary or clustered; pod unknown. Habitat, Lachlan and Macquarie Rivers.

Timber handsome, light, firm, and tough; used by the natives for making their spears.

10. A. ELATA.—A fine tree, attaining a height of 60 feet and a diameter of 15 inches, the young shoots often tinged with a golden-yellow pubescence; leaves bipinnate, pinnæ 2 to 4 distant pairs, 6 to 3 inches long; leaflets 8 to 12 pairs, lanceolate, acuminate, 1 to 2 inches long, minutely silky; flower heads globular, in racemes often 6 inches long, the upper ones forming a large terminal panicle, the flowers numerous; pod 4 to 6 inches long, about ½ inch broad. Habitat, scrub forests and shaded ravines on the Blue Mountains and Grose River, southwards to Illawarra.

Timber close-grained, hard, and tough.

11. A. FALCATA.—*Hickory; Sally; Lignum-vitæ; Willow.*—A small handsome tree, about 25 feet high and 15 inches in diameter, glabrous, the branchlets angular; leaves reduced to phyllodia, lanceolate-falcate, acuminate, narrowed towards the base, 3 to 6 inches long, or more, one-nerved, obliquely penniveined, with the margins slightly thickened; flowers pedunculate in racemes shorter than the phyllodia, with 10 to 20 small globular heads of about 20 small flowers each; pod flat, 2 to 3 inches long, about 3 lines broad. Habitat, open forests and banks of streams, Port Jackson to the Blue Mountains, southwards to Illawarra.

Timber close-grained, hard, and tough. The bark is rich in tannin, and was formerly used by the aborigines to poison fish, and also for curing skin diseases.

12. A. GLADIIFORMIS.—A small tree, quite glabrous, with the branchlets angular; leaves reduced to phyllodia, linear lanceolate or almost spathulate, curved, obtuse with a small hooked point, 3 to 6 inches long, narrowed at the base, coriaceous, one-nerved, smooth and shining; flowers mostly pentamerous, in globular heads of about 30, forming short racemes, the rhachis rigid and flexuose; pod elongated, flat but flexuose, about 3 lines broad, coriaceous. Habitat, scrub forests, Blue Mountains, and in the interior.

Timber similar to that of the preceding species.

13. A. GLAUCESCENS.—*Bastard Myall.*—A large tree, sometimes attaining 80 feet in height and 24 inches in diameter, the foliage ashy or hoary with a minute close pubescence or the young shoots yellowish; leaves reduced to phyllodia, oblong-falcate or lanceolate, 4 to 6 inches long, coriaceous, and striate with numerous

very fine veins ; flowers distinct or distant in spikes nearly sessile or shortly pedunculate, often clustered in the upper axils ; pod linear, twisted or coiled, about 2 lines broad. Habitat, scrub forests, Blue Mountains, Nepean, Hunter, Clarence, and Richmond Rivers, southwards to Illawarra.

Timber dark, handsome, finely grained, and hard ; very suitable for cabinet-makers and turners.

14. A. HOMALOPHYLLA.—*Spearwood ; Myall.*—A small tree, glabrous, or the foliage sometimes minutely hoary or pale ; leaves reduced to phyllodia, lanceolate-falcate, narrow, oblong or linear, obtuse with a small point, narrowed at the base, 1 to 3 inches long, 1 to 4 lines broad, thick and very finely striate with parallel nerves ; flowers mostly pentamerous, numerous, in dense globular heads, pedunculate in pairs or clusters on a common peduncle ; pod linear, usually glaucous, slightly curved, 2 to 3 lines broad, longitudinally veined. Habitat, salt-bush plains on the Murray, and barren scrubs from the Lachlan to the Barrier Range.

Timber hard, dark, and fragrant ; very suitable for cabinet-making ; used by the aborigines for making spears.

15. A. IMPLEXA.—A glabrous tree, sometimes slightly glaucous, the branchlets terete or nearly so ; leaves reduced to phyllodia, lanceolate-falcate, acuminate, narrowed at the base, 5 to 6 inches long or more, with several longitudinal nerves and fine veins ; flowers mostly pentamerous, numerous, in small dense heads on peduncles in short slender racemes ; pod narrow-linear, curved and twisted, 2 to 3 lines broad. Habitat, open forests, Port Jackson, northwards to the Clarence River and Mount Lindsay, southwards to Illawarra and Shoalhaven.

Timber hard and close-grained, but seldom used.

16. A. LEPROSA.—A small tree with pendulous branchlets, more or less glutinous, otherwise glabrous or the young shoots pubescent ; leaves reduced to phyllodia, narrow, linear-lanceolate, acute or obtuse with a small callous point, narrowed at the base, 1½ to 3 inches long, one-nerved, with anastomosing veins ; flowers mostly pentamerous, numerous, in globular heads on peduncles clustered or in pairs, hoary-pubescent; pod falcate or rarely straight, flat, 2 to 2½ lines broad. Habitat, Port Jackson.

Timber not much used.

17. A. LONGIFOLIA.—A small tree, sometimes low and bushy, glabrous or slightly pubescent when young, the branchlets angular ; leaves reduced to phyllodia, from broadly-oblong to oblong-lanceolate or linear, obtuse or acuminate, narrowed at the base, 2 to 3 or 5 to 6 inches long, with prominent longitudinal nerves and reticulate ; flowers always tetramerous, in loose and interrupted axillary spikes ; pod linear, often several inches long, 2 to 4 lines

broad. Habitat, scrub forests, Port Jackson to the Blue Mountains, northwards to the Clarence River and New England, southwards to Twofold Bay.

Timber light, tough, and hard, but seldom used.

18. A. MELANOXYLON.—*Blackwood*; *Lightwood*.—A fine tree, attaining a very large size, but sometimes flowering when uuder 20 feet, glabrous, or the young shoots minutely pubescent; leaves reduced to phyllodia, falcate-oblong or almost lanceolate, 3 to 4 inches long, ½ to 1 inch broad, obtuse or acute, narrowed towards the base, coriaceous, with several longitudinal nerves and numerous anastomosing veins; flowers mostly pentamerous, in very dense globular heads on peduncles 3 to 4 lines long, few together in a short raceme or sometimes solitary; pod elongated, flat, often curved into a circle, 3 to 4 lines broad, with thickened nerve-like margins. Habitat, Port Jackson to the Blue Mountains.

Timber hard, dark in colour, finely veined, very durable, and celebrated for cabinet work.

19. A. NERIIFOLIA.—A small handsome tree, with slender branchlets, angular, glaucous or mealy-tomentose when young, but soon glabrous; leaves reduced to phyllodia, linear-lanceolate, falcate, with a callous and often recurved point, narrowed towards the base, 3 to 5 inches long, 2 to 4 lines broad, one-nerved and penniveined; flowers mostly pentamerous, in small globular heads of 30 to 40, in simple rather slender racemes, the rhachis and peduncles usually tomentose; pod flat, straight or nearly so, several inches long, about 4 lines broad. Habitat, whinstone hills, Liverpool Plains, and open forests, New England and Gwydir River.

Timber close-grained, hard and tough, but seldom used.

20. A. NOTABILIS.—A very handsome tree, glabrous and often glaucous, the branchlets terete or nearly so; leaves reduced to phyllodia, from lanceolate-falcate to almost linear, narrowed at the base, oblique, 4 to 8 inches long, coriaceous, one-nerved and veined; flowers mostly pentamerous, in globular heads of about 50, forming short racemes; pod straight, flat, glaucous, 1½ to 3 inches long, 4 to 5 lines broad, coriaceous. Habitat, scrub forests of the interior towards the Barrier Range.

Qualities of *timber* not known.

21. A. PENDULA.—*Myall*; *Boree*.—A beautiful tree, attaining a height of 40 feet and a diameter of 18 inches, the foliage pale or ash-coloured with a minute pubescence, the branchlets slightly angular and usually pendulous, but soon terete; leaves reduced to phyllodia, linear-lanceolate, falcate, acuminate, narrowed towards the base, 2 to 3 inches long, rigidly coriaceous, and very finely striate; flowers on peduncles on a short common peduncle about

2 lines long, each bearing a small globular head of about 12 to to 20 flowers; pod linear, very flat, fully 5 lines broad, thinly coriaceous. Habitat, open plains, Illawarra, Liverpool Plains, and in the interior. "The only timber tree of the Lachlan morasses."

Timber close-grained, hard, violet-scented, and beautifully marked; used by cabinetmakers and turners; also for tobacco pipes and stockwhip handles, and by the aborigines for *boomerangs.*

22. A. PENNINERVIS.—*Blackwood.*—A tree sometimes attaining a height of 40 feet, but usually smaller, glabrous in all its parts, with the branchlets angular; leaves reduced to phyllodia, from oblong to lanceolate-falcate, acuminate, 3 to 4 inches long, sometimes twice that length, narrowed towards the base, one-nerved and penniveined; flowers mostly pentamerous, in globular heads of about 20, forming short but loose racemes, usually axillary; pod flat, straight or curved, 4 to 5 inches long, nearly $\frac{1}{2}$ inch broad. Habitat, Blue Mountains, Macquarie River, northwards to the Hastings, and southwards to Twofold Bay.

Timber handsome, close-grained, and hard; suitable for cabinet work, &c.; bark used for tanning.

Var. falciformis.—Phyllodia longer and more falcate, the young shoots and inflorescence hoary or golden-pubescent; pod $\frac{3}{4}$ inch broad. Habitat, coast districts generally, New England, Blue Mountains, and Lachlan River.

23. A. POLYBOTRYA.—A beautiful small tree, with the foliage more or less pubescent; leaves bipinnate, pinnæ usually 2 or 3 pairs, leaflets 6 to 10 pairs, narrow-oblong, obtuse, 3 to 4 lines long, with a prominent nerve near the lower edge, the rhachis terminating in a recurved deciduous point; flowers mostly pentamerous, in numerous small heads in racemes, the upper ones forming a terminal panicle; pod unknown. Habitat, Gwydir River, and boggy forest land in the north-western interior. "The most beautiful of all the Acacias." (*Fraser.*)

Qualities of *timber* unknown.

24. A. SALICINA.—*Cuba ; Native Willow.*—A small tree, with the branches often pendulous, and the foliage pale or of a glaucous hue, quite glabrous; leaves reduced to phyllodia, straight or nearly so, oblong-linear or lanceolate, obtuse or acuminate, narrowed at the base, 2 to 5 inches long, about $\frac{1}{2}$ inch broad, sometimes broader and falcate, the mid-rib and veins scarcely prominent; flowers 20 or more, mostly pentamerous, in racemes of 2 or 3 globular heads or sometimes a single head; pod straight, 1 to 3 inches long, about 3 lines broad. Habitat, open forests, Liverpool Plains, and scrub forests from the Lachlan to the Barrier Range.

Timber close-grained, hard, and tough, but not often used.

25. A. SENTIS.—A divaricately-branched small tree, sometimes shrubby, with the branchlets nearly terete, glabrous or pubescent when young; leaves reduced to phyllodia, lanceolate-oblong or linear, oblique falcate or curved, one-nerved, penniveined, ¾ to 2 inches long, usually glabrous; flowers mostly pentamerous, in globular heads of 20 to 30 on slender peduncles, solitary or in pairs, axillary or by the abortion of the phyllodia in terminal racemes; pod unknown. Habitat, low sand hills and arid salt-bush plains, Murray and Darling Rivers, extending towards the Barrier Range.

Qualities of *timber* unknown.

25. A. STENOPHYLLA.—A moderately large tree, quite glabrous, with the branchlets angular; leaves reduced to phyllodia, long-linear, acuminate or falcate, narrowed at the base, 6 inches to 1 foot long, 2 to 2½ lines broad, coriaceous, finely striate, with numerous parallel nerves; flowers mostly pentamerous, in globular heads of 20 to 30 or more in pedunculate racemes of 3 to 6, but sometimes solitary; pod long, moniliform, 4 to 5 lines broad. Habitat, scrub forests, Murray, Lachlan, and Darling Rivers, also towards the Barrier Range.

Timber exceedingly hard, firm, and close-grained.

27. A. SUBPOROSA.—A tree attaining a height of about 40 feet, with slender branchlets, viscid when young, and scarcely angular; leaves reduced to phyllodia, linear-lanceolate or linear, often falcate, acute with the point incurved, 1½ to 3 or rarely 4 inches long, 1 to 3 or 4 lines broad, with 2 or 3 prominent nerves, and often marked with glandular dots; flowers mostly pentamerous, in globular heads of 20 to 30 on slender peduncles, solitary or in pairs; pod not seen. Habitat, near Mount Imlay, Twofold Bay.

Timber light, close-grained, and tough.

28. A. TETRAGONOPHYLLA.—A small spreading tree, glabrous, with the branchlets terete; leaves reduced to phyllodia, clustered on the old nodes, linear-subulate, rigid, pungent-pointed, ½ to 1 inch long or rarely more; flowers pentamerous, numerous, in globular heads on peduncles, solitary or two together; pod curved and twisted, flat with thickened margins, nearly 3 lines broad. Habitat, Darling River and towards the Barrier Range.

Qualities of *timber* unknown.

29. A. UNDULIFOLIA.—A tree sometimes low and busy, but frequently of great size and very handsome from its long pendulous garland-like flowering branches, the branchlets slightly angular but soon terete, pubescent, hirsute or rarely glabrous; leaves reduced to phyllodia, numerous, ovate or orbicular, obliquely truncate and narrowed at the base, often petiolate, from a ¼ to

nearly 1 inch long, coriaceous, undulate, one-nerved, penniveined, with the margins thickened and terminating in a fine point; flowers mostly pentamerous, in globular heads of 20 to 30 on slender peduncles; pod stipulate, 7 to 9 lines broad, very flat, with nerve-like margins. Habitat, scrub forests, Blue Mountains, Cox's River, near Bathurst, Liverpool Plains, and north-west interior.

Timber light, strong, and tough, but not much used.

Var. dysophylla.—Softly villous; phyllodia large. Habitat, Pine Ridge, near Croker's Range.

Var. humilis—Diffuse and low, glabrous; phyllodia 3 to 4 lines long and nearly as broad, oblique and often recurved. Habitat, north-west interior.

Var. sertiformis.—More glabrous, with larger, phyllodia, not contracted at the base. Habitat, Liverpool Plains.

. III. ACHRAS.

(Natural Order SAPOTACEÆ.)

30. A. AUSTRALIS.—*Black Apple; Native Plum.*—A beautiful tree with a milky juice, frequently attaining a height of 100 feet, and a diameter of 36 inches, quite glabrous except a slight appressed pubescence on the very young shoots; leaves alternate, petiolate, entire, from elliptical-oblong and shortly and obtusely acuminate to broadly obovate-oblong and very obtuse, 3 to 4 inches long, sometimes larger, usually reticulate; flowers in axillary clusters or almost solitary on short pedicels; fruit a berry or drupe, resembling a plum but insipid, about 1 inch diameter, indehiscent. Habitat, brush forests, Illawarra to the Tweed.

Timber close-grained, firm, beautifully veined, and suitable for cabinet work; used also for staves and laths.

31. A. MYRSINOIDES.—*Nut Apple.*—A tall but rather slender and twiggy tree, with the young branches and leaves more or less pubescent or villous, the full-grown leaves glabrous above or sometimes on both sides; leaves alternate, petiolate, entire, mostly ovate or broadly elliptical, sometimes obovate, obtuse, narrowed at the base, 1 to 2 or rarely 3 inches long, usually with prominent veins; flowers rather few, in axillary clusters or almost solitary on pedicels, tomentose-pubescent; fruit (a berry or drupe) not seen. Habitat, brush forests, Richmond and Tweed Rivers.

Timber firm and elastic, rather hard but easily worked, and used for dray poles and shafts.

IV. ACKAMA.

(Natural Order SAXIFRAGEÆ.)

32. A. MUELLERI.—A moderately large tree, glabrous or nearly so, except the inflorescence ; leaves opposite, pinnate, leaflets usually 5, rarely 7 or 3, ovate-elliptical or ovate-lanceolate, acuminate, obtusely and very shortly serrate, usually 3 to 4 inches long, but sometimes much larger, narrowed at the base and more or less petiolulate, somewhat coriaceous, penniveined with usually a minute tuft of hairs in the axils of the principal primary veins underneath ; flowers very small but numerous, in compound panicles, the branchlets all minutely pubescent ; fruit a capsule, ovoid-globular, 1 to 1½ line long.   Habitat, brush forests, Hastings and Clarence Rivers.

Qualities of *timber* not known.

V. ACRONYCHIA.

(Natural Order RUTACEÆ.)

33. A. BAUERI.—*Brush Ash.*—A small tree, quite glabrous or the young shoots and inflorescence minutely hoary-tomentose ; leaves opposite, of a single leaflet on a rather long petiole, ovate, elliptical or obovate, obtuse or very shortly and obtusely acuminate, narrowed at the base, 3 to 4 or very rarely 5 inches long, thinly coriaceous ; flowers small, few, in axillary oblong panicles ; fruit a drupe, nearly globular or 4-angled, obtuse or acuminate, about ½ inch diameter, somewhat succulent.   Habitat, brush forests of coast districts, from Illawarra to the Clarence River.

Qualities of *timber* unknown.

34. A. LÆVIS.—*Yellowwood.*—A tree attaining a height of 60 feet, glabrous except the stamens ; leaves opposite or alternate, of a single leaflet, obovate-oblong to oblong-elliptical, obtuse, 1½ to 4 inches long, coriaceous when old ; flowers in dichotomous or trichotomous cymes, few, and usually pedunculate ; fruit a drupe, succulent, with a crustaceous endocarp, obtusely 4-angled, truncate at the top and depressed in the centre, about ½ inch diameter. Habitat, brush forests, Port Jackson to the Blue Mountains, northward to the Clarence River. southward to Yowaka and Lake King.

Qualities of *timber* unknown.

VI. ÆGICERAS.

(Natural Order MYRSINEÆ.)

35. Æ. MAJUS.—*Mangrove.*—A glabrous small tree or shrub ; leaves alternate, obovate, very obtuse, 2 to 3 inches long, entire, narrowed into a petiole, coriaceous and evergreen ; flowers white, small, on pedicels in axillary and terminal umbels, nearly sessile ; ovary very acute, growing out into a curved horn-like fruit. Habitat, Port Jackson, Hunter, Hastings, and Clarence Rivers.

Qualities of *timber* unknown.

VII. AILANTHUS.

(Natural Order Simarubeæ.)

36. A. IMBERBIFLORA.—"*Agundigundie.*"—A moderately large tree, glabrous in all its parts ; leaves alternate, pinnate, leaflets 15 to 17, petiolulate, ovate-lanceolate, 2 to 3 inches long; flowers small in terminal panicles; fruit a *samara*, about 2 inches long and 1½ inch broad. Habitat, Clarence River.

Qualities of *timber* unknown.

VIII. AKANIA.

(Natural Order Sapindaceæ.)

37. A. HILLII.—An elegant tree, 30 to 40 feet high, glabrous except the panicles, leaves alternate, pinnate, often above 2 feet long, leaflets numerous, lanceolate, acutely acuminate, often above 8 inches long, bordered with acute sometimes pungent serratures, rounded at the base, petiolulate, coriaceous, light green, shining above, marked underneath within each areola of the smaller reticulations with three or four round ovate or reniform dots ; flowers pedicellate in elongated panicles ; fruit not seen. Habitat, brush forests, Clarence and Richmond Rivers.

Qualities of *timber* unknown.

IX. ALCHORNEA.

(Natural Order Euphorbiaceæ.)

38. A. ILICIFOLIA.—A small straggling tree, attaining a height of 15 feet, quite glabrous ; leaves alternate, ovate or rhomboidal, sinuate-toothed or lobed, the teeth or lobes terminating in prickly points, coriaceous, penniveined and reticulate, resembling those of a holly, 1½ to 3 inches long, tapering into a petiole; flowers diœcious, pedicellate in axillary or lateral racemes, the males slender and often several together on a common rhachis, the females solitary ; fruit a capsule, depressed-globular, 2- or 3-celled, 3 or 4 lines diameter. Habitat, brush forests of the coast districts, from Illawarra to the Clarence River.

Qualities of *timber* unknown.

(Under the name of *Cœlebogyne ilicifolia*, the above tree has been the subject of numerous papers by English and Continental *savans*, having reproduced itself from seed in European gardens through several generations from female plants alone, without the intervention of any male flowers.)

X. ALPHITONIA.

(Natural Order RHAMNEÆ.)

39. A. EXCELSA.—*Red Ash*; *Leatherjacket.* A fine large tree, attaining a height of 100 feet, the young branches, petioles and inflorescence hoary or rusty with a close tomentum ; leaves alternate, petiolate, varying from broadly ovate or almost orbicular and very obtuse to ovate or lanceolate and acute or acuminate, usually 3 to 6 inches long, entire, coriaceous, glabrous or slightly hoary above, white or rarely rust-coloured underneath with a close tomentum, the parallel pinnate veins very prominent ; flowers 2 to 3 lines in diameter, in umbel-like cymes or dichotomous in the upper axils or in a terminal corymbose panicle ; fruit a drupe, 3 to 4 lines in diameter. Habitat, brush forests of the coast districts, from Illawarra to the Clarence River.

Timber hard, firm, and close-grained ; used for a variety of purposes.

XI. ALSOPHILA.

(Natural Order FILICES.)

40 A. AUSTRALIS.—A large tree fern, with a trunk attaining from 10 to 70 feet in height, slender or stout, covered with the bases of old fronds ; fronds 5 to 12 feet long, twice or thrice pinnate, the secondary pinnæ 3 to 4 inches long ; sori globular without indusium ; spore-cases numerous, sessile or nearly so. Habitat, valley of the Grose River, and shaded and permanently damp ravines in the brush forests from Illawarra to the Richmond River, also in New England.

Valuable as an article of export to Europe, where it is cultivated for ornamental purposes.

41. A. LEICHHARDTIANA.—A large tree fern, not easily distinguished from *A. australis*, but the trunk is generally more slender, and the fronds of a more elegant aspect ; sori small, close to the mid-rib ; base of the stipes covered with long brown setaceous hairs. (Synonym : *A. Macarthurii.*) Habitat, brush forests from Illawarra to the Tweed River ; also, Blue Mountains and New England.

Exported to Europe, where it is much in demand for ornamental purposes.

42. A. LODDIGESII.—A large tree fern, the fronds shorter than in *A. australis* ; secondary pinnæ 2 to 3 inches long, deeply pinnatifid ; sori rather small. Habitat, brush forests, Richmond and Tweed Rivers.

Exported to Europe, where it is valued for ornamental purposes.

XII. ALSTONIA.

(Natural Order APOCYNEÆ.)

43. A. CONSTRICTA.—*Bitterbark ; Feverbark.*—A tree attaining 40 feet in height, quite glabrous, with a milky juice and a bark of intensely bitter taste, similar to quinine ; leaves opposite, on long petioles, mostly oblong-falcate, but varying from almost ovate to narrow-lanceolate, acute or acuminate, 3 to 5 inches long ; flowers numerous, in corymbose cymes ; the fruit consisting of a double follicle, from 3 to 4 inches long, sometimes twice that length, dehiscent. Habitat, scrub forests, Hastings and Clarence Rivers ; also on the Darling.

Qualities of *timber* unknown. A decoction of the bark is sometimes sold as bitters.

XIII. AMOORA.

(Natural Order MELIACEÆ.)

44. A. NITIDULA.—A fine tall tree, quite glabrous ; leaves alternate or rarely opposite, pinnate, leaflets 2 to 4, opposite, without a terminal odd one, elliptical-oblong, 3 to 4 inches long or more, obtuse or acuminate, coriaceous and shining, narrowed at the base, the common petiole slightly dilated towards the end ; flowers small in loose axillary panicles ; fruit a capsule, obovoid, hard and woody. Habitat, brush forests, Clarence and Richmond Rivers.

Qualities of *timber* unknown.

XIV. ANGOPHORA.

(Natural Order MYRTACEÆ.)

45. A. CORDIFOLIA.—*Apple-tree.*—A small tree, more or less pubescent or glaucous, the older bark smooth and falling off in layers or large flakes ; leaves opposite or here and there alternate, ovate or oblong, deeply cordate, 2 to 4 inches long, glabrous and shining above, glaucous or pubescent underneath ; flowers large, umbels forming a dense terminal corymb ; fruit a capsule, enclosed in and adnate to the hard and persistent calyx-tube, about ¾ inch in diameter at the top.—Habitat, open forests, Port Jackson.

Timber hard and heavy, but seldom used.

46. A. INTERMEDIA.—*Apple-tree.*—A tree attaining a height of 80 feet and a diameter of 36 inches, with a rough persistent bark, quite glabrous, or slightly pubescent or rarely with a few bristles on the inflorescence ; leaves opposite or here and there alternate, petiolate, lanceolate or sometimes ovate-lanceolate, acutely acuminate, 2 to 4 inches long or more ; flowers rather small, in loose

corymbs or trichotomous panicles ; fruit a capsule, enclosed in and adnate to the persistent calyx-tube, 3 to 4 lines in diameter and about as long. Habitat, open forests, from Twofold Bay to the Clarence, westward to Bathurst and New England.

Timber strong and heavy, but subject to the defect of "gum-veins"; used by wheelwrights for naves, and sometimes for slabs, rough buildings, and firewood.

47. A. LANCEOLATA.—*Apple-tree; Red Gum.*—A tree of considerable size, with a rough persistent fibrous bark, glabrous or slightly pubescent ; leaves opposite or here and there alternate, lanceolate, acuminate, 2 to 4 inches long ; flowers small, in loose corymbs or trichotomous panicles ; fruit a capsule, enclosed in and adnate to the calyx-tube, usually thick and very smooth. Habitat, open forests, Port Jackson and Grose River, northwards to the Clarence and New England, southwards to Twofold Bay.

Timber similar to that of the preceding species.

48. A. SUBVELUTINA.—*Apple-tree.*—A large wide-spreading tree, with a rough persistent bark, the foliage and young shoots glaucous or minutely pubescent, with often a few bristles on the flowering branches and inflorescence ; leaves opposite or here and there alternate, sessile or nearly so, ovate or ovate-lanceolate, mostly acute, cordate at the base, with rounded auricles, 2 to 4 inches long; flowers small, in loose corymbs or trichotomous panicles ; fruit a capsule, enclosed in and adnate to the persistent calyx-tube, 3 to 4 lines in diameter. Habitat, open forests, from Illawarra to the Tweed, westward to Bathurst and throughout the interior.

Timber strong, heavy, and very durable, but subject to "gum-veins"; used by wheelwrights for naves, and also for other purposes.

XV. ANOPTERUS.

(Natural Order SAXIFRAGEÆ.)

49. A. MACLEAYANUS.—A handsome tree, attaining sometimes 40 feet in height ; leaves alternate, chiefly at the end of the branches, from elliptical-lanceolate to almost obovate, but usually narrow, shortly acuminate, mostly 4 to 8 inches long, obtusely or callously serrate, narrowed into a very short petiole, coriaceous and shining, penniveined ; flowers in racemes. 3 to 6 inches long, somewhat drooping ; fruit a capsule, oblong-conical, from 1 to 1½ inch long. Habitat, brush forests, Hastings and Clarence Rivers.

Qualities of *timber* unknown.

XVI. APHANANTHE.

(Natural Order URTICEÆ.)

50. A. PHILIPPINENSIS.—*Elm ; Tulipwood.*—A tree sometimes attaining a height of 80 feet, glabrous or scabrous-pubescent ; leaves alternate, shortly petiolate, from broadly ovate to elliptical, acute or almost obtuse, rigidly membraneous or coriaceous, scabrous, penniveined, 1 to 2 inches long ; flowers in cymes, the males almost sessile, but loose ; fruit a drupe, ovoid, acuminate, about 3 lines long, the endocarp crustaceous. Habitat, brush forests, Clarence and Richmond Rivers.

Timber elastic and tough, but little used.

XVII. APHANOPETALUM.

(Natural Order SAXIFRAGEÆ.)

51. A. RESINOSUM.—*White Myrtle; Blue Ash.*—A tree sometimes of great beauty and attaining a height of 120 feet, sometimes a tall straggling or climbing shrub, quite glabrous, the smaller branches scabrous with raised dots said to be resinous ; leaves opposite, simple, ovate, lanceolate or elliptical, obtuse or scarcely acuminate, obtusely serrate, 1½ to 3 inches long, on petioles, coriaceous, smooth and shining ; flowers in axillary peduncles, or the inflorescence developed into a short dense more or less leafy panicle ; fruit small, acid, hard and indehiscent. Habitat, brush forests, from Twofold Bay to the Macleay River.

Timber close-grained and easily wrought ; likely to be useful.

XVIII. ARAUCARIA.

(Natural Order CONIFERÆ.)

52. A. CUNNINGHAMII.—*Moreton Bay Pine ; Colonial Pine ; Hoop Pine.*—A noble tree with a pyramidal or somewhat flattened head, attaining sometimes 200 feet in height and 5 feet in diameter, but sometimes much smaller ; leaves crowded in dense spires, rigidly acicular and very acute ; male amenta sessile, cylindrical, dense, 2 to 3 inches long and 3 to 4 lines in diameter ; fruit-cones ovoid, about 3 inches long and 2 inches diameter. Habitat, brush and open forests, Clarence, Richmond, and Tweed Rivers.

Timber valuable, white, light, easily wrought, and durable ; much used for cabinet-work and interior fittings, that grown inland or on the mountains being the strongest.

C

XIX. ARDISIA.

(Natural Order MYRSINEÆ.)

53. A. PSEUDOJAMBOSA.—A tree attaining a height of about 30 feet, quite glabrous ; leaves alternate, obovate-oblong, acuminate, narrowed into a petiole, entire or sinuate, pinnately veined, 3 to 5 inches long ; flowers small, pedicellate in umbels, several in a terminal panicle, sometimes sessile, sometimes pedunculate, longer, looser, and with divaricate branches ; fruit a drupe, globular, about 4 lines diameter. Habitat, brush forests on the Richmond River.

Qualities of *timber* unknown.

XX. AVICENNIA.

(Natural Order VERBENACEÆ.)

54. A. OFFICINALIS.—*Mangrove.*—An erect low-branching tree, varying much in height, but sometimes attaining from 30 to 40 feet, the branches, inflorescence and underside of the leaves white or silvery with a very close tomentum, more silky on the flowers, the upper side of the leaves usually glabrous when full-grown, black and shining when dry ; leaves opposite, undivided, coriaceous, usually lanceolate, acute, 2 to 3 inches long ; flowers in cymes on peduncles in the upper axils or in a small terminal thyrsus. Habitat, saltwater estuaries all along the coast.

Timber valuable for stonemasons' mallets on account of its inlocked and tenacious fibre.

XXI. BACKHOUSIA.

(Natural Order MYRTACEÆ.)

55. B. MYRTIFOLIA.—*Native Myrtle.*—A tree attaining a height of 40 feet, the young shoots and the underside of the leaves as well as the inflorescence more or less pubescent or softly hirsute, the older foliage glabrous ; leaves opposite, ovate, acutely acuminate, penniveined, 1 to 2 inches long ; flowers white, in small cymes, sometimes forming leavy panicles ; fruit a capsule, enclosed in the persistent calyx-tube, but not seen ripe. Habitat, brush forests, from Port Jackson to the Tweed River.

Timber close-grained, soft to the touch, and easily wrought.

XXII. BALOGHIA.

(Natural Order EUPHORBIACEÆ.)

56. B. LUCIDA.—*Brush Bloodwood ; Roger Gough.*—A tree attaining a height of 80 feet, and a diameter of 18 inches, perfectly glabrous ; leaves opposite, oblong or elliptical, obtuse or acuminate, rigidly coriaceous, veined and shining ; flowers large,

few together in short loose sessile terminal racemes; fruit a capsule, globular, hard, $\frac{1}{2}$ to $\frac{3}{4}$ inch diameter. Habitat, brush forests, from Illawarra to the Tweed River.

Timber soft but close-grained; much liked for many purposes; burns freely when green, and seems to contain an oily secretion.

XXIII. BANKSIA.

(Natural Order PROTEACEÆ. Sub-Order *Folliculares*.)

57. B. COCCINEA.—*Honeysuckle.*—A small, erect, and beautiful tree, attaining a height of 20 feet, the branches densely tomentose; leaves alternate, sessile or shortly petiolate, broadly oblong or orbicular, often cordate at the base, bordered by small irregular prickly teeth, $1\frac{1}{2}$ to $2\frac{1}{2}$ inches long. flat, rigid, penniveined and reticulate underneath; flowers in globular spikes about 2 inches diameter; fruiting cone after the fall of the perianths ovoid, 1 to $1\frac{1}{2}$ inch diameter, tomentose-villous. Habitat, scrub forests of southern districts (Sir William Macarthur).

Qualities of *timber* unknown.

58. B. INTEGRIFOLIA.—*Honeysuckle.*—A tree sometimes of considerable size but low-branching, the young shoots closely tomentose; leaves scattered, sometimes irregularly verticillate, oblong, cuneate or lanceolate, entire or irregularly toothed, tapering into a short petiole, 3 to 4 inches long, sometimes twice that length, $\frac{1}{2}$ to 1 inch broad, white underneath; flowers in oblong and cylindrical spikes, 3 to 6 inches long; fruiting cone oblong, cylindrical. Habitat, scrub forests, from Twofold Bay to the Richmond River; also New England.

Timber close-grained and strong; used for ribs and knees in boat-building.

59. B. SERRATA.—*Honeysuckle.*—A low-branching tree, often of crooked growth, attaining a height of 30 feet and a diameter of 24 inches, the young shoots tomentose or villous; leaves alternate, oblong-lanceolate, acute or truncate, regularly and deeply serrate, tapering into a petiole, 3 to 6 inches long, $\frac{1}{2}$ to 1 inch broad, coriaceous, flat, hoary or white underneath; flowers in oblong-cylindrical or rarely globular spikes, 3 to 6 inches long, very thick; capsules very prominent, tomentose, thick and hard, above 1 inch broad. Habitat, scrub forests, from Illawarra to the Tweed River.

Timber very handsome, close-grained and strong; used for gun-stocks and ribs of boats, &c.

XXIV. BOSISTOA.

(Natural Order RUTACEÆ.)

60. B. SAPINDIFORMIS.—*Union Nut.*—A small tree with the habit of a *Cupania*, the young shoots, petioles, and inflorescence, pubescent; leaves opposite, pinnate, leaflets 7 to 11, opposite in pairs, the terminal odd one sometimes wanting, oblong-lanceolate, 4 to 8 inches long, more or less serrate-toothed, narrowed at the base, shortly petiolate or nearly sessile; flowers in terminal trichotomous panicles, shorter than the leaves; fruit separating into distinct cocci, large, coriaceous, 2-valved. Habitat, brush forests, Richmond and Tweed Rivers.

Timber close-grained, beautifully marked, and easily wrought; very suitable for cabinet-making.

XXV. BRIEDELIA.

(Natural Order EUPHORBIACEÆ.)

61. B. EXALTATA.—A tree attaining a height of 70 feet, perfectly glabrous; leaves alternate, petiolate, ovate-lanceolate, acute or obtuse, with numerous veins, 2 to 4 inches long, glaucous underneath; flowers monœcious, small, few together, and almost sessile in axillary clusters; fruit a berry, black, globular, rather large. Habitat, brush forests, Clarence, Richmond, and Tweed Rivers.

Qualities of *timber* unknown.

XXVI. BURSARIA.

(Natural Order PITTOSPOREÆ.)

62. B. SPINOSA.—A tree attaining a height of 40 feet, but often shrubby, generally glabrous and, when young, very bushy, the smaller branches often reduced to short subulate thorns; leaves very variable, most frequently clustered, obovate, oblong or cuneate, obtuse, truncate or notched, ½ to 1 inch long, narrowed at the base, sometimes petiolate, green on both sides, but sometimes oblong-lanceolate, and 1 to 2 inches long, rarely with a few coarse teeth at the top; flowers white, usually numerous, in broad pyramidal terminal panicles, arranged along the branches in short racemes on pedicels of 1 to 3 lines, but occasionally the panicles are reduced to short racemes, or to 1 or 2 terminal flowers; fruit a capsule, 3 to 4 lines broad. Habitat, open and scrub forests, especially in the interior.

Timber close-grained, but seldom used.

Var. incana.—Young shoots, inflorescence and underside of leaves white or hoary with tomentum; leaves sometimes 2 to 3 inches long; flowers and fruit larger than in the normal type. Habitat, Snowy River, Murray Desert, and Lachlan River.

XXVII. CADELLIA.

(Natural Order SIMARUBEÆ.)

63. C. PENTASTYLIS.—A tree attaining 40 feet in height, with a bitter bark, the smaller branches very slender and minutely pubescent ; leaves alternate, from obovate-oblong to elliptical or lanceolate, obtuse, 1½ to 2 inches long, entire, petiolate, glabrous, penniveined and reticulate, without any dots ; flowers small in pedunculate slender racemes in the upper axils ; fruit a drupe, nearly globular, about 1½ line diameter, with a crustaceous endocarp. Habitat, Severn River, near Tenterfield, New England. Qualities of *timber* unknown.

XXVIII. CALLICOMA.

(Natural Order SAXIFRAGEÆ)

64. C. SERRATIFOLIA.—*Black Wattle* (of the early colonists), *Native Beech.* A slender-growing tree attaining a height of 70 feet, the young shoots often tomentose or villous, the branches soon glabrous ; leaves opposite, simple, from elliptical-oblong to ovate-lanceolate, acuminate, serrate, 2 to 4 inches long, coriaceous, glabrous and shining above, white or softly tomentose or villous and rust-coloured underneath ; flowers small, numerous, in dense globular heads on peduncles of ½ to 1 inch long ; fruit a capsule, small, tomentose or villous, separating into distinct carpels. Habitat, brush forests, Port Jackson to the Blue Mountains, Hastings River, and New England.

Timber close-grained, elastic, and easily split ; used for making baskets.

XXIX. CALLISTEMON.

(Natural Order, MYRTACEÆ.)

65. C. BRACHYANDRUS.—*Tea-tree.*—A small tree, often stiff and bushy, the young shoots softly hairy ; leaves scattered, linear-subulate, terete and channelled above, rigid and pungent-pointed, ¾ to 1½ inch long ; flowers in loose and interrupted spikes, sometimes dense, rarely 2 inches long, the rhachis and calyxes loosely hairy ; fruit a capsule, enclosed in and more or less adnate to the fruiting-calyx. Habitat, open and scrub forests, from the Darling River to the Barrier Range.

Timber hard and close-grained.

66. C. LANCEOLATUS.—*Water Gum.*—A small tree, sometimes low and bushy, the young shoots silky, the inflorescence pubescent or glabrous ; leaves scattered, lanceolate, variable in width, usually acute, 1 to 3 inches long, rather rigid and more or less distinctly

penniveined ; flowers showy, in spikes 2 to 4 inches long, not very dense ; fruit a capsule, enclosed in and more or less adnate to the truncate fruiting-calyx. Habitat, Port Jackson to the Blue Mountains, northward to the Clarence River, southward to Bargo.

Timber very tough and strong; used for boats' knees, axe and chisel handles ; shavings will bind like a ribbon.

67. C. LINEARIS.—*Tea-tree.*—A small tree, very similar to *C. rigidus,* but differing in the leaves being all much narrower or quite linear, 2 to 5 inches long, concave or almost flat, obtuse or acute ; flowers large, the rhachis of the spikes usually pubescent or villous; fruiting-calyx globular, about 4 lines diameter, enclosing the capsule. Habitat, Port Jackson to the Blue Mountains.

Timber hard and tough.

68. C. PINIFOLIUS.—*Tea-tree.*—A small tree, usually quite glabrous ; leaves scattered, linear-subulate, terete, more or less channelled above, rigid, obtuse, acute or pungent-pointed, 2 to 4 inches long ; flowers rather large, similar to those of *C. lanceolatus* except in colour. Habitat, Port Jackson and Hunter River.

Timber similar to that of the last species.

69. C. RIGIDUS.—*Tea-tree.*—A small tree attaining a height of about 30 feet, and similar to *C. lanceolatus* in habit and inflorescence; leaves scattered, linear or very narrowly linear-lanceolate, flat, rigid, acute and almost pungent-pointed, penniveined, 2 to 5 inches long, rarely above 2 lines wide ; flowers in dense spikes, rather showy ; fruit a capsule, enclosed in and more or less adnate to the truncate fruiting-calyx. Habitat, Lane Cove River.

Timber scarcely to be distinguished from that of the two preceding species.

70. C. SALIGNUS.—*Broad-leaved Tea-tree* ; *White Water Gum* ; *River Tea-tree.*—A small tree, attaining a height of 40 feet and a diameter of 20 inches, the young shoots silky and the infloresence usually pubescent, but sometimes glabrous ; leaves scattered, lanceolate, variable in breadth, acute, 1 to 3 inches long, rather rigid ; flowers showy, in cylindrical spikes, 2 to 4 inches long, not very dense ; fruit a capsule, enclosed in and more or less adnate to the truncate fruiting-calyx. Habitat, open forests, from Illawarra to the Tweed River.

Timber very close-grained and durable, even underground, but apt to split if carelessly seasoned ; used for fencing-posts and sleepers ; also for wood engraving.

Var. angustifolia.—Leaves linear-lanceolate, very rigid, almost pungent, 1 to 2 inches long ; the flowers glabrous. Habitat, New England and north-west interior.

Var. Sieberi.—Leaves almost linear, crowded, $\frac{1}{2}$ to $\frac{3}{4}$ inch long ; the flowers small, in short spikes. Habitat, Shoalhaven.

XXX. CAPPARIS.

(Natural Order CAPPARIDEÆ.)

71. C. MITCHELLI.—*Native Pomegranate ; Native Lemon.*—A much-branched small tree, more or less clothed with a minute yellowish or whitish tomentum, sometimes disappearing on the old leaves, and with short prickly stipules; leaves alternate or rarely opposite, petiolate, ovate or oblong, obtuse, 1 to 1½ inch long, coriaceous ; flowers rather few, pedicellate in the axils ; fruit a berry, globular, about 2 inches in diameter when ripe. Habitat, Liverpool Plains, Bogan and Darling Rivers.

Qualities of *timber* unknown.

72. C. NOBILIS.—*Mock Orange.*—A small or dwarf tree, perfectly glabrous or the young shoots and underside of the leaves slightly pubescent, with short conical stipulary prickles ; leaves alternate or very rarely opposite, simple, ovate-oblong or oblong, acute, acuminate or obtuse, 2 to 4 inches long, coriaceous and often shining above, on petioles of 3 to 6 lines ; flowers on solitary pedicels in the upper axils or rarely two together, about 1 inch long; fruit a berry, globular, about 1 inch diameter, with a small protuberance at the top. Habitat, brush forests, Hastings, Clarence, Richmond, and Tweed Rivers.

Timber close-grained and hard, quite yellow when fresh.

XXXI. CARGILLIA.

(Natural Order EBENACEÆ).

73. C. AUSTRALIS.—*Black Plum ; Illawarra Plum.*—An erect slender tree, attaining a height of 40 feet and a diameter of 15 inches, glabrous or the young parts mealy-pubescent ; leaves alternate, entire, without stipules, from oblong to oval-elliptical, obtuse, narrowed into a short petiole, coriaceous, penniveined and reticulate, 1½ to 3 inches long; flowers solitary or several together, in little axillary clusters or dense cymes ; fruit a berry, globular, eaten by the aborigines. Habitat, brush forests, Port Jackson to the Blue Mountains, Hastings and Macleay Rivers, Berrima and Illawarra.

Timber close-grained and hard, but apt to get discoloured and to rend in seasoning.

74. C. PENTAMERA.—*Black Myrtle ; Grey Plum.*—A tree attaining a height of 100 feet and a diameter of 3 feet, glabrous or the young shoots slightly silky ; leaves alternate, oblong-lanceolate or elliptical, acuminate, contracted into a short petiole, coriaceous, shining and reticulate above, opaque and less veined underneath,

1½ to 2½ inches long ; male flowers in pedunculate clusters of 3 to 5 ; fruit a berry, globular, about ½ inch diameter, eaten by the aborigines. Habitat, brush forests, Illawarra, Clarence, Richmond, and Tweed Rivers.

Timber soft when fresh, but exceedingly tough and strong, said to be durable.

XXXII. CARISSA.

(Natural Order APOCYNEÆ).

75. C. OVATA.—An erect, much-branched, small tree, quite glabrous, or the young shoots rarely pubescent, more or less armed with opposite axillary spines ; leaves opposite, ovate, rhomboidal or almost orbicular, obtuse or acute, coriaceous, usually ½ to ¾ inch long, sometimes 3 inches ; flowers in small compact sessile or pedunculate axillary cymes ; fruit ovoid, ½ to ¾ inch long. Habitat, mountain brushes, Clarence River.

Timber close-grained and finely veined.

XXXIII. CASTANOSPERMUM.

(Natural Order LEGUMINOSÆ. Sub-Order *Papilionaceæ*.)

76. C. AUSTRALE —*Moreton Bay Chestnut* ; *Bean Tree.*—A beautiful tree, attaining a height of 130 feet and a diameter of 5 feet, quite glabrous ; leaves alternate or opposite, large, unequally pinnate, 1 to 1½ foot long, leaflets 11 to 15, ovate-elliptical or broadly oblong, 3 to 5 inches long ; flowers large, yellow, in loose axillary or lateral racemes ; pod 8 or 9 inches long, 2 inches broad, falcate, terete, containing 3 to 5 large chestnut-like seeds, eaten when roasted by the aborigines. Habitat, brush forests, Clarence, Richmond, and Tweed Rivers.

Timber very handsome, dark and veined, not unlike walnut ; suitable for cabinet work, but hitherto seldom used except for staves.

XXXIV. CASUARINA.

(Natural Order CASUARINEÆ.)

77. C. CUNNINGHAMIANA.—*Belah* ; *Scrub She Oak.*—A tall tree, with slender leafless branches, closely resembling *C. equisetifolia* and *C. suberosa* in aspect and number of parts of the whorls, but the fruiting-cones much smaller, about 4 lines in diameter, globular, regular and glabrous. Habitat, open and scrub forests, from Twofold Bay to the Hastings River, and from the Darling to the Barrier Range.

Timber light, tough, and strong ; used for shingles and staves.

78. C. DISTYLA.—*Oak.*—A small tree, with leafless glabrous or pubescent branches, erect or spreading, whorls usually heptamerous, but the parts varying from 6 to 8; flowers diœcious, male spikes on deciduous branchlets of 1 to 3 inches, or almost sessile on the persistent branches, 1 to 2 inches long, more or less moniliform; fruit-cones sessile or nearly so, oblong, ½ to 1 inch long. Habitat, open forests, Port Jackson to the Blue Mountains, and Lachlan River.

Timber similar to that of the last species.

Var. paludosa.—*Swamp Oak.*—More shrubby, the branchlets more slender; male spikes ½ to 1 inch long, and the cones ½ to ¾ inch long. Habitat, Hunter River, Port Jackson, Blue Mountains, Argyle, Twofold Bay.

79. C. EQUISETIFOLIA, *Var. incana.*—*Bull Oak; Forest Oak.*— A large tree with leafless branches, the principal ones elongated and spreading or ascending, the smaller ones often pendulous, the young shoots very tomentose, the whorls usually heptamerous but the parts varying from 6 to 8; flowers diœcious, the male spikes about ¾ inch long, terminating slender deciduous branchlets; fruit-cones shortly pedunculate on the persistent branches, globular, about ½ inch diameter. Habitat, Port Macquarie and Lachlan River.

Timber used for shingles, staves, and veneers for cabinet-making.

80. C. GLAUCA.—*Belah; Bull Oak; River She Oak.*—A tree of considerable size, with leafless robust branches, the branchlets usually pendulous, the whorls usually 10 to 12 merous, but the parts varying from 9 to 16; flowers diœcious, the male spikes rather dense, ½ to 1 inch long; fruit-cones usually subglobose, flat-topped, about ½ inch diameter. Habitat, open forests, Port Jackson to the Blue Mountains, Liverpool Plains, New England, Lachlan and Darling Rivers, and towards the Barrier Range.

Timber tough and strong; used for shingles and staves, &c.

81. C. NANA.—*Dwarf Oak.*—A densely-branched small and scrubby tree, the branchlets short, slender, and terete, the whorls usually pentamerous, but varying from 4 to 6; flowers diœcious, the male spikes slender, compact, ¼ to ½ inch long, fruit-cones sessile, from globular and 4 lines diameter to oblong-cylindrical and ¾ inch long, glabrous or slightly hispid. Habitat, rocky hills, Blue Mountains.

Timber tough and strong, but seldom used.

82. C. STRICTA.—*Oak; Forest Swamp Oak.*—A tree sometimes of considerable size, sometimes reduced to a tall dense shrub, with leafless robust branches, the branchlets usually if not always pendulous, in whorls of 9 to 12 parts, the internodes ½ inch long or more, the ribs prominent, the sheath-teeth acute or acuminate; flowers diœcious, in spikes, sometimes terminating deciduous branchlets of several inches, sometimes almost sessile on the

permanent branch, often more than 2 inches long; fruit-cones globular or ovoid, often 1 inch in diameter or more. Habitat, open forests, Lachlan River and Twofold Bay.

Timber strong, durable, and easily wrought; used for shingles, staves, &c.

83. C. SUBEROSA.—*Swamp Oak ; Black Oak ; Shingle Oak.*—A tree attaining a height of 50 feet and a diameter of 24 inches, with leafless branches, the principal ones elongated and spreading or ascending, seldom if ever corky, the smaller ones often pendulous, usually slender and quite glabrous, the whorls heptamerous or the parts varying from 6 to 8; flowers often monœcious, the males in spikes, slender and interrupted; fruit-cones ovoid or oblong, truncate at both ends. Habitat, Port Jackson, Argyle, Hastings, Macleay, Clarence, and Richmond Rivers, and New England.

Timber handsome, strong and durable ; largely used for shingles, staves, and cabinet work; very useful for veneers.

84. C. TORULOSA.—*Forest Oak; Beefwood; River Oak.*—A tree attaining a height of 80 feet, and a diameter of 2 feet, but some-times much smaller, with leafless branches, the branchlets very slender, the whorls tetramerous or rarely pentamerous, the sheath-teeth very short; flowers diœcious or sometimes monœcious, the male spikes very slender, ½ to 1 inch long, terminating deciduous branchlets; fruit-cones nearly globular but flat-topped, about ¾ inch diameter. Habitat, open forests, from Illawarra to the Richmond River, westward to Bathurst and New England.

Timber handsome, sometimes remarkably heavy and of great strength ; valuable for cabinet work, shingles, &c.

XXXV. CEDRELA.

(Natural Order MELIACEÆ.)

85. C. TOONA.—*Red Cedar.*—A magnificent and most valuable timber tree, attaining a height of 150 feet and a diameter of 10 feet, quite glabrous or the young shoots pubescent; leaves alternate or very rarely opposite, large, pinnate, deciduous, leaflets 11 to 17, opposite or alternate, ovate-lanceolate, acuminate, 3 to 5 inches long, petiolulate, membraneous; flowers numerous, small, in large pyramidal panicles; fruit a capsule, glabrous, oblong, 1 to 1½ inch long, the seeds flattened and winged. Habitat, brush forests, from Shoalhaven to the Tweed River.

Timber very valuable, dark red, light, easily wrought, and durable; extensively used for furniture, cabinet-making, patterns, and all kinds of internal fittings in house and ship building; now to be obtained only from the northern rivers.

Var. parviflora.—Flowers smaller, the petals scarcely 2 lines long. Habitat, Clarence River.

XXXVI. CELASTRUS.

(Natural Order CELASTRINEÆ.)

86. C. CUNNINGHAMII.—A small tree, quite glabrous and somewhat glaucous; leaves alternate, linear or narrow-lanceolate, mucronate, from 1 to 3 inches long, entire, rigid, the mid-rib prominent underneath; flowers small, pedicellate in short loose axillary or lateral racemes, occasionally growing out into leafy branches; fruit a capsule, globular or ovoid, about 2 lines diameter and 2-valved. Habitat, brush forests, Port Jackson to the Clarence River; also New England, Blue Mountains, and open forests, Lachlan River.

Qualities of *timber* unknown.

XXXVII. CELTIS.

(Natural Order URTICEÆ.)

87. C. PANICULATA.—A large tree, quite glabrous; leaves alternate, from ovate-lanceolate to elliptical-oblong, acuminate, cuneate at the base and often slightly falcate, entire, coriaceous, smooth, penniveined and 3-nerved at the base; flowers in cymes, sometimes dense, sometimes loose and 1 inch broad; fruit a small drupe. Habitat, brush forests, from Illawarra to the Richmond River.

Qualities of *timber* unknown.

XXXVIII. CERATOPETALUM.

(Natural Order SAXIFRAGEÆ.)

88. C. APETALUM.—*Coachwood; Lightwood; Leatherjacket.*—A beautiful tree, with a cylindrical stem and shining silvery bark, attaining a height of 130 feet and a diameter of 3 feet; leaves opposite, digitate, leaflets usually solitary (occasionally three on luxuriant shoots or young trees) from ovate-lanceolate to narrow-lanceolate, 3 to 5 inches long, or nearly twice that size on luxuriant barren branches, serrate, coriaceous and shining, on a petiole of ½ to 1 inch long; flowers small, numerous, in dense corymbose cymes, sometimes pubescent; fruit small, hard and indehiscent. Habitat, brush forests, from Illawarra to the Hastings River.

Timber fragrant, soft, light, and tough, but close-grained; extensively used for coach-making, and also by joiners and cabinet-makers.

89. C. GUMMIFERUM.—*Christmas Bush; Lightwood; Officer Plant.*—A small tree, sometimes attaining a height of 40 feet and a diameter of 15 inches; leaves opposite, digitate, leaflets 3, lanceolate, sometimes under 1½ inch long, sometimes twice that

size, obtuse or acuminate, serrulate, narrowed at the base, coriaceous, shining, penniveined and reticulate; flowers small, in cymes or panicles loosely trichotomous, the common peduncle shorter or longer than the leaves; fruit small, of a brilliant red colour, hard and indehiscent. Habitat, scrub forests, Illawarra and Port Jackson to the Blue Mountains.

Timber close-grained, soft, and light, but seldom used, except with the foliage for decorative purposes.

XXXIX. CHRYSOPHYLLUM.
(Natural Order SAPOTACEÆ.)

90. C. PRUNIFERUM.—A small tree, the branches and under side of the leaves tomentose-villous with rust-coloured stellate hairs; leaves alternate, petiolate, ovate-elliptical or obovate-oblong, acuminate, penniveined, reticulate, glabrous above, 3 to 4 inches long or more; flowers small, closely sessile in axillary clusters; fruit a berry or drupe, about 1 inch diameter, the exocarp succulent, the endocarp crustaceous and veined. Habitat, brush forests, Bellinger River.

Qualities of *timber* unknown.

XL. CLAOXYLON.
(Natural Order EUPHORBIACEÆ.)

91. C. AUSTRALE.—A straggling tree of 25 to 30 feet, sometimes shrubby, the young shoots and inflorescence more or less pubescent, rarely quite glabrous; leaves alternate, oblong, broad or narrow, rarely ovate, obtuse or acuminate, dentate, tapering into a petiole, 3 to 6 inches long, green on both sides, or rarely reddish-purple underneath; flowers diœcious, small, pedicellate, the males few together in clusters, the females solitary, in axillary racemes, solitary or two together; fruit a capsule, nearly 3 lines diameter, usually pubescent. Habitat, brush forests, from Illawarra to the Clarence River; also Blue Mountains and New England.

Qualities of *timber* unknown.

Var. dentata.—Leaves coarsely and deeply toothed. Habitat, Macleay River.

Var. laxiflora.—Leaves long and narrow; racemes longer and looser. Habitat, Tweed River.

XLI. CLERODENDRON.
(Natural Order VERBENACEÆ.)

92. C. TOMENTOSUM.—A small tree attaining a height of 15 feet and a diameter of 6 inches, the foliage and inflorescence usually velvety-pubescent; leaves opposite or in whorls on rather long

petioles, ovate-elliptical or almost lanceolate, acuminate, acute or rounded at the base, 2 to 4 inches long ; flowers usually numerous, in compact terminal corymbs, or rarely axillary ; fruiting-calyx expanding to ¾ inch diameter, the drupe black and shining. Habitat, brush forests, from Illawarra to the Clarence River ; also Blue Mountains.

Qualities of *timber* unknown.

XLII. CODONOCARPUS.

(Natural Order PHYTOLACCACEÆ.)

93. C. AUSTRALIS.—A tree of 30 feet, with numerous slender flexuose branches ; leaves alternate, lanceolate, tapering into a petiole, 1½ to 3 inches long ; flowers in leafless racemes, axillary or terminal, or the females on the leafless bases of the year's shoots ; fruit pear-shaped, 7 to 8 lines long.   Habitat, Richmond River.

Qualities of *timber* unknown.

94. C. COTINIFOLIUS.—A remarkable denizen of the scrub forests and deserts of the far interior, sometimes attaining a height of 40 feet, of a pale or glaucous green ; leaves alternate, from broadly obovate or ovate to elliptical-oblong or lanceolate, obtuse or pointed, contracted into a petiole, 1 to 2 inches long ; flowers diœcious or monœcious but usually the two sexes in separate racemes in the upper axils, sometimes forming a terminal panicle, the males on short and the females on long pedicels ; fruit obconical or obovoid, about 5 lines diameter.   Habitat, scrub forests of the Lachlan and Darling Rivers, and deserts on the Murray.

Qualities of *timber* unknown.

XLIII. COMMERSONIA.

(Natural Order STERCULIACEÆ.)

95. C. ECHINATA.—*Brown Rurrajong.*—A small tree, with the young branches and inflorescence whitish-tomentose ; leaves alternate or irregularly opposite, ovate or cordate, acuminate, 3 to 6 inches long or more, irregularly toothed or nearly entire ; flowers small, numerous, in pedunculate cymes ; fruit a capsule, beset with soft pubescent setæ, 5-valved.   Habitat, brush forests on the Clarence River.

Timber soft and spongy, but the bark furnishes a strong fibre which is used by the aborigines for making kangaroo and fishing nets.

96. C. FRASERI.—*Brown Kurrajong.*—A small tree, with tomentose or hirsute branches ; leaves alternate or irregularly opposite, cordate-ovate, acuminate, 3 to 6 inches long, toothed,

oblique at the base, glabrous or pubescent above, white-tomentose or hirsute underneath, the lower ones in young plants broad and 3 or 5 lobed; flowers small, numerous, in loosely dichotomous cymes, terminal, leaf-opposed or axillary; fruit a capsule, large and densely beset with soft villous setæ. Habitat, brush forests, from Twofold Bay to the Macleay River.

Timber soft, brittle, and spongy. The fibre furnished by the bark is used by the aborigines for making dilly-bags and fishing-nets.

XLIV. CROTON.

(Natural Order EUPHORBIACEÆ.)

97. C. INSULARIS.—A small straggling tree, the branches, inflorescence, and underside of the leaves silvery-white or reddish with a close tomentum; leaves alternate or rarely opposite, ovate to lanceolate, obtuse, entire or sinuate, finely penniveined, green above, mostly 2 to 3 inches long, petiolate; flowers monœcious, on pedicels, clustered along the rhachis of a terminal raceme; fruit, a capsule, about 3 lines diameter. Habitat, Breakfast Creek, Blue Mountains.

Qualities of *timber* unknown.

98. C. PHEBALIOIDES.—A small tree, with slender weak and often pendulous branches, silvery-white as well as the inflorescence and the underside of the leaves with a close tomentum; leaves alternate or rarely opposite or almost verticillate immediately under the inflorescence, petiolate, lanceolate, obtuse or almost acute, entire or with small distant teeth, green above, 1½ to 3 inches long; flowers numerous, usually clustered along the rhachis of a terminal raceme, 1 to 3 inches long; fruit a capsule, 3 to 4 lines diameter, hirsute with stellate hairs, separating into three deciduous 2-valved cocci. Habitat, brush forests, Clarence and Richmond Rivers.

Qualities of *timber* unknown.

99. C. VERREAUXII.—*Cascarilla.*—A small tree, quite glabrous or the smaller branches and foliage sprinkled with stellate hairs; leaves alternate or rarely opposite, from ovate to oblong-elliptical or lanceolate, obtuse or acuminate, entire or dentate, green on both sides, 2 to 4 inches long, but occasionally twice that size, petiolate; flowers monœcious, clustered along the rhachis of a terminal raceme; fruit a capsule, nearly globular, variable in size, sprinkled with hairs or at length glabrous. Habitat, brush forests, from Illawarra to the Tweed; also Blue Mountains.

Qualities of *timber* unknown.

XLV. CRYPTOCARYA.

(Natural Order LAURINEÆ.)

100. C. GLAUCESCENS.—*Native Lurel; Sycamore; Whitewood.*—A noble tree, attaining a height of 120 feet and a diameter of 30 inches, the young branches pubescent, the older ones glabrous, the inflorescence hoary-pubescent; leaves alternate or rarely irregularly opposite, ovate, elliptical or oblong, obtuse or acuminate, contracted at the base, flat, penniveined and reticulate, green on both sides or somewhat glaucous, rarely more than 4 inches long on flowering specimens, but larger on luxuriant barren shoots; flowers small, numerous, pedunculate in thyrsoid panicles, the upper ones often forming a large terminal panicle; fruit a drupe, depressed globular, $\frac{1}{2}$ to $\frac{3}{4}$ inch diameter. Habitat, brush forests, from Illawarra to the Tweed River.

Timber fragrant when fresh, soft, easily wrought; said to be fairly durable, and useful for many purposes.

101. C. OBOVATA.—*Sycamore; Flindosa.*—A lofty but bushy-headed tree, attaining a height of 130 feet and a diameter of 5 feet, the young shoots and inflorescence tomentose and ferruginous; leaves alternate or rarely irregularly opposite, from oblong to ovate, obtuse, 2 to 4 inches long, sometimes larger and acuminate, thick, the margins often recurved, glabrous above, often glaucous or pubescent underneath when young, penniveined and reticulate; flowers small, numerous, in loose thyrsoid panicles, the upper ones forming a terminal panicle; fruit a drupe, globular, about $\frac{1}{2}$ inch diameter. Habitat, brush forests, from Illawarra to the Tweed River.

Timber, soft, white, useful for many purposes.

102. C. TRIPLINERVIS.—A tall handsome tree, about 80 feet in height and 30 inches in diameter; leaves alternate or rarely irregularly opposite, ovate-elliptical or oblong-lanceolate, acuminate, glabrous above, pubescent underneath, rarely more than 4 inches long, triplinerved or penniveined; flowers numerous, in dense short thyrsoid axillary panicles, hoary-pubescent or hirsute; fruiting perianth ovoid, about $\frac{1}{2}$ inch long. Habitat, brush forests, from Illawarra to the Richmond River.

Timber light and soft; much in request for decking small craft.

XLVI. CUDRANIA.

(Natural Order URTICEÆ.)

103. C. JAVANENSIS.—*Cockspur Thorn; Dyewood.*—A dwarf straggling tree, sometimes scandent and shrubby, nearly allied botanically to the famous "Upas-tree" (*Antiaris toxicaria*) of Java, glabrous except the inflorescence, and armed with straight or recurved axillary spines, about $\frac{1}{2}$ inch long; leaves alternate, petiolate, oblong

or elliptical, acute or acuminate, sometimes obtuse, entire, 1½ to 3 inches long, penniveined and reticulate ; flowers diœcious, in globular heads, solitary or two together on peduncles of one to three lines, intermixed with small bracts, the receptacle more or less fleshy ; fruit a syncarp, formed of the enlarged perianth and receptacle, the nuts free, the pericarp crustaceous.   Habitat, thin brush forests of the coast districts.

Timber yellow, the centre very hard ; used chiefly by dyers for dyeing yellow and brown.

XLVII. CUPANIA.

(Natural Order SAPINDACEÆ.)

104. C. ANACARDIOIDES.—A slender tree, sometimes attaining a height of 80 feet and a diameter of 2 feet, glabrous or with a minute hoariness on the inflorescence ; leaves alternate, pinnate, leaflets 6 to 10, alternate or opposite, from broadly ovate to elliptical-oblong, very obtuse, 2½ to 4 inches long, petiolulate, entire, coriaceous ; flowers rather large, in pedunculate cymes along the branches of loose axillary panicles ; fruit a capsule, glabrous, coriaceous, 3-lobed, 6 to 8 inches broad. Habitat, brush forests, from Port Jackson to the Richmond River.

Timber close-grained ; used occasionally in house carpentry.

105. C. PSEUDORHUS.—A spreading tree of moderate size, the young branches and petioles densely rusty-tomentose ; leaves alternate, pinnate, crowded under the panicles, leaflets 13 to 21 or more, alternate or opposite, lanceolate or ovate-lanceolate, acuminate, serrate, 1½ to 3 inches long, oblique or almost falcate, nearly glabrous and shining above, tomentose or pubescent underneath ; flowers small on short pedicels, in much-branched dense tomentose axillary or terminal panicles ; fruit a capsule, globular, slightly lobed, almost woody, densely hirsute, about ½ inch diameter.   Habitat, brush forests, from the Hastings to the Tweed River.

Timber close-grained and of a yellow colour ; hitherto not much used.

106. C. SEMIGLAUCA.—*Black Ash.*—A small tree, sometimes of very crooked growth ; leaves alternate, pinnate, leaflets 2 to 4 or 6, alternate or opposite, oblong-elliptical or from ovate to lanceolate, obtuse, acute or mucronate, 2 to 4 inches long, entire, petiolulate, coriaceous, glabrous and shining above, glaucous underneath ; flowers small, on short pedicels in panicles either small and axillary or terminal and much branched, glabrous or pubescent ; fruit a capsule, 4 to 5 lines in diameter, glabrous and lobed. Habitat, brush forests, from Kiama to the Clarence River ; also Blue Mountains.

Timber hard and compact.

107. C. SERRATA.—A very ornamental tree, flowering when still shrubby, the young branches rusty with a close tomentum ; leaves alternate, pinnate, leaflets 6 to 10, alternate or opposite, ovate-lanceolate or lanceolate, acute or acuminate, 3 to 6 inches long, serrate, nearly sessile, rigid, thin, shining above, penniveined and reticulate underneath ; flowers rather large, on short pedicels in panicles in the upper axils, little branched or almost reduced to dense racemes of 2 or 3 inches, tomentose or pubescent ; fruit a capsule, not seen. Habitat, brush forests, Clarence and Richmond Rivers.

Timber similar to that of the last species, but seldom used.

108. C. XYLOCARPA.—A large tree, the young branches rusty-tomentose ; leaves alternate, pinnate, leaflets 2 to 6 or rarely more, alternate or opposite, ovate, obovate or elliptical-oblong, obtuse or acuminate, 2 to 3 inches long or rarely more, slightly toothed or entire, glabrous and shining above, pubescent underneath or rarely almost glabrous, with hairy tufts in the axils of the primary veins ; flowers small, in short and little-branched axillary or terminal panicles, sometimes reduced to simple racemes, about 2 inches long, shortly tomentose ; fruit a capsule, nearly globular, triangular, about ½ inch broad, woody, glabrous or tomentose outside, the valves villous inside. Habitat, brush forests on the Clarence and Richmond Rivers.

Timber close-grained and hard.

XLVIII. CYATHEA.

(Natural Order FILICES.)

109. C. MEDULLARIS.—A large tree fern, the trunk sometimes attaining 50 feet in height, densely covered with matted fibres in the lower part, naked higher up with the scars of fallen fronds, and muricate at the top with the bases of old fronds ; fronds 10 to 20 feet long, twice or thrice pinnate, the rhachis and primary branches sprinkled with small tubercles, secondary pinnæ 4 to 6 inches long, with numerous pinnules, the lower ones distinct, 6 to 9 lines long, crenate or pinnatifid, the upper ones short and confluent into a pinnatifid point ; sori globular, one to each lobe of the pinnule ; indusium broad and short under the sorus, irregularly lobed ; sporecases numerous. Habitat, brush forests, Richmond River.

Valuable as an article of export to Europe, where it is cultivated for ornamental purposes.

D

XLIX. DAPHNANDRA.

(Natural Order MONIMIACEÆ.)

110. D. MICRANTHA.—*Satin-wood ; Light Yellow-wood.*—A remarkably handsome tree, attaining a height of 80 feet and a diameter of 3 feet, quite glabrous or the young inflorescence minutely hoary; leaves opposite, petiolate, oblong-lanceolate or elliptical, acuminate, serrate, green on both sides, 3 to 4 inches long; flowers rather few, in panicles; fruit (a drupe or nut) not seen. Habitat, brush forests, Clarence, Richmond, and Lansdowne Rivers.

Timber fragrant, quite yellow when fresh, taking a fine polish, and very suitable for cabinet-making.

L. DENHAMIA.

(Natural Order CELASTRINEÆ.)

111. D. PITTOSPOROIDES.—A tree of moderate size, with a beautifully striated bark ; leaves alternate, lanceolate or ovate-lanceolate, obtuse, 2 to 4 inches long, serrate, narrowed into a petiole, coriaceous, prominently veined and reticulate ; flowers small, rather few, in pedunculate cymes, on short leafless branches on the old wood or at the base of young leafy branches ; fruit a capsule, globular, about ½ inch diameter, opening in thick woody valves bearing the placentas in their centre. Habitat, brush forests, Clarence River.

Qualities of *timber* unknown.

LI. DICKSONIA.

(Natural Order FILICES.)

112. D. ANTARCTICA. —*Valley Tree Fern.*—A large tree fern, attaining a height of 50 feet, covered with matted rootlets, giving it a diameter sometimes of 4 feet ; fronds 6 to 12 feet long, twice or thrice pinnate, secondary pinnæ 2 to 3 inches long; sori solitary on each lobe ; indusium globular. Habitat, brush forests, Port Jackson to the Blue Mountains, northward to the Clarence River, and southward to Twofold Bay.

Valuable for ornamental purposes, and largely exported to Europe.

113. D. YOUNGIÆ.—A large arborescent fern, with the trunk from 10 to 30 feet in height and from 2 to 4 feet in diameter, marked by the bases of old fronds ; fronds large, compound, coriaceous, and glossy, the stipes covered with glossy brown hair, the rhachis ferruginous-pubescent or glabrous, secondary pinnæ 2 to 3 inches long, pinnules 3 to 6 inches long, deeply divided into

rounded lobes; indusium 1 line in diameter, the upper valve entirely adnate. Habitat, brush forests, Richmond and Tweed Rivers; also New England.

Exported to Europe, where it is cultivated for ornamental pur poses.

LII. DIOSPYROS.

(Natural Order EBENACEÆ.)

114. D. HEBECARPA.—*Native Ebony.*—A tree attaining a height of about 25 feet, the adult foliage and branches quite glabrous; leaves alternate, entire, broadly ovate to oval-oblong, obtuse or obtusely acuminate, reticulate, slightly coriaceous, contracted into a short petiole, 2 to 3 inches long; flowers axillary, the females often solitary, the males clustered or in small cymes; fruit a berry on a very short pedicel, ¾ to 1 inch diameter, covered with short hairs. Habitat, brush forests, Clarence River.

Timber soft, of a very dark colour when fresh, becoming lighter on exposure; hitherto not much used.

LIII. DIPLOGLOTTIS.

(Natural Order SAPINDACEÆ.)

115. D. CUNNINGHAMII.—*Native Tamarind.*—A remarkable tree, attaining a height of 80 feet, and a diameter of 3 feet, with habit and fruit similar to those of a *Cupania* and flowers like those of a *Paullinia*, the young branches, petioles and inflorescence densely clothed with a soft rust-coloured tomentum; leaves very large, sometimes exceeding 2 feet, alternate, pinnate, leaflets 8 to 12, opposite or irregularly alternate, oblong-elliptical to ovate-lanceolate, acute or obtuse, usually 6 to 8 inches long, but sometimes above 1 foot, glabrous above, pubescent underneath, with raised pinnate veins; flowers rather large, numerous, on pedicels of 1 to 2 lines, clustered along the branches of ample axillary panicles; fruit a capsule, ½ inch diameter, fleshy, tomentose, 3-valved, sub-acid and edible. Habitat, brush forests, from Illawarra to the Tweed River.

Timber whitish, rather coarse in the grain, but said to be fairly strong and durable. The fruit makes an excellent preserve.

LIV. DORYPHORA.

(Natural Order MONIMIACEÆ.)

116. D. SASSAFRAS.—*Sassafras*—A beautiful aromatic tree, attaining a height of 120 feet, and a diameter of 3 feet, often of irregular growth, glabrous except the inflorescence, or the young shoots hoary-tomentose; leaves opposite, petiolate, ovate-elliptical

or oblong-lanceolate, acuminate, toothed, 2 to 4 inches long, smooth above, penniveined and reticulate underneath; flowers 3 together on short axillary peduncles; fruit not seen. Habitat, brush forests, from Illawarra to the Clarence River; also Blue Mountains.

Timber highly fragrant, but soft and weak; occasionally used for indoor work and packing-cases. The bark contains a bitter principle which may be extracted by infusion and used as a simple tonic.

LV. DRIMYS.

(Natural Order MAGNOLIACEÆ.)

117. D. DIPETALA.—*Pepper Tree.*—A small ornamental tree; leaves alternate, entire, oblong-lanceolate or oval-oblong, acute or acuminate, 3 to 5 inches long, narrowed towards the base, but generally obtuse or minutely biauriculate at the very base, on a short broad petiole or almost sessile; flowers greenish yellow or white, rather large, on peduncles; fruit a berry, ovoid, succulent, about ½ inch long. Habitat, brush forests, from Illawarra to the Clarence River; also Mount Lindsay and various parts of the interior.

Qualities of *timber* unknown.

LVI. DUBOISIA.

(Natural Order SCROPHULARINEÆ.)

118. D. MYOPOROIDES.—*Corkwood.*—A small low-branching tree, attaining a height of 30 feet, and a diameter of 16 inches, with a rough cork-like bark, quite glabrous; leaves alternate, entire, from ovate-oblong to oblong-lanceolate, obtuse or rarely acute, contracted into a petiole, 2 to 4 inches long; flowers small, in terminal panicles, sometimes leafy at the base, much branched, pyramidal or corymbose; fruit an indehiscent berry, small, nearly globular. Habitat, brush forests, Port Jackson to the Blue Mountains, northward to the Richmond River, southward to Illawarra.

Timber white, close-grained and firm, but soft; excellent for wood-engraving and carving.

LVII. DYSOXYLON.

(Natural Order MELIACEÆ.)

119. D. FRASERANUM.—*Rosewood.*—A tree attaining a height of 130 feet, and a diameter of 4 feet, the young leaves and shoots pubescent, glabrous when old; leaves alternate or rarely opposite, pinnate, leaflets 5 to 9, oblong-lanceolate or elliptical, acuminate, 3 to 6 inches long, narrowed at the base, with occasionally tufts of

hair in the axils of the principal veins underneath ; flowers rather large, in axillary panicles, loose, divaricately branched, and slightly pubescent; fruit globular or pear-shaped (not seen). Habitat, brush forests, from Illawarra to the Tweed River.

Timber of a deep red colour, rose-scented ; very valuable for cabinet-making, wood-engraving, turning and carving ; also for all kinds of interior fittings in house and ship building.

120. D. LESSERTIANUM.—A tree attaining a height of 100 feet, and a diameter of 3 feet, quite glabrous or the young shoots and panicles minutely pubescent ; leaves alternate or rarely opposite, pinnate, leaflets 4 to 10, usually without a terminal odd one, elliptical or lanceolate, shortly acuminate, 4 to 5 inches long ; flowers rather large, in loose extra-axillary panicles, 3 to 4 inches long; fruit hard, obovoid, about ½ inch long. Habitat, brush forests, from the Hunter to the Tweed River.

Timber close-grained and easily worked, sometimes beautifully marked ; suitable for cabinet work, &c.

Var. pubescens.—Young shoots, petioles, underside of the leaflets, and the inflorescence softly pubescent. Habitat, Clarence River.

121. D. MUELLERI.—*Pencil Cedar ; Turnipwood.*—A large tree, attaining a height of 100 feet, and a diameter of 4 feet, glabrous or nearly so, except the very young shoots and inflorescence ; leaves alternate or rarely opposite, pinnate 1 to 2 feet long, leaflets 11 to 21, from ovate to almost lanceolate, acuminate, 3 to 6 inches long, oblique at the base, one side rounded, the other truncate and shorter, almost coriaceous ; flowers rather large, numerous, in pyramidal panicles, ¾ to 1 foot long, much-branched ; fruit not seen in a ripe state. Habitat, brush forests, Clarence, Richmond, and Tweed Rivers.

Timber of a red colour and easily wrought ; suitable for cigar-boxes, cabinet-making, and interior fittings in general ; when fresh it emits an odour similar to that of a Swedish turnip.

122. D. RUFUM.—*Bastard Pencil Cedar.*—A slender tree of 30 to 40 feet, the young branches, petioles, and underside of the leaves clothed with a soft often rust-coloured pubescence ; leaves alternate or rarely opposite, 1½ to 2 feet long, pinnate, leaflets numerous, petiolate, ovate-lanceolate or lanceolate, acuminate, 3 to 6 inches long, oblique at the base, glabrous above ; flowers sessile, in axillary or lateral pubescent panicles, not much branched ; fruit depressed-globular, 1 inch diameter, densely hirsute with short, rigid, almost golden hairs. Habitat, brush forests, from Port Macquarie to the Tweed River.

Timber similar to that of the preceding species, but inferior.

LVIII. ECHINOCARPUS.*

(Natural Order TILIACEÆ.)

123. E. AUSTRALIS.—*Maiden's Blush.*—A beautiful tree, sometimes attaining a height of 150 feet, the trunk frequently irregular, glabrous in all its parts ; leaves alternate or rarely opposite, ovate-oblong, $\frac{1}{2}$ to 1 foot long, acuminate, sinuate-toothed, obtuse or slightly cordate at the petiole, coriaceous ; flowers pendulous, on erect pedicels of 1 to 2 inches, the upper ones forming terminal racemes ; fruit a capsule, opening in four hard almost woody valves, about $\frac{1}{2}$ inch long, covered with short exceedingly dense setæ. Habitat, brush forests, from Illawarra to the Tweed River.

Timber of a delicate rosy tint, close-grained, but soft and easily wrought; likely to prove useful for many purposes.

* This genus includes the genus *Sloanea* of various authors.

LIX. EHRETIA.

(Natural Order BORAGINEÆ.)

124. E. ACUMINATA.—A deciduous tree of about 60 feet in height, quite glabrous except the inflorescence, which is slightly pubescent ; leaves alternate or rarely opposite, petiolate, oval or elliptical-oblong, obtusely acuminate, narrowed at the base, serrate, 3 to 6 inches long ; flowers rather small, usually white, sessile and crowded on the branchlets of dense thyrsoid panicles, terminal and in the upper axils ; fruit globular, 2 to 3 lines diameter, the endocarp separating into two hard 2-celled pyrenes. Habitat, Port Jackson, Emu Plains, and Blue Mountains.

Timber of a yellowish colour, soft, and seldom used.

Var. laxiflora.—Inflorescence much looser. Habitat, brush forests, from Illawarra to the Tweed River.

LX. ELÆOCARPUS.

(Natural Order TILIACEÆ.)

125. E. CYANEUS.—*Native Olive ; White Boree ; White-bark.*— A tree usually small, but sometimes attaining a height of 60 feet or more, glabrous in all its parts ; leaves alternate or rarely opposite, elliptical-oblong or oblong-lanceolate, acuminate, 3 to 4 inches long or more, serrate, acute at the base, coriaceous and reticulate; flowers rather small, in loose axillary racemes ; fruit a drupe, globular or ovoid, blue outside, the putamen 4 to 6 lines long, hard and rugose. Habitat, brush and scrub forests, from Twofold Bay northward to the Tweed River and Mount Lindsay. (Specimens growing at Illawarra are remarkable for their thick branches and leaves 6 to 8 inches long.)

Timber close-grained, but soft ; suitable for wood engraving and carving

126. E. GRANDIS.—*Blue Fig.*—A tall slender tree, glabrous except the young shoots, which are slightly silky-hairy ; leaves alternate or rarely opposite, on short petioles, oblong or lanceolate, obtuse or acuminate, 4 to 6 inches long, crenulate, narrowed at the base, scarcely coriaceous, the smaller veins not conspicuous ; flowers large, in short dense axillary racemes ; fruit a drupe, globular, about 1 inch diameter. Habitat, brush forests, Clarence and Richmond Rivers.

Timber close-grained and soft, but little used.

127. E. HOLOPETALUS.—*Blueberry Ash ; Prickly Fig.*—A beautiful tree, attaining a height of 80 feet, the young shoots rusty-tomentose or villous ; leaves alternate or rarely opposite, on very short petioles, oblong-lanceolate or slightly obovate, acute or acuminate, 2 to 4 inches long, sinuate-serrate, coriaceous, reticulate and glabrous above, loosely tomentose underneath or almost glabrous with age ; flowers in racemes in the upper axils, tomentose-villous, the pedicels rather long ; fruit a drupe, not seen. Habitat, brush forests, Wingecarribee, Hastings, Bellinger, Macleay, and Clarence Rivers ; also New England.

Timber close-grained and easily wrought; very suitable for joiners' work.

128. E. OBOVATUS.—*Ash ; Pigeon-berry Tree.*—A noble tree, attaining sometimes a height of 130 feet and a diameter of 5 feet, glabrous in all its parts ; leaves alternate or rarely opposite, from oval-elliptical to ovate-oblong or almost lanceolate, obtuse or acuminate, 2 to 4 inches long, sinuate-crenate, narrow at the base, thinly coriaceous, the smaller veins not very conspicuous ; flowers numerous, in axillary racemes, solitary or clustered ; fruit a drupe, globular or ovoid, often blue, the putamen rugose or tuberculate. Habitat, brush forests, from Illawarra to the Clarence River.

Timber light and tough ; extensively used for oars, &c.

(The above tree was formerly abundant on Ash Island, near Newcastle, to which it gave its name.)

LXI. ELÆODENDRON.

(Natural Order CELASTRINEÆ.)

129. E. AUSTRALE.—*Blue Ash.*—A slender-growing tree, about 35 feet in height and 10 inches in diameter; leaves opposite or here and there alternate, ovate, obovate, elliptical or oblong-lanceolate, obtuse or acuminate, 2 to 4 inches long, entire or broadly crenate, narrowed into a short petiole, coriaceous and reticulate ; flowers small, tetramerous, in slender dichotomous cymes, usually axillary

or lateral, often clustered ; fruit a drupe, ovoid or globular, about ½ inch long, of a bright red colour, the putamen hard and woody. Habitat, brush forests, from Illawarra to the Tweed River.

Timber close-grained and beautifully marked, but liable to split if carelessly seasoned.

LXII. ENDIANDRA.
(Natural Order LAURINEÆ.)

130. E. GLAUCA.—*Teakwood.*—A noble lofty tree, with a cylindrical stem and ample head, the young shoots and inflorescence ferruginous-tomentose ; leaves alternate, elliptical-oblong, acuminate, contracted at the base, 3 to 5 inches long, glabrous and green above, glaucous or white underneath, the primary veins sometimes ferruginous-tomentose; flowers in axillary thyrsoid panicles, rather loose and short ; fruit a berry, oblong or globular, resting on the persistent but not enlarged perianth. Habitat, brush forests, Brisbane Water.

Timber very fragrant, hard, close, and fine in the grain, the duramen dark-coloured and very handsome; said to be very valuable.

131. E. PUBENS.—A large tree, attaining a height of 100 feet, the branches and petioles velvety-tomentose and ferruginous ; leaves alternate, from oval to elliptical-oblong, acuminate or obtuse, narrowed at the base, 4 to 8 inches long, glabrous above, veined and pubescent or villous underneath ; flowers in axillary panicles, broadly thyrsoid, usually 1 inch long, ferruginous-hirsute ; fruit globular, ½ to ¾ inch diameter. Habitat, brush forests, Bellinger, Clarence, and Richmond Rivers.

Timber close-grained and easily wrought.

132. E. VIRENS.—*Native Pomegranate ; Native Orange ; Bat and Ball Tree.*—A tree sometimes attaining considerable size, glabrous in all its parts ; leaves alternate, oblong, usually narrow, rarely broader and elliptical, obtuse, contracted at the base, 2 to 3 inches long or twice that length, thin, green and reticulate on both sides, somewhat shining above; flowers small, in slender axillary panicles, glabrous, short, on rather long pedicels; fruit globular, ½ to ¾ inch diameter, resting on the thickened pedicel. Habitat, brush forests, Clarence and Richmond Rivers.

Qualities of *timber* unknown.

LXIII. EREMOPHILA.
(Natural Order MYOPORINEÆ.)

133. E. BIGNONIÆFLORA.—A strong-scented small tree, quite glabrous and often glutinous ; leaves alternate or scattered, lanceolate, acuminate, entire, narrowed into a petiole, 2 to 6 inches long ; flowers large, solitary, pedicellate in the axils ; fruit a drupe,

ovate, acute, ½ inch long or more, succulent, the putamen hard and bony, separating into four pyrenes.   Habitat, deserts and scrub forests, Murray and Darling Rivers.
Qualities of *timber* unknown.

134. E. LONGIFOLIA.—*Berrigan.*—A small erect-growing tree, the young shoots hoary-tomentose, the older foliage nearly glabrous; leaves scattered, linear or linear-lanceolate, obtuse or tapering into a recurved point, 2 to 5 inches long, contracted into a petiole; flowers large, solitary or two together on pedicels in the axils; fruit a drupe, ovoid or globular, succulent, with a hard putamen. Habitat, thickets, Liverpool Plains, Murray, Lachlan, and Darling Rivers, extending towards the Barrier Range.
Qualities of *timber* unknown.

135. E. MITCHELLI.—*Sandalwood ; Rosewood.*—A small tree, attaining a height of about 30 feet, glabrous, viscid, and strongly scented ; leaves alternate or scattered, linear-lanceolate, obtuse or with a hooked point, entire, narrowed into a petiole, one-nerved, 1 to 2 inches long; flowers large, pedicellate, solitary in the axils ; fruit a drupe, ovoid, almost acuminate, 2 to 3 inches long, the exocarp thin and membraneous, the endocarp separating into four pyrenes or nuts.   Habitat, scrub forests, Lachlan, Bogan, and Castlereagh Rivers.
Timber beautiful, close-grained, and probably valuable for wood engraving, &c.

136. E. OPPOSITIFOLIA.—*Berrigan.*—A small spreading and elegant tree of 20 to 30 feet, quite glabrous or the young shoots hoary or yellowish, with a minute tomentum ; leaves scattered or here and there opposite, linear-lanceolate, acuminate and often ending in a hooked point, contracted into a petiole, 1 to 2 inches long ; flowers large, solitary, on pedicels in the axils ; fruit a drupe, separating into four dry cocci.   Habitat, scrub forests and barren wastes on the Murray, Lachlan, and Darling Rivers.
Qualities of *timber* unknown.

LXIV. ERYTHRINA.

(Natural Order LEGUMINOSÆ.   Sub-Order *Papilionaceæ.*)
137. E. VESPERTILIO.—*Coral Tree ; Bat's Wing Coral Tree ; Heilaman Tree.*—A small but most remarkable tree, with leaves resembling a bat's wing extended, and the branches prickly ; leaves alternate or opposite, pinnately trifoliate, leaflets 3, broadly cuneate at the base, spreading to 3 or 4 inches in breadth, often but not always broader than long, usually 3-lobed, the lateral lobes spreading or recurved, obtuse, the middle triangular or lanceolate, usually acute or disappearing altogether, leaving the leaf divided into two long narrow lobes ; flowers red, large,

numerous, pendulous in showy erect racemes ; pod elongated, torulose, with a few large red seeds. Habitat, open forests bordering on the brush forests, Clarence and Richmond Rivers ; also Mount King.

Timber very tough ; used by the aborigines for making their " heilamans " or shields.

LXV. EUCALYPTUS.

(Natural Order MYRTACEÆ.)

138. E. ALBENS.—*White Gum* (of the interior).—A tree attaining a height of 60 to 80 feet, with a dull green persistent bark, separating in smooth laminæ or strips, the foliage usually very glaucous or almost mealy-white ; leaves alternate or opposite, usually large, broad, ovate-lanceolate or lanceolate, often 6 inches long or more, with oblique veins, the intramarginal one some distance from the edge ; flowers 4 to 8, rather large, in lateral pedunculate umbels, the operculum conical, acuminate, about as long as the calyx-tube ; fruit obovoid-oblong, truncate, nearly ½ inch long, the capsule deeply sunk. Habitat, open forests, New England, Macquarie River, and other parts of the interior.

Timber not much valued.

139. E. AMYGDALINA.—*Messmate ; Stringybark; Almond-leafed Eucalyptus.*—A tree usually of small or moderate size, but occasionally of colossal dimensions, the bark sometimes persistent and fibrous, sometimes more or less deciduous in large flakes, the branches slender ; leaves on flowering branches alternate, otherwise sometimes opposite, from linear to broadly lanceolate, straight or falcate, mostly acuminate, 2 to 4 inches long, the veins few and oblique, the intramarginal one usually at some distance from the edge ; flowers 4 to 8, rather small, in axillary or lateral pedunculate umbels, terete or nearly so, the operculum hemispherical, shorter than the calyx-tube, obtuse and umbonate ; fruit subglobose-truncate, usually under 3 lines in diameter, but sometimes larger, the capsule scarcely sunk. Habitat, open forests, Port Jackson to the Blue Mountains, Argyle, southward to Twofold Bay, and northward to the Clarence River.

Timber used in house carpentry, but not in much repute.

Var. radiata.—*River White Gum.*—Trunk smooth and nearly white, the bark generally hanging from the upper branches in long strips ; leaves sometimes both opposite and alternate on the same tree, broader than in the normal form, 3 to 4 inches long ; flowers more numerous, sometimes nearly 20 ; fruit almost pear-shaped. Habitat, banks of the Neapean River, Bent's Basin, and south of Argyle.

140. E. BICOLOR.—*Bastard Box; Yellow Box; Slaty Gum.*—A tree sometimes attaining a height of 160 feet with a smooth white bark, sometimes reduced to 30 or 40 feet with a persistent ash-grey or blackish bark ; leaves alternate or opposite, lanceolate, narrow or rarely passing into ovate-lanceolate, mostly 3 to 4 inches but sometimes 5 or 6 inches long, thin, often glaucous or pale-coloured, the veins fine, oblique, not close, the marginal one at some distance from the edge, sometimes very prominent towards the base ; flowers small but rather striking, from 3 to 8 together, in pedunculate umbels, forming axillary or terminal panicles, the operculum thin, hemispherical, obtuse or umbonate, shorter than the calyx-tube ; fruit globular-truncate or pear-shaped, from 2 to 3 lines diameter, the capsule somewhat depressed. Habitat, open forests, Port Jackson, Williams River, Maranoa, Blue Mountains, Macquarie and Darling Rivers, extending towards the Barrier Range.

Timber very hard and durable, but difficult to split, and frequently hollow or decayed at heart ; used for fencing, plough-beams, poles, shafts of drays and carts, spokes of wheels, cogs, &c. The "Slaty Gum" of Mudgee is said to be next to "Ironbark" in point of durability, and excellent for weatherboards, fencing, and wheelwrights' work ; does not crack from exposure to the sun.

(The above tree is supposed by sawyers and carpenters to be a cross between the "Box" and the "Gray Gum," having in youth the appearance of the former, and in old age that of the latter.)

141. E. BOTRYOIDES.—*Bastard Mahogany;* "*Bangalay*" (of carpenters).—A tree of crooked growth and gnarled appearance, never attaining any considerable height, with a rough furrowed persistent bark ; leaves usually alternate, ovate-lanceolate or lanceolate, acuminate, straight or rarely falcate, 4 to 6 inches long or more, with numerous fine diverging parallel veins, the intramarginal one very close to the edge; flowers 4 to 10, rather large, sessile or nearly so, in pedunculate umbels, axillary or lateral, the operculum obtuse and shorter than the calyx-tube, or broadly conical and nearly that length; fruit obovoid-oblong, 4 to 5 lines long, the capsule more or less deeply sunk. Habitat, open forests, Paterson River, Baulkham Hills, and Port Jackson ; plentiful at Manly Beach.

Timber strong and durable ; used for knees and ribs of vessels in ship-building, and for firewood.

142. E. BRACHYPODA.—*Dwarf Box;* "*Goborro*" ; "*Coorkaroo*" ; "*Bimbil.*"—A small or moderate-sized tree, sometimes reduced to a shrub, the bark varying from smooth and whitish to dark and rugged, persistent or shedding in large patches, or dark and rough on the trunk, smooth, whitish, and deciduous on the branches ; leaves alternate or opposite, from ovate-obtuse and under 2

inches to long-lanceolate, obtuse, acute, or acuminate, and 6 to
8 inches long, pale or glaucous, finely veined, the marginal vein
close to the edge ; flowers 3 to 6 or more, small, in pedunculate
umbels, usually three or four together in panicles, either terminal
or in the upper axils, or rarely the lower one solitary and axillary,
the operculum conical or obtuse, not longer than the calyx-tube ;
fruit almost hemispherical, about 2 lines diameter, the capsule
sunk.   Habitat, plains subject to inundation, seldom on the banks
of running streams, Lachlan and Darling Rivers, extending
towards the Barrier Range.

Qualities of *timber* unknown.

143. E. CAPITELLATA.—*Stringybark.*—A large tree, sometimes
attaining a height of 400 feet, with a dark-grey furrowed fibrous
bark ; leaves of the flowering branches alternate, otherwise
opposite, from ovate-lanceolate to long-lanceolate, generally
oblique and falcate, from 3 to 6 inches long, thick and shining,
with oblique anastomosing veins, the intramarginal one at some
distance from the edge; flowers 5 to 10, small, sessile in
pedunculate umbels, axillary or lateral, the operculum very
obtuse and about as long as the calyx-tube, or rather longer
and obtusely conical ; fruit depressed-globose, 4 to 5 lines in
diameter, the valves of the capsule usually protruding.   Habitat,
open forests, Cumberland, Camden, and Blue Mountains, constituting the main mass of the timber trees growing on the more
barren ridges and mountain spurs.

Timber excellent for house-carpentry, and largely used for
flooring-boards, battens, joists, and rafters, as well as for fencing
material and firewood.   The bark is useful for making paper, and
for thatching rural dwellings.

144. E. CINEREA.—*Argyle Apple.*—A moderately large tree,
similar in appearance to the *Angophora subvelutina*, with a
whitish-brown persistent bark, somewhat fibrous, the foliage more
or less glaucous or mealy-white ; leaves opposite, sessile, cordate,
ovate or ovate-lanceolate, obtuse or acute, 2 to 4 inches long ;
flowers 3 to 7, pedicellate in pedunculate axillary umbels, or
short terminal corymbs, the operculum conical and shorter than
the calyx-tube ; fruit semi-globose or subglobose-truncate, about 3
lines in diameter, the capsule scarcely sunk.   Habitat, rocky and
stony places near Berrima ; also near Bathurst and Lake George,
and on the Lachlan River.

Qualities of *timber* unknown.

145. E. CORIACEA.—*White Gum.*—A tree attaining sometimes a
height of 80 feet, the exterior bark deciduous, the inner smooth
and whitish ; leaves of the flowering branches alternate and
petiolate, otherwise opposite, ovate-lanceolate or lanceolate,
acuminate and falcate, 3 to 4 inches long, or sometimes twice

that length, thick, smooth and shining, the veins not numerous, oblique, a few almost parallel to the mid-rib; flowers 5 to 10, in pedunculate umbels, axillary or lateral, the operculum hemispherical, obtuse or with a small point, or conical, shorter than the calyx-tube; fruit often nearly sessile, smooth, pear-shaped, truncate, 3 to 4 lines diameter, the capsule somewhat sunk. Habitat, open forests, Port Jackson, Blue Mountains, Argyle, Berrima, and New England.

Timber not much valued, but the foliage is eaten by cattle and horses in dry seasons.

146. E. CORYMBOSA.—*Bloodwood.*—A small or middle-sized tree near the coast, but inland attaining sometimes a great height, with a persistent furrowed bark and of rapid growth; leaves alternate or opposite, ovate-lanceolate or lanceolate, acuminate; 3 to 6 inches long, with fine transverse parallel veins, sometimes scarcely visible; flowers rather large, on pedicels in pedunculate loose umbels, several-flowered, mostly in a terminal corymbose panicle, the operculum short, hemispherical, umbonate or shortly acuminate; fruit urceolate, $\frac{1}{2}$ to $\frac{3}{4}$ inch long, the capsule sunk. Habitat, open forests, from Twofold Bay to the Richmond River.

Timber soft when young, but harder when old; used for fencing and firewood; that growing on the Clarence and Richmond Rivers is said to be very strong and durable, even under ground, but subject to the defect of "gum-veins."

147. E. CREBRA.— *White or Pale Ironbark; White Narrow-leaved Ironbark.*—A small or middle-sized or large tree, with a hard blackish rough persistent bark; leaves alternate or opposite, oblong-lanceolate or linear, straight or falcate, obtuse, mucronate-acute or acuminate, 4 to 6 inches long, sometimes thick and glaucous or yellowish when dry, with numerous fine veins, the intramarginal one very close to the edge; flowers 3 to 6, small, on short pedicels in pedunculate umbels, usually 3 to 4 together in short terminal or axillary panicles, or the lower ones rarely solitary in the axils, the operculum conical or hemispherical, about as long as the calyx-tube; fruit obovoid-truncate, less than 2 lines in diameter, the capsule sunk, but the tips of the valves often protruding when open. Habitat, open forests, from Port Jackson to the Clarence River and New England, also Berrima.

Timber very valuable, hard, tough, inlocked and strong; much esteemed by coachbuilders and wheelwrights for poles and shafts of carriages and spokes of wheels; also for piles and railway sleepers.

148. E. DEALBATA.— *White Gum.*—A small stunted tree, sometimes attaining a height of 50 feet, the foliage often glaucous-white, and the bark rugose or separating in scales, leaving the inner bark white and smooth, or white or purplish when young, getting

brownish with age, and shedding once in three years; leaves
alternate, from ovate to ovate-lanceolate and under 4 inches long or
sometimes lanceolate and longer, obtuse or acute, the veins oblique
and conspicuous, the intramarginal one at some distance from the
edge; flowers 3 to 6, pedicellate in axillary or lateral pedunculate
umbels, the operculum hemispherical or conical, longer than the
calyx-tube; fruit almost hemispherical, about 3 lines diameter.
Habitat, rocky places near Mudgee and Bathurst, and open forests
of the interior and New England.

Timber of a light colour, but too soft to be of much use except
for firewood.

149. E. DIVES.—*Peppermint.*--A small tree of about 12 feet, leaves
opposite, sessile, cordate or ovate, acute or acuminate, rather large,
sometimes alternate and oblique; flowers 8 to 12 or more, in
dense umbels or peduncles, mostly on the stem below the leaves,
the operculum short, obtuse, and hemispherical; fruit globose-
truncate, about 2 lines diameter, 4-celled with a broad brim, the
capsule sunk. Habitat, Port Jackson, Blue Mountains, Bargo
Brush, and Mittagong.

Timber not much esteemed.

150. E. DUMOSA.—*"Mallee"* (of the Lachlan and Darling Rivers).
—A dwarf or shrubby species, with a smooth whitish persistent
bark, and exceedingly dense growth, forming impenetrable "scrubs";
leaves usually alternate, from oblong or almost ovate and obtuse to
lanceolate falcate and acuminate, 3 to 4 inches long, thick and
smooth, the veins not conspicuous; flowers 4 to 8, sessile or shortly
pedicellate on short axillary or lateral peduncles, the operculum
hemispherical, umbonate or conical, shorter than the calyx-tube;
fruit obovoid-truncate or almost oblong, about 3 lines long, the
capsule more or less sunk. Habitat, scrubs and deserts on the
Lachlan and Darling Rivers; also the Euryalean Scrub and the
Blue Mountains.

Timber of no use, but the leaves are said to contain an essential
oil, and may therefore some day be turned to account.

(Sir Thomas Mitchell regarded the above as "the most unpleasing
of shrubs to a traveller," and describes it as " a lofty bush with a
great number of stems, each 2 or 3 inches in diameter; and the
bushes grow thickly together, having between them nothing but
the prickly grass in large tufts.")

151. E. EXIMIA.—*Bloodwood.*—A large tree, with the bark
sometimes smooth, sometimes furrowed and wrinkled; leaves
alternate or opposite, falcate-lanceolate, acuminate, 4 to 6 inches long,
with numerous fine parallel veins, scarcely visible; flowers usually
large, several together, closely sessile, in heads on thick peduncles
in terminal corymbs or panicles, the operculum double, conical or
acuminate, shorter than the calyx-tube; fruit urceolate, ¾ to 1 inch

long, the capsule deeply sunk. Habitat, open forests, Cumberland, Camden, Grose River, Blue Mountains, Clarence and Richmond Rivers.

Timber used for posts and rails.

152. E. GLOBULUS. *Blue Gum.*—A lofty tree of rapid growth, sometimes exceeding 200 feet in height, but often flowering when not above 10 feet, the young shoots and foliage often glaucous-white, the bark somewhat fibrous but deciduous, leaving the inner bark on the trunk smooth ; leaves of the young tree opposite, sessile and cordate, of the full-grown tree lanceolate or ovate-lanceolate, acuminate, falcate, often $\frac{1}{2}$ to 1 foot long, the veins conspicuous, oblique and anastomosing, the intramarginal one at some distance from the edge ; flowers, large axillary, solitary or 2 or 3 together, closely sessile on the stem or on peduncles, the calyx-tube broadly turbinate, thick, woody, and replete with oil-receptacles, generally ribbed, rugose or warty, $\frac{1}{2}$ to $\frac{3}{4}$ inch diameter, the operculum thick, hard and warty, depressed-hemispherical with an umbonate or conical centre, shorter than the calyx-tube ; fruit semi-globular, $\frac{3}{4}$ to 1 inch diameter, the capsule scarcely sunk. Habitat, open forests, near Araluen, and most likely other localities in the southern districts.

Timber of a pale colour, heavy, strong and durable; equal to English oak in transverse strength, and eminently useful in ship-building, coachbuilding, and house construction.

(The credit of first discovering this tree in New South Wales belongs to the Rev. Robert Collie, F.L.S., who found it growing in the above-mentioned locality about four years ago.)

153. E. GONIOCALYX.—*Cumberland Blue Gum*; *Clarence Flooded Gum.*—A tree of rapid growth, attaining a height of 80 feet, and a diameter of 7 feet, with the bark rough and persistent on the trunk, at least when the tree is large, deciduous in the upper part, or usually deciduous, but sometimes persistent; leaves alternate or opposite, ovate-lanceolate to lanceolate, falcate, often above 6 inches long, pale-coloured, with pellucid dots, the veins oblique and numerous, the intramarginal one at some distance from the edge; flowers 3 to 7, sessile or tapering into short pedicels in pedunculate umbels, the operculum conical or hemispherical, much shorter than the calyx-tube ; fruit ovoid-truncate, about 4 lines long and rather less in diameter, the capsule sunk. Habitat, open forests and near rivers on good soil, from Twofold Bay northward to the Clarence.

Timber one of the most valuable in the Colony; extensively used for building purposes, scantling, battens, flooring-boards, posts and rails, ships' planks, naves and felloes of wheels, &c.; of less specific gravity than the timber of any other Gum. Some trees of its species yield from 6,000 to 7,000 feet of timber, worth 18s. per hundred.

154. E. GRACILIS.—A small tree or tall shrub, with a silvery-grey smooth bark; leaves alternate or opposite, narrow-lanceolate or oblong-linear, mucronate, under 3 inches long, thick and densely dotted, the veins scarcely visible ; flowers 4 to 8, small, in pedunculate umbels, axillary or the upper ones in a short terminal panicle, the operculum hemispherical, conical or acuminate, shorter than the calyx-tube ; fruit oblong or narrow-urceolate, about 3 lines long, the capsule deeply sunk. Habitat, deserts of the Murray and Darling Rivers.

Timber not used for any purpose.

155. E. HÆMASTOMA.—*White Gum* ; *Spotted Gum.*—A tree of stunted growth near the sea, but attaining inland a height of 160 feet and a diameter of 5 feet, with a smooth deciduous bark, bearing a spotted or variegated trunk, or the bark sometimes smooth and sometimes half-barked like the "*Blackbutt*"; leaves alternate or opposite, usually oblique or falcate, lanceolate, 4 to 6 inches long, coriaceous, the veins very oblique and often anastomosing; flowers 4 to 8, on axillary or lateral peduncles or a few in a short terminal oblong panicle, the operculum very short, hemispherical and obtuse ; fruit globular-truncate or pear-shaped, 3 to 4 lines in diameter, the capsule slightly depressed. Habitat, open forests, Illawarra, Cumberland, and in the interior.

Timber of doubtful value, some authorities stating that it is excellent for ship-building and wheelwrights' work, while others say that it is useless even as firewood.

Var. micrantha.—Flowers and seed-vessels smaller. Habitat, interior.

156. E. HEMIPHLOIA.—*Box.*—A large tree, attaining a height of 180 feet and a diameter of 6 feet, with the bark on the lower part of the trunk persistent, wrinkled, and full of clefts, but on the upper part and on the branches rendered smooth by the shedding of the outer layers; leaves alternate or opposite, ovate-lanceolate, falcate or nearly straight, 3 to 5 inches long, thick and rigid, with very oblique distant veins; flowers 4 to 8, in pedunculate umbels, mostly forming short terminal panicles, the fruiting ones usually lateral below the leaves, the operculum conical, acuminate, as long as the calyx-tube or rarely shorter; fruit ovoid-oblong, 3 to 4 lines long, the capsule deeply sunk. Habitat, open forests, Illawarra, Camden, Cumberland, &c., indicating good grazing country.

Timber of first-rate quality, obtainable in large scantlings, white, and generally very hard, tough and durable, but liable to suffer from "dry rot" and the attacks of the "white ant," and does not stand long in the ground. It is excellent for fuel, burning with great brilliancy and generating a large amount of heat.

Var. parviflora.—Flowers smaller. Habitat, Mount Elliott.

157. E. INCRASSATA.—"*Mallee*" (of the Murray, in part).—A shrub or small tree, sometimes 25 feet, of dense growth, and with a smooth bark, persistent or shedding in large patches; leaves alternate or opposite, ovate, ovate-lanceolate or lanceolate, obtuse or acuminate, under 4 inches long, very thick, with oblique veins; flowers 3 to 8, rather large, sessile or pedicellate in pedunculate umbels, axillary or lateral, the operculum acuminate or rostrate, as long as or longer than the calyx-tube; fruit ovoid-cylindrical, ½ to 1 inch long, the capsule deeply sunk. Habitat, deserts on the Murray River; also towards the Barrier Range.

Timber of no use, but the foliage contains an essential oil which may some day be utilized.

158. E. LEUCOXYLON.—*Red-flowering Ironbark; Black Ironbark; Red Ironbark.*—A tree usually from 60 to 80 feet in height, but in the interior sometimes attaining a height of 100 feet and a diameter of 4 feet, with a persistent rough dark iron-grey bark, or dark grey or spongy on the trunk and soft and white on the branches; leaves alternate or opposite, lanceolate, acuminate, often falcate, 3 to 6 inches long, thick and coriaceous, the veins very oblique and irregular; sometimes scarcely conspicuous, the intramarginal one close to the edge, except when the leaf is broad; flowers 3 to 5, large, red, on pedicels in pedunculate axillary umbels, the operculum conical or acuminate, about as long as the calyx-tube; fruit obovoid or subglobular, truncate, 3 to 4 lines in diameter, the capsule slightly depressed. Habitat, open forests, generally in poor soil, from Twofold Bay northward to the Hastings River and New England; also near Mudgee, Lachlan River, and other parts of the interior.

Timber remarkable for its dark colour and great strength and durability, though inferior to two other kinds of Ironbark; much used for fencing and house-carpentry.

(A variety of this species, with *white* flowers, grows near Mudgee.)

159. E. LONGIFOLIA.—*Woollybutt.*—A large tree, sometimes attaining a height of 200 feet, with a rough fibrous persistent or partially deciduous bark, or somewhat smooth or fibrous and wrinkled, according to the age of the tree; leaves alternate, lanceolate, usually long and falcate, often more than 6 inches long, the veins fine and divergent, the intramarginal one close to the edge; flowers 3 or 4, rather large, pedicellate in axillary or lateral peduncles, usually recurved, the operculum conical, about as long as the calyx-tube or rather longer; fruit pear-shaped, truncate, about ¾ inch long, the capsule slightly sunk. Habitat, open forests, from Twofold Bay to Port Jackson, and most likely in other parts of the Colony.

Timber (about Sydney) not much esteemed except for firewood, and sometimes for fencing. In Illawarra and Gippsland the

E

timber is said to be strong and durable, and employed for wheel-wrights' work and fencing. The bark yields over 8 per cent. of Kino-tannic acid, and the fibre is made into packing-paper. The leaves yield a valuable volatile oil.

160. E. MACRORHYNCHA.—*Stringybark.*—A lofty tree, with a dark dull-grey furrowed and fibrous bark; leaves of the flowering branches alternate and petiolate, otherwise opposite, falcate, rather narrow and acuminate, 3 to 5 inches long, the lower ones broader, thick and coriaceous, the veins oblique and prominent; flowers 6 to 8, pedicellate in pedunculate axillary or lateral umbels, the operculum conical or acuminate, longer than the calyx-tube; fruit depressed-globose, 4 to 6 lines diameter. Habitat, open forests, New England.

Timber excellent for house-carpentry, flooring-boards, battens, and fencing. The bark may be made into paper, and is also employed for thatching.

161. E. MACULATA.—*Spotted Gum.*—A lofty handsome tree, attaining a height of more than 100 feet, with a smooth bark falling off in patches and giving the trunk a spotted or mottled appearance; leaves alternate or opposite, ovate-lanceolate or lanceolate, straight or falcate, acuminate, 4 to 6 inches long or more, with oblique veins, rather coarse, the intramarginal one close to the edge; flowers 3, rather large, pedicellate in pedunculate umbels, usually several together on short leafless branches, forming a panicle or corymb, the operculum much shorter than the calyx-tube, umbonate or acuminate; fruit ovoid-urceolate, about ½ inch long and nearly as much in diameter, the capsule deeply sunk. Habitat, open forests, from Illawarra to the Clarence River; also on the Lachlan River.

Timber, according to some authorities, equal to English oak in point of utility, but according to others only fit for firewood. Sir William Macarthur says it is "a good timber, in increasing reputation for ship-building, but not to be compared for strength and durability with the best description of Gums." Many practical men say it may be used for staves of casks and the upper portions of railway bridges. It is not a favourite for fencing, the posts and rails decaying soon, perhaps because the sap-wood has not been removed. It grows only in poor soil.

162. E. MELANOPHLOIA.—*Silver-leaved Ironbark; Broad-leaved Ironbark.*—A small tree, with a blackish persistent deeply furrowed bark, the foliage more or less glaucous or mealy-white-leaves opposite, sessile, from cordate-ovate or orbicular to ovate; lanceolate, obtuse or acute; flowers 3 to 6, in pedunculate umbels-axillary or several in a short terminal corymb, the operculum, conical and shorter than the calyx-tube; fruit pear-shaped or

globular-truncate, 2 to 3 lines in diameter, the capsule nearly level. Habitat, open forests, Liverpool Plains, near Cassilis, and on the Narran River.

Timber as yet little known, but supposed to be inferior to the other Ironbarks.

163. E. MELLIODORA.—*Yellow Box; Red Gum.*—A moderate-sized tree of irregular growth, with a smooth bark of a pale lead colour, scaling of in flakes in the upper parts of the tree, or furrowed and persistent; leaves alternate or opposite, lanceolate, usually narrow, acuminate and often falcate, 3 to 4 inches long, thick, with fine oblique veins, the intramarginal one at some distance from the edge; flowers 4 to 8, rather small, pedicellate in pedunculate axillary or lateral umbels, the operculum hemispherical or conical, with a small point, about as long as the calyx-tube; fruit subglobose, truncate, rarely ovoid, the capsule more or less depressed. Habitat, open forests, Lachlan River, near Bathurst, New England, Gwydir River, and north-west interior.

Timber hard, tough, and durable.

164. E. MICROCORYS.—*Tallowwood ; Mahogany.*—A tall tree, with a persistent furrowed fibrous bark ; leaves alternate or opposite, ovate-lanceolate or broad-lanceolate, acuminate, straight or unequal at the base, 3 to 4 inches long, thin, the veins divergent, fine, distant, prominent ; flowers 4 to 8, in pedunculate umbels or short terminal corymbs, the operculum broad, flat, obtuse or umbonate, much shorter than the calyx-tube ; fruit obovoid-oblong, about 3 lines long and 2 lines in diameter, the capsule sunk. Habitat, open forests, Myall Lakes, on the Hastings River, and in the north-west interior ; also at Brisbane Water (?)

Timber strong, handsome, and durable ; very useful for building purposes, staves, palings, &c.

165. E. OBLIQUA.—*Stringbark ; Messmate.*—An immense tree, often more than 250 feet in height and 7 feet in diameter, but flowering already when young and small, with a very tenacious rugged fibrous bark ; leaves of the flowering branches alternate, otherwise opposite, mostly ovate-lanceolate, falcate and very oblique at the base, acuminate, 4 to 6 inches long, thick, with oblique anastomosing veins, the intramarginal one at some distance from the edge ; flowers 4 to 8, on pedicels in pedunculate axillary or lateral umbels, the operculum hemispherical or flattened, obtuse, shorter than the calyx-tube ; fruit pear-shaped, truncate at the top, 3 to 5 lines in diameter, the capsule more or less sunk. Habitat, open forests in the Berrima district, and south-eastern portions of the Colony.

Timber excellent for house-carpentry, flooring-boards, battens, and other scantlings, and for fencing. The bark may be used for thatching, and for making paper.

166. E. OBTUSIFLORA.—*Box ; Blackbutt.*—A tree of moderate size, with the bark fibrous and persistent on the lower part of the trunk, on the upper part and on the branches smooth ; leaves alternate or opposite, mostly straight, oblong-elliptical or lanceolate, acuminate, often all under 3 inches long, but sometimes more falcate and 5 inches long, thick and rigid, with oblique veins, the intramarginal one at some distance from the edge ; flowers 4 to 8, rather large, on pedicels in lateral or axillary peduncles, the operculum broadly hemispherical, obtuse or umbonate, shorter than the calyx-tube ; fruit hard and woody, ovoid-truncate, above ½ inch long, the capsule depressed. Habitat, Port Jackson, Bargo Brush, and Blue Mountains.

Timber similar to that of the " White Gum," and of little value.

167. E. OLEOSA.—" *Mallee* " (of the Murray, in part).—A small tree or shrub of dense growth, the bark of the trunk rough and persistent, that of the branches smooth ; leaves alternate, mostly lanceolate, obtuse or acuminate, under 4 inches long, thick and smooth, the oblique veins scarcely perceptible ; flowers 4 to 8 or more, on pedicels in pedunculate axillary or lateral umbels, the operculum conical or acuminate, usually longer than the calyx-tube ; fruit ovoid or globose, truncate, about 3 lines long, the capsule sunk. Habitat, deserts on the Murray River.

Timber of no use, but the essential oil of the foliage may perhaps some day be turned to account.

168. E. PANICULATA.—*White Ironbark ; Pale Ironbark ; She Ironbark.*—A moderate-sized or large tree, attaining sometimes a height of 150 feet and a diameter of 5 feet, with the character of the bark uncertain, but generally persistent, deeply furrowed, and solid within ; leaves alternate or opposite, lanceolate, falcate, acuminate, rather broad, 3 to 5 inches long, coriaceous and smooth, with fine oblique scarcely perceptible veins ; flowers 3 to 6 or more, on short peduncles, usually in a short terminal corymbose panicle or a few solitary in the upper axils, the operculum obtuse and short or conical, about as long as the calyx-tube ; fruit from subglobose to obovoid-oblong, truncate, 2 to 4 lines in diameter, the capsule more or less sunk. Habitat, open forests on poor or indifferent soil, Cumberland and Coast districts.

Timber very valuable, hard, tough, inlocked and strong, highly esteemed by coachbuilders and wheelwrights for poles and shafts of carriages and spokes of wheels ; also for piles and railway sleepers.

Var. angustifolia.—*Narrow-leaved Ironbark.*—Leaves narrower and thinner ; umbels loose and paniculate. Habitat, Cumberland.

169. E. PILULARIS.—*Blackbutt ; Flintwood.*—A large tree of rapid growth, attaining on good soil a height of 200 feet and a diameter of 15 feet, with a dark-coloured rough and somewhat

furrowed persistent bark ; leaves alternate or opposite, mostly lanceolate, falcate or nearly straight, acuminate, 3 to 6 inches long, thick and smooth, with fine rather oblique veins ; flowers 6 to 12, on pedicels in pedunculate axillary or lateral umbels, or the upper ones forming a terminal panicle, the operculum conical or acuminate, longer than the calyx-tube ; fruit semiglobose or subglobose, truncate, 4 to 5 lines diameter, the capsule somewhat sunk or nearly level. Habitat, open forests, from Twofold Bay to the Hastings River, extending a considerable distance inland.

Timber excellent for house-carpentry, ship-building, and for any purpose where strength and durability are required ; as regards crushing in the direction of the fibre there is none stronger except the " Rough Ironbark."

(There is a fine specimen of the above growing on the Bulli Mountain, not far from the road, a little below the " Elbow," which is perhaps the largest tree in New South Wales.)

Var. acmenioides.— White Mahogany.—Bark wrinkled, furrowed, persistent, similar to that of *"Stringybark"*; veins of the leaves finer, distinct ; peduncles less flattened, the pedicels longer and more slender, the operculum rather shorter, and the fruit smaller. Habitat, Cumberland, northward to the Hastings River ; plentiful north of Parramatta.

Timber much heavier than that of the normal form, useful for building purposes, palings, &c.; when nicely planed it has a beautiful satin-like surface, with the grain sometimes prettily veined or marked.

170. E. PIPERITA.—*Peppermint.*—A tree attaining sometimes a height of 200 feet and a diameter of 6 feet, with a persistent fibrous bark at least on the trunk ; leaves of the flowering branches alternate, otherwise opposite, from ovate-lanceolate and very oblique to lanceolate and nearly straight, rarely above 1 inch long, thick and rigid, the veins very oblique and fine ; flowers 6 to 12, on pedicels in axillary or lateral pedunculate umbels, the operculum conical or acuminate, about as long as the calyx-tube ; fruit obovoid-globular, 2 to 3 lines in diameter, the capsule sunk. Habitat, open forests, from Twofold Bay to the Clarence River, New England, Blue Mountains, Argyle, &c.

Timber used for various purposes, but inferior to Stringybark.

Var. brachycorys.—Stringybark.—Operculum short and hemispherical. Habitat, Twofold Bay.

Var. eugenioides.—Mountain Blue Gum ; Bathurst Blue Gum ; Stringybark.—Bark smooth ; leaf-veins more regular and divergent ; pedicels longer ; buds broader ; fruit less contracted at the orifice. Habitat, Blue Mountains, Bathurst Plains, and Twofold Bay.

Var. laxiflora.—Peppermint ; Stringybark.—Pedicels longer ; fruit more obovoid. Habitat, Manly Beach, Twofold Bay, Camden, Macleay and Clarence Rivers.

171. E. POLYANTHEMOS.—*Lignum-vitæ ; Poplar-leaved Gum ; Bastard Box.*—A tree attaining a height of 50 feet, with an ash-grey persistent rough and furrowed bark; leaves alternate or opposite, on rather long petioles, broadly ovate-orbicular or rhomboidal, obtuse or rarely shortly acuminate, mostly under 3 inches long, in older trees ovate-lanceolate, obtuse and longer, rigid, with fine diverging anastomosing veins, the intramarginal ones distant from the edge; flowers 3 to 6, small, on pedicels in pedunculate umbels, usually several together in short oblong or corymbose panicles in the upper axils or at the ends of the branches, the operculum conical or hemispherical, nearly as long as the calyx-tube; fruit turbinate, 2 to 3 lines in diameter, the capsule sunk. Habitat, open forests, Cumberland, Camden, Nepean River, Goulburn Plains, Bathurst Plains, near Mudgee, Lachlan River, and other parts of the interior.

Timber of a brown colour towards the centre, very hard and tough; used for naves, felloes, and spokes of wheels, &c.

172. E. PULVERULENTA.—*Argyle Apple.*—A small tree, similar in appearance to the *Angophora subvelutina*, with the bark furrowed and wrinkled, the foliage more or less glaucous or mealy-white; leaves opposite, sessile, cordate, orbicular or broadly ovate, obtuse or almost acute, always quite entire; flowers 3, rather small, sessile or nearly so in pedunculate axillary umbels, the operculum conical or acuminate, about as long as the calyx-tube; fruit subglobose-truncate, about 4 lines diameter, the capsule scarcely depressed. Habitat, Cox's River, Argyle, and rocky and stony places near Berrima.

Qualities of *timber* unknown.

173. E. RESINIFERA.—*Red Mahogany ; Forest Mahogany ; Red Gum.*—A tall tree with a rough persistent bark on the trunk, but more or less deciduous on the branches; leaves alternate or opposite, ovate-lanceolate to lanceolate, acuminate, straight or falcate, 4 to 6 inches long, thick, with fine transverse veins, sometimes faint, the intramarginal one close to the edge; flowers 6 to 8 or more, on pedicels in pedunculate axillary or lateral umbels, the operculum conical or acuminate, much longer than the calyx-tube; fruit obconical, subglobose-truncate or almost hemispherical, the capsule somewhat sunk or nearly level. Habitat, open forests, from Illawarra to the Clarence River; also New England, Blue Mountains, Argyle, and in the interior.

Timber red in colour, very strong and durable; used extensively for fencing, beams, rafters, and rough carpentry. In building St. John's Church, at Parramatta, in 1798, rafters of this timber were used, which were found to be quite sound when the church was pulled down in 1852.

174. E. ROBUSTA.—*Swamp Mahogany.*—A large tree, attaining a height of more than 100 feet and a diameter of 5 feet, with a rough furrowed bark ; leaves usually alternate, ovate-lanceolate, nearly straight or the upper ones narrower and falcate, 4 to 6 inches long or more, with numerous fine transverse veins, the intra-marginal one close to the edge ; flowers 4 to 12, large, on pedicels in pedunculate axillary or lateral umbels, the operculum thick, obtusely acuminate, usually rather longer than the calyx-tube ; fruit ovoid-oblong, truncate, smooth, about ½ inch long, the capsule much sunk. Habitat, open forests, generally in low and marshy plains, from Illawarra to the Clarence River ; also Blue Mountains.

Timber used for rough furniture and inside work, but supposed by some not to be durable.

175. E. ROSTRATA.—*Flooded Gum ; Red Gum ; White Gum ; " Yarrah."*—A tall tree, attaining a height of over 100 feet, with a greyish-white bark, smooth and separating in thin layers, or rarely persistent and rough ; leaves alternate or opposite, lanceo-late, mostly falcate or acuminate, 3 to 6 inches long or more, the lower ones sometimes ovate or ovate-lanceolate and straight, thin, the veins regular and oblique, the intramarginal one distant from the edge and sometimes thick ; flowers 4 to 8, on pedicels in pedunculate umbels, the operculum usually hemispherical, about as long as the calyx-tube without the point or beak ; fruit nearly globular, about 3 lines diameter, the capsule not sunk. Habitat, open forests, generally on the banks of rivers, from Cumberland and Camden to the Clarence River, and most of the rivers of the interior.

Timber strong and durable, impervious to the "white ant" and the "*teredo*," used in railway construction, and in ship-building for heavy deck-framing, beams and knees, planking, &c.

176. E. SALIGNA.—*Grey Gum ; Flooded Gum ; Grey Box.*—A tall tree with a smooth silvery-grey shining bark, shedding in thin longitudinal strips ; leaves alternate or opposite, from ovate-lanceolate to long-lanceolate, but usually narrow, acuminate, 4 to 6 inches long, with fine transverse parallel veins, the intramarginal one close to the edge ; flowers 4 to 8, nearly sessile in pedunculate umbels, the operculum conical, about as long as the calyx-tube ; fruit subglobose-truncate, the capsule scarcely sunk. Habitat, open forests, from Camden and Cumberland to the Richmond River ; also Cox's River.

Timber useful for various purposes, but inferior to that of the true "Grey Gum" (*E. tereticornis*).

177. E. SIDEROPHLOIA.—*Red Ironbark ; Large-leaved Ironbark ; She Ironbark.*—A tall tree, with a hard, persistent, rough, and furrowed bark ; leaves alternate or opposite, ovate-lanceolate or lanceolate, much acuminate, straight or more frequently falcate,

about 3 to 6 inches long, often rather thick, with numerous fine diverging veins, the intramarginal one close to the edge; flowers 6 to 12, on angular pedicels in pedunculate axillary umbels or in terminal corymbose panicles, the operculum conical or acuminate, rather longer than the calyx-tube; fruit globular-truncate or obovoid, 3 to 4 lines diameter, the capsule scarcely sunk, but the valves frequently protruding. Habitat, open forests, from Shoalhaven to the Richmond River, and many parts of the interior.

Timber dark in colour and inferior to that of *E. crebra* and *E. paniculata*, but still a most valuable timber; extensively employed for large beams in building stores, railway sleepers, poles for bullock drays, &c. The inspissated juice of this tree is the wellknown Botany Bay "*Kino*."

Var. rostrata.—Operculum longer; valves of capsule more prominent. Habitat, Port Jackson.

178. E. STELLULATA.—*White Gum; Lead Gum; Grey Gum.*—A small tree, the furrowed bark coming off at length in layers, sometimes rugose below, very smooth above and of a lead colour; leaves of the flowering branches alternate and petiolate, otherwise opposite, elliptical, lanceolate or the lower ones ovate, rarely more than 3 inches long, usually straight or nearly so, acuminate and narrowed towards the base, the veins very oblique and anastomosing, a few almost parallel with the mid-rib; flowers small and numerous, nearly sessile in very shortly pedunculate umbels, lateral or axillary, the operculum conical, about as long as the calyx-tube; fruit globular-truncate or pear-shaped, rarely more than 2 lines in diameter, the capsule scarcely sunk. Habitat, open forests, from Illawarra to the Clarence River, New England, Mudgee, Bathurst, Berrima, and Goulburn Plains.

Timber of doubtful value, some authorities stating that it is in high repute for ship-building and other purposes, while others say it is of no use except for firewood.

Var. angustifolia.—Bark sometimes white, sometimes lead-coloured, leaves narrow, thick, and smooth, scarcely showing the venation. Habitat, Blue Mountains.

179. E. STRICTA.—*Blue Mountain Brush Gum.*—A shrub or small tree, sometimes not more than 3 feet high, with the bark stringy; leaves alternate or opposite, linear-lanceolate or linear, straight or falcate, obtuse or acuminate, 2 to 4 inches long, thick and shining, the veins scarcely visible; flowers 4 to 8, small, pedicellate in pedunculate umbels, the operculum hemispherical and mucronate or conical, not longer than the calyx-tube; fruit globose-truncate, smooth, 3 to 4 lines diameter, the capsule sunk. Habitat, Blue Mountains, forming "brushes" in the more elevated regions.

Timber of no use.

180. E. STUARTIANA.—*Bastard Box ; Yellow Gum ; Turpentine
Gum ; Hickory.*—A tree attaining a height of 80 feet, the bark of
the branches smooth and deciduous, that of the trunk rough and
rigid and somewhat stringy ; leaves alternate or opposite, from
broadly ovate-lanceolate to narrow-lanceolate, 3 to 6 inches long,
narrowed at the base, equal or nearly so, but sometimes oblique,
thick, the nerves divergent but not conspicuous ; flowers 4 to 8,
pedicellate in axillary or lateral pedunculate umbels, the operculum
conical, sometimes acuminate, about as long as the calyx-tube ;
fruit almost turbinate, 2 to 4 lines diameter, the capsule level or
scarcely sunk. Habitat, Blue Mountains and Bathurst Plains.

Timber of little value, perhaps the worst of all, decaying rapidly
if exposed.

Var. longifolia.—Yellow Gum.—Leaves long (4 to 8 inches),
acuminate, falcate, thick, the intramarginal vein near the edge.
Habitat, Bong Bong, Berrima, Wingeecarribee, and interior ; also
Cumberland ("Grey Gum" or "Bastard Box"), and Twofold Bay
("Turpentine Gum" or "Hickory.")

Timber, according to Sir William Macarthur, good; but according to the Rev. Dr. Woolls, only fit for fencing and fuel.

181. E. TERETICORNIS.—*Grey Gum ; Bastard Box ; Red Gum ;
Blue Gum.*—A large tree, attaining a height of 150 feet and a
diameter of 4 feet, with a smooth whitish or ash-coloured bark
shedding in thin layers ; leaves alternate or opposite, lanceolate,
mostly falcate and acuminate, often more than 6 inches long, the
veins numerous and oblique, often coarse, the intramarginal one
distant from the edge ; flowers 4 to 8, pedicellate in pedunculate
axillary or lateral umbels, the upper ones sometimes forming a
short panicle, the operculum conical or acuminate, about $\frac{1}{2}$ inch
long, always much longer than the calyx-tube ; fruit ovoid or
almost globular, 3 to 4 lines diameter, the capsule not sunk.
Habitat, open forests, from Twofold Bay to the Richmond River.

Timber valuable, but more prized in some districts than in
others ; where "Ironbark" cannot be procured it is always used
for posts and rails, as well as for fuel ; very durable, whether
exposed or not.

Var. brachycorys.—Hickory ; Leather-jacket.—Operculum more
obtuse, 3 to 4 lines long. Habitat, Manly, Parramatta, Blue
Mountains, Hastings, and Macleay.

Timber exceedingly tough and durable, excellent for fencing and
firewood ; said to be *next to Ironbark for railway sleepers.* Fencing posts made of this timber have been found to be perfectly sound
after standing fifty years in the ground.

Var. brevifolia.—Red Gum.—Leaves ovate or oblong, obtuse.
Habitat, New England, in exposed situations in the mountains.

Timber prized not only for ordinary carpentry, but for its beautiful grain, similar to English Oak, and taking a fine polish.

182. E. UNCINATA.—"*Mallee.*"—A tall shrub rarely more than 12 feet high, with a smooth red or ash-grey bark, coming off in coriaceous plates; leaves alternate or opposite, narrow-lanceolate or linear, under 3 inches long, thick, the veins scarcely visible, always black-dotted, especially underneath; flowers 6 to 8, small, in pedunculate axillary umbels, the operculum conical or acuminate, as long as or rather longer than the calyx-tube; capsule globular-truncate or pyriform, 2 to 3 lines diameter. Habitat, deserts of the Murray and Darling Rivers, the Euryalean Scrub, and other parts of the interior.

Timber of no value, but the roots run along considerable distances underground, retaining a copious supply of fresh water, which is sometimes a great boon to the aborigines and travellers.

183. E. VIMINALIS.—*Manna Gum; Drooping Gum; White Gum; Flooded Gum.*—An elegant tree, attaining a height of 150 feet and a diameter of 8 feet, with a rough persistent bark, at least on the trunk and main branches, that of the smaller branches often smooth and deciduous, or sometimes the whole deciduous; leaves alternate or opposite, lanceolate or more or less falcate and acuminate, 3 to 6 inches long, the veins numerous and diverging, the intramarginal one near the edge; flowers 3 or 4 to 6, pedicellate in pedunculate axillary or lateral umbels, the operculum conical, about as long as the calyx-tube, or rarely longer and acuminate; fruit subglobose-truncate, 3 to 5 lines diameter, the capsule not sunk. Habitat, Argyle, Camden, Illawarra, northward to the Hastings and New England, westward to Bathurst, &c.

Timber not much valued.

(Bentham refers *E. diversifolia*, Bonpl., the "Camden Woolly-butt," to the above species, but Dr. Woolls says it is quite distinct, having the lower part of the trunk covered with fibrous bark, and the upper branches smooth. It is a beautiful tree, common near Berrima, about 80 feet in height, the timber indifferent.)

184. E. VIRGATA.—*Mountain Ash; White-top.*—A tree of considerable size, sometimes attaining a height of 150 feet and a diameter of 4 feet, with the trunk covered with a furrowed persistent fibrous bark, with the branches smooth; leaves of the flowering branches alternate and petiolate, otherwise opposite, lanceolate, narrow falcate and acuminate, 4 to 6 inches long or more, thick and shining, with the veins oblique and often indistinct; flowers several, pedicellate in pedunculate umbels, the operculum hemispherical and short, more frequently conical and as long as or longer than the calyx-tube; fruit narrow pear-shaped,

4 to 6 lines long, the capsule somewhat sunk. Habitat, open forests, Cumberland, northward to Twofold Bay; also Blue Mountains, &c.

Timber tough and durable, used for shafts of drays and carts, rough carpentry, and fencing; said to make better staves for casks than the timber of the "Spotted Gum."

LXVI. EUCRYPHIA.

(Natural Order SAXIFRAGEÆ.)

185. E. MOOREI.—*White Sallow; "Acacia."*—A handsome ornamental tree of moderate size, the young shoots and foliage pubescent, the buds very gummy; leaves opposite, pinnate, leaflets usually 9 to 11, narrow-oblong, entire, coriaceous, the terminal one often 1½ to 2 inches long, the lateral ones shorter, the veins prominent; flowers large, white, very showy, solitary in the upper axils; fruit a capsule, hard, ovoid or oblong, dehiscent, about ½ inch long. Habitat, brush forests on hill slopes, Clyde and Shoalhaven Rivers.

Timber tough and durable, but little used.

LXVII. EUGENIA.

(Natural Order MYRTACEÆ.)

186. E. EUCALYPTOIDES.—*Large-leaved Water Gum.*—A small tree, glabrous and somewhat glaucous, with pendulous branches; leaves opposite, entire, lanceolate, often falcate, 4 to 6 inches long or more, narrowed into a very short petiole, remotely and irregularly penniveined and reticulate, the principal veins more or less confluent at some distance from the edge; flowers rather large, few, in compact terminal cymes; fruit globular, 1-seeded. Habitat, banks of the Clarence and Richmond Rivers.

Timber very hard and tough; used for boats' knees and braces, and axe and chisel handles.

187. E. JAMBOLANA.—*"Durobbi."*—A tree attaining sometimes a height of 100 feet and a diameter of 3 feet, quite glabrous; leaves opposite, entire, oval-oblong, obtuse, 4 to 6 inches long, 2 to 3 inches broad, firm, shining, penniveined and reticulate; flowers small, numerous, in broad trichotomous panicles; fruit a berry, rounded, from the size of a cherry to that of a pigeon's egg. Habitat, Tweed River.

Timber of a red colour when fresh; not much used.

188. E. MYRTIFOLIA.—*Brush Cherry; Myrtle.*—A small tree, sometimes attaining a height of 80 feet and a diameter of 2 feet, quite glabrous; leaves opposite, entire, petiolate, from oval-oblong to oblong-elliptical or almost lanceolate, obtuse or acuminate, 2 to

3 inches long, penniveined; flowers in peduncles, axillary, lateral, or terminating short leafy shoots, bearing 3 or 5 or more flowers in a loose trichotomous panicle; fruit red, ovoid or nearly globular, edible. Habitat, brush forests, from Illawarra to the Tweed. *Timber* not much used.

189. E. SMITHII.—*"Lilly Pilly"*—A tree, sometimes small and slender, sometimes large, quite glabrous; leaves opposite, entire, petiolate, from ovate to ovate-oblong or ovate-lanceolate, obtuse or more or less acuminate, narrowed at the base, mostly 2 or 3 inches long, smooth and finely penniveined; flowers small and numerous, in a terminal panicle, sometimes corymbose, sometimes pyramidal; fruit white or purple, globular, $\frac{1}{4}$ to $\frac{1}{2}$ inch diameter, the endocarp thick and hard. Habitat, brush forests, from Two-fold Bay to the Clarence River.

Timber hard and close-grained; useful for carpenters' work, flails, and handles of tools; also for staves.

190. E. VENTENATII.—*Large-leaved Water Gum; Hickory; Lignum-vitæ.*—A tall spreading tree, quite glabrous; leaves opposite, entire, petiolate, oblong-lanceolate, acuminate, 3 to 5 inches long; flowers in compound thyrsoid or oblong panicles; fruit a berry, not seen. Habitat, brush forests, Hastings, Macleay, Clarence, and Richmond Rivers.

Timber very hard and tough, beautifully marked; used in boat-building, and for handles of tools, dray-poles, &c.

LXVIII. EUPOMATIA.

(Natural Order ANONACEÆ.)

191. E. LAURINA.—An erect small tree, with weak branches, quite glabrous; leaves alternate, entire, oblong or almost elliptical, shortly acuminate, 3 to 5 inches long, narrowed into a short petiole; flowers solitary, on short lateral or nearly axillary peduncles; fruit urceolate-globular, nearly $\frac{3}{4}$ inch diameter. Habitat, brush forests, from Twofold Bay to the Clarence River.

Timber yellowish-brown, soft, but close-grained.

LXIX. EUROSCHINUS.

(Natural Order ANACARDIACEÆ.)

192. E. FALCATUS—*Jemmy Donnelly.*—A tree attaining sometimes 150 feet in height and a diameter of 4 feet, glabrous or the young shoots minutely hoary; leaves alternate or rarely opposite, pinnate, leaflets 4 to 8, very oblique or falcate, ovate to lanceolate, acuminate, 2 to 3 inches long, on petiolules of 1 to 3 lines, penniveined and reticulate; flowers numerous, small, almost sessile,

clustered along the branches in divaricate terminal or lateral
panicles; fruit a drupe, at first ovate, oblong when ripe, attaining about ½ inch in length.   Habitat, brush forests, Hastings,
Clarence, Richmond, and Tweed Rivers.

Timber resembling " Red Cedar," useful for various purposes.

LXX. EVODIA.

(Natural Order RUTACEÆ.)

193. E. MICROCOCCA.—*Mountain Ash.*—A tree often of considerable size, quite glabrous; leaves opposite, digitately trifoliate,
with long petioles, leaflets ovate-oblong, obtuse, 1½ to 3 inches
long, entire, narrowed at the base; flowers small, in dense cymes
or trichotomous panicles on short lateral peduncles below the young
shoots; fruit separating more or less into 2-valved cocci. Habitat,
brush forests, from Illawarra to the Richmond River and New
England; also Blue Mountains.

Qualities of *timber* unknown.

LXXI. EXOCARPUS.

(Natural Order SANTALACEÆ.)

194. E. CUPRESSIFORMIS.—*Native Cherry.*—A tree usually
about 20 feet in height, the very numerous, green, wiry, rigid or
filiform apparently leafless branches sometimes collected in a dense
conical head, sometimes loose and pendulous at the extremities, all
terete, but more or less furrowed; leaves alternate or rarely opposite, reduced to minute scales; flowers minute, in little terminal
or lateral pedunculate spikes of 1½ to 3 lines, each one sessile in a
notch of the rhachis or in the axil of a minute bract; fruit a
drupe, ovoid or nearly globular, resting on the enlarged succulent
pedicel, the epicarp thin, the endocarp crustaceous.   Habitat,
open and brush forests, from Illawarra to the Hastings, and New
England.

Timber close-grained; used by turners for making cornice-poles,
map-rollers, &c.

195. E. LATIFOLIA.—A small tree, the young parts slightly
hoary with a minute pubescence; leaves alternate, petiolate, from
broadly ovate to oval-oblong, very obtuse, coriaceous, more or less
distinctly nerved, 1 to 2 inches long; flowers minute in slender
pedunculate spikes, solitary or several in a short raceme in the
upper axils; fruit ovoid, 3 to 4 lines long, on a turbinate truncate
pedicel.   Habitat, brush forests, Tweed River.

Qualities of *timber* unknown.

196. E. SPARTEA.—A small tree, from 15 to 20 feet in height, the branches slender, erect or horizontal and pendulous at the ends; leaves alternate, distant, linear-subulate, 1 to 2 lines long, acute and recurved at the end, sometimes thicker and 4 to 6 lines long, often deciduous; flowers minute, in spikes 2 to 4 lines long, often more than one in the same axil, and generally flowering from near the base; fruit ovoid or oblong, red, the succulent pedicel usually shorter than the fruit itself. Habitat, deserts on the Murray and Darling Rivers.

Qualities of *timber* unknown.

LXXII. FAGUS.

(Natural Order CUPULIFERÆ.)

197. F. MOOREI.—*Negrohead Beech.*—A beautiful tree, attaining a height of 150 feet and a diameter of 4 feet, often 80 feet to the branches, glabrous or the branches minutely pubescent, the foliage dark green and very dense; leaves evergreen, alternate, ovate or ovate-lanceolate, acute or a few of the lowest obtuse, 1 to 2 inches long on the barren shoots, ¾ to 1 inch on the flowering branches, flat and coriaceous, with numerous prominent veins; flowers monœcious, but not seen; fruiting involucre about 5 lines long; nuts usually 2 with 3 wings and a central flat one with 2 wings. Habitat, mountain slopes at the heads of the Bellinger and Macleay Rivers, forming dense forests.

Timber close-grained and firm, of a pink colour when fresh, likely to prove valuable, but hitherto scarcely known. Nearly allied to the English Beech (*Fagus sylvatica*).

LXXIII. FICUS.

(Natural Order URTICEÆ).

198. F. ASPERA.—*Rough-leaved Fig.*—A large tree, attaining sometimes a height of 100 feet, sometimes small, the young branches, petioles, and inflorescence hispid with short hairs; leaves alternate, on short petioles, entire, oblong-elliptical, acuminate, often toothed above the middle, rounded, oblique or acuminate at the base, 3 to 6 inches long, 1½ to 2½ inches broad, scabrous above, pubescent or hispid underneath, penniveined and reticulate; flowers in axillary receptacles on peduncles solitary or in pairs, ovoid-globular or urceolate, 4 to 6 lines in diameter, the male flowers mixed with the females; fruit a fig or *synœcium*, formed by the enlarged fruiting receptacle. Habitat, brush forests, from Twofold Bay to the Clarence River and New England.

Timber brittle and spongy, of little value.

199. F. EUGENIOIDES.—*Native Fig.*— A small tree, quite glabrous; leaves alternate, on petioles, oblong, lanceolate or elliptical-oblong, obtuse or acuminate, tapering at the base, 1½ to 2½ inches long, ½ to 1 inch broad, entire, coriaceous, finely veined; flowers unisexual, minute, mixed, in sessile receptacles, mostly in pairs in the lower axils or at the nodes below the leaves, globular, about 3 lines diameter, growing into a fig or *synæcium.* Habitat, brush forests, Tweed River.

Timber similar to that of the preceding species, of no value.

Var. puberula.—Young shoots slightly pubescent. Tweed River.

200. F. MACROPHYLLA.—*Moreton Bay Fig* ; *Large-leaved Fig.*— A magnificent tree, attaining a height of 120 feet and a diameter of 12 feet, the trunk often with buttress-like processes, the branches and foliage forming a broad and ample head, quite glabrous ; leaves alternate, entire, oval-elliptical or broadly oblong, obtuse or acuminate, 4 to 10 inches long, 3 to 4 inches broad, coriaceous, penni-veined, the stipules often above 2 inches long ; flowers in axillary receptacles, nearly globular or pear-shaped, ¾ to 1 inch diameter, on peduncles of 3 to 4, the fruiting ones growing into a fig or *synæ-cium.* Habitat, brush forests, from Twofold Bay to the Tweed River.

Timber brittle and spongy, and difficult to season, but sometimes used for packing-cases.

201. F. MUELLERI.—*Native Fig.*—A glabrous tree ; leaves alternate, on petioles, ovate or elliptical-oblong, acuminate, rounded at the base, 2 to 3 inches long, entire, coriaceous, finely veined and reticulate ; flowers unisexual, mixed in receptacles, in pairs, sessile or shortly pedunculate, globular, about ½ inch diameter, growing into a fig or *synæcium.* Habitat, brush forests, on the Hastings River.

Timber brittle and spongy, seldom used for any purpose.

202. F. OPPOSITA.—*Native Fig.*—A small tree, the young branches and underside of the leaves pubescent ; leaves mostly opposite, on petioles, broadly cordate-ovate and about 2 inches long, or ovate, ovate-oblong or ovate-lanceolate and 6 to 8 inches long, all obtuse or acuminate, entire or undulate-crenulate, scabrous above, penniveined and reticulate underneath, on barren branches some-times hastately 3-lobed ; flowers mixed in receptacles, axillary, solitary or in pairs, at first pear-shaped, but at length nearly globular and about ½ inch in diameter, forming a fig or *synæcium.* Habitat, brush forests, Clarence River and New England.

Timber of no use.

203. F. RUBIGINOSA.—*Small-leaved Fig.*—A tree of considerable size, sometimes attaining a height of 200 feet and a diameter of 15 feet, with spreading branches, throwing out woody roots which

descend to the ground, forming pillars as in the Indian Banyan tree (*F. indica*), the young shoots and petioles more or less ferruginous-pubescent ; leaves alternate, entire, on petioles of ½ to 1 inch, oval or elliptical, obtuse or acuminate, rounded or slightly cordate at the base, 3 to 4 inches long, 2 to 2½ inches broad, coriaceous, glabrous above, ferruginous-pubescent underneath, penniveined, the stipules narrow-acuminate ; male and female flowers mixed in axillary receptacles, mostly in pairs, on thick peduncles, globular, about 4 to 5 lines in diameter, growing into a fig or *synœcium*. (Synonym : *F. australis.*) Habitat, brush forests, from Illawarra to the Clarence River ; also Blue Mountains and New England.

Timber brittle and spongy, but used sometimes for making packing-cases.

LXXIV. FLINDERSIA.

(Natural Order MELIACEÆ.)

204. F. AUSTRALIS.—*Ash*; *Cugerie*; *Bulboro*; *Flindosa*; *Flintamendosa.*—A tree attaining a height of 100 feet, and a diameter of 4 feet, with a dark brown rugged and scaly bark ; leaves alternate, pinnate, crowded at the end of short barren branches, glabrous ; leaflets 3 to 6, broadly lanceolate or oblong-elliptical, obtuse or scarcely acuminate, 3 to 4 inches long, scarcely oblique, marked with pellucid dots ; flowers numerous, in much-branched panicles, terminating short branches without leaves ; fruit almost woody, 2 or 3 inches long, the seeds flat, winged at the upper end. Habitat, brush forests, Clarence, Richmond, and Tweed Rivers.

Timber very hard, close-grained and compact ; used in house-building, but not a favourite with workmen on account of its hardness.

205. F. BENNETTIANA.—"*Bogum Bogum.*"—A large smooth-stemmed tree ; leaves opposite, pinnate, crowded under the panicles, leaflets 3 to 5, from ovate to ovate-lanceolate or oblong-elliptical, obtuse or rarely acuminate, from 2 to 5 inches long, glabrous, very coriaceous, not oblique, and scarcely petiolulate, marked with pellucid dots ; flowers numerous, in terminal ample panicles, minutely pubescent ; fruit muricate, 2 to 3 inches long, the seeds winged at the upper end. Habitat, brush forests, Clarence, Richmond, and Tweed Rivers.

Timber close-grained, said to be durable.

206. F MACULOSA.—"*Spotted Tree.*"—A small tree, with the trunk remarkably spotted by the falling off of the outer bark in patches ; leaves opposite or nearly so, glabrous, coriaceous, the glandular dots often visible only on the young ones, sometimes all simple, linear-oblong or lanceolate, obtuse or emarginate and mucronate, 1 to 2 inches long or more, sometimes a few of the leaves break out into 2 or 3 narrow continuous lobes, sometimes again

all pinnate, with 3 or 5 leaflets, like the simple leaves but smaller, and with a winged petiole; flowers in terminal panicles, rather dense; fruit a capsule, oblong and muricate, often not more than 1 inch long. Habitat, Tweed River; also Darling River. Qualities of *timber* unknown.

207. F. OXLEYANA.—*Light Yellowwood.*—A tall much-branched tree, aften attaining 100 feet in height; leaves opposite, pinnate, crowded under the panicles, leaflets 4 to 10, with or without a terminal odd one, broadly lanceolate, obtuse or shortly acuminate, 2 to 4 inches long, oblique and almost falcate, narrowed into a distinct petiolule, glabrous or sprinkled with minute stellate hairs underneath, thinly coriaceous, rather sparingly glandular-dotted; flowers numerous in loose terminal panicles; fruit woody, 3 to 4 inches long, muricate, the seeds winged at both ends. Habitat, brush forests, Clarence, Richmond, and Tweed Rivers.

Timber hard, close-grained, and of a clear yellow colour when fresh; very suitable for cabinet and fancy work.

208. F. SCHOTTIANA.—*Stavewood.*—A tree attaining a height of 100 feet and a diameter of 3 feet; leaves opposite, pinnate, crowded under the panicles, leaflets 8 to 12, with or without a terminal odd one, ovate-lanceolate, obtuse or acuminate, 4 to 5 inches long, more or less falcate, sessile, with a broad very oblique base, coriaceous, glabrous on both sides or softly pubescent underneath when young, marked with pellucid dots; flowers numerous, in ample terminal panicles; fruit not seen. Habitat, brush forests, Bellinger, Macleay, Clarence, and Richmond Rivers.

Timber used for shingles and staves of tallow casks.

· LXXV. FRENELA.

(Natural Order CONIFERÆ.)

209. F. ENDLICHERI.—*Red Pine*; *Black Pine.*—A tree attaining a height of 60 to 100 feet, and a diameter of 2 feet, the branches rather slender, often drooping, sometimes erect and dense, angular when young; leaves in whorls of 3 or rarely 4, reduced to minute acute scales, those of the young plants sometimes acicular; male amenta usually solitary, short and compact; fruit-cones usually clustered on short branches, ovoid or oblong, almost $\frac{1}{2}$ inch diameter, the seeds winged. Habitat, scrub and open forests, near Berrima, Liverpool Plains, Lachlan and Darling Rivers, and other places in the interior.

Timber valuable, of a dark colour, close-grained, strong, and easily wrought; used for telegraph posts, interior fittings and mouldings, and cabinet-making, taking a fine polish.

Var. mucronata. Cone-valves produced into a thick, almost terminal point. Mount Mitchell.

F

210. F. Macleayana.—*Port Macquarie Pine.*—A tall pyramidal tree, with spreading branches; leaves in whorls of 4 or sometimes 3, developed on the lower or sometimes on nearly all the branches into rigid linear-triquetrous almost pungent-pointed spreading laminæ of 2 to 4 lines, reduced in some of the upper branches to minute scales or teeth; male amenta 2 to 4 lines long; fruit-cones sessile, nearly globular or slightly pyramidal, about $\frac{3}{4}$ inches diameter, the seeds winged. Habitat, Port Macquarie, Hastings River.

Timber light and useful; cut up into weatherboards, deals, batters, and other small scantlings.

211. F. Muelleri.—*Blue Mountain Pine.*—A small tree, attaining 20 to 30 feet in height, with stout branches, sometimes erect and dense; leaves in whorls of 3 or rarely 4, reduced to minute acute scales; male amenta very small, usually 3 together; fruit-cones solitary or few together, globular, $\frac{3}{4}$ to 1 inch diameter. Habitat, Blue Mountains.

Timber soft and easily wrought, but seldom used.

212. F. rhomboidea.—*Illawarra Mountain Pine.*—A tree of 20 to 25 feet, sometimes double that height, the branches rather slender, often drooping, angular when young; leaves in whorls of 3 or rarely 4, reduced to minute very acute scales; male amenta solitary or 3 together, small or loose; fruit-cones often clustered on short branches, globular, not exceeding $\frac{1}{2}$ inch in diameter, the seeds 2-winged. Habitat, Twofold Bay, Illawarra, and New England.

Timber strong and durable; used for planks, weatherboards, battens, &c.

213. F. robusta.—*White Pine; Cypress Pine.*—A tree of considerable size, often exceeding 100 feet, but sometimes reduced to a tall shrub, the crowded branchlets short and erect, often slender and glaucous, the internodes terete or with very obtuse angles; leaves in whorls of 3 or rarely 4, reduced to minute and acute scales or teeth; male amenta solitary or 3 together, 2 to 4 lines long, slender and loose; fruit-cones solitary or few together, nearly globular, and usually about 1 inch in diameter, neither angled nor furrowed, the valves 6, smooth or more or less verrucose on the back, without any dorsal point, the seeds usually 2-winged, the central columella often prominent. Habitat, scrub forests on sandy barren lands, Blue Mountains, New England, Murray, Lachlan, and Darling Rivers, extending towards the Barrier Range.

Timber very strong and durable; used for telegraph posts, planks, weatherboards, rafters, battens, &c., but inferior to the red or black pine.

Var. microcarpa.—Richmond White Pine.—Cones small, from ½ to ¾ inch diameter, the valves more unequal and the central columella more developed and triangular. Habitat, Clarence and Richmond Rivers.

Timber very valuable and useful, the root-stock furnishing excellent veneers for cabinet-making.

Var. verrucosa.—White Cypress Pine of the interior.—Cones large, with large warts on the back of the valves. Habitat interior generally (together with the smooth-valved form).

Timber excellent for many purposes; similar to the last two kinds.

LXXVI. FUSANUS.

(Natural Order SANTALACEÆ.)

214. F. ACUMINATUS.—*"Quondong."*—A small tree of 20 to 30 feet; leaves opposite, lanceolate, acute, with a short hooked point, 2 or 3 inches long; flowers numerous, in a terminal pyramidal panicle; fruit globular, ½ to ¾ inch in diameter, the epicarp succulent, the endocarp hard and bony. Habitat, scrub forests on the Murray and Darling Rivers, and interior generally.

Timber handsome and close-grained; suitable for wood-engraving and carving.

LXXVII. GEIJERA.

(Natural Order RUTACEÆ.)

215. G. SALICIFOLIA.—*Balsam Copaiba Tree.*—A moderate-sized tree, sometimes 40 feet, glabrous or with a minute hoary pubescence on the inflorescence, and sometimes on the underside of the leaves; leaves alternate, from ovate to ovate-lanceolate or rarely oblong-lanceolate, obtuse or acuminate, 3 to 4 inches long, entire, coriaceous, narrowed or rarely rounded at the base, with a rather long petiole; flowers numerous, small, white, in terminal loose panicles, broadly pyramidal, and alternately branched; cocci often reduced to 1 or 2, obovoid, not beaked, 2 to 3 lines long. Habitat, brush forests, from Port Jackson to the Clarence River.

Timber firm and close-grained, but seldom used. Ink of a good quality has been made from the bark of this tree, which has a taste similar to that of the drug from which it has received its local name.

LXXVIII. GEISSOIS.

(Natural Order SAXIFRAGEÆ.)

216. G. BENTHAMII.—A beautiful tree, with a straight stem and round head, attaining a height of 120 feet, often 40 or 50 feet to the branches; leaves opposite, trifoliate, ovate, 6 to 10 inches long, 3 to 5 inches broad, coriaceous, remotely and not deeply

toothed, glabrous, green on both sides; flowers purple or red, large, in simple lateral racemes; fruit a capsule, cylindrical, about ¾ inch long, on a short pedicel, the endocarp minutely tomentose. Habitat, brush forests, from the Hastings to the Tweed River.

Timber close-grained, firm, and easily wrought, but little known.

LXXIX. GMELINA.

(Natural Order VERBENACEÆ.)

217. G. LEICHHARDTII.—*Native Beech ; White Beech.*—A noble tree, attaining a height of 150 feet and a diameter of 4 feet, the young branches and inflorescence tomentose ; leaves opposite, ovate, acute, rounded or cuneate at the base, 3 to 6 inches long, coriaceous, glabrous and almost rugose on the upper side, reticulate and densely tomentose underneath, petiolate ; flowers white, with purple markings, numerous, in opposite pedunculate cymes forming loose ovoid or pyramidal terminal panicles ; fruit a succulent drupe, 6 to 8 lines in diameter, the putamen hard or bony. Habitat, brush forests, from Illawarra to the Tweed River.

Timber very valuable, white, of a fine silvery grain ; highly esteemed for decks of vessels and flooring of verandahs, as it neither shrinks nor warps when seasoned ; used also for wood-engraving and ornamental carving.

LXXX. GREVILLEA.

(Natural Order PROTEACEÆ. Sub-Order *Folliculares*.)

218. G. ASPLENIFOLIA.—A small and slender tree of 12 to 15 feet, the branches pubescent when young ; leaves alternate, lanceolate or linear-lanceolate, mucronate-acute, entire, acutely toothed or pinnatifid with short broad acute lobes contracted into a short petiole, 4 to 10 inches long, glabrous and penniveined above, silky-silvery or fulvous underneath, the mid-rib prominent ; flowers pedicellate in pairs in sessile or pedunculate racemes, terminal or in the upper axils, secund, 1 to 2 inches long ; fruit a follicle, usually oblique, with the ventral suture curved. Habitat, Port Jackson to the Blue Mountains.

Timber close-grained and handsome, but seldom used ; splits freely, in planes radiating from the centre.

219. G. HILLIANA.—*Silky Oak.*—A large tree, the young branches tomentose ; leaves alternate, petiolate, either entire, obovate-oblong or elliptical, very obtuse, tapering at the base, and 6 to 8 inches long or more, and deeply divided at the end into 2 or 3 diverging lobes, or deeply pinnatifid with 5 to 7 oblong or lanceolate lobes of several inches, the whole leaf then sometimes above 1 foot long, glabrous above, penniveined, reticulate, with an intramarginal nerve and silvery-silky underneath ; flowers small,

numerous, on pedicels, pubescent as well as the rhachis, in dense cylindrical racemes on short axillary shoots often accompanied by 1 or 2 smaller racemes ; fruit a follicle, slightly compressed, nearly 1 inch long. Habitat, brush forests, Clarence, Richmond, and Tweed Rivers.

Timber valuable for superior kinds of coopers' work.

220. G. ROBUSTA.—*Silky Oak.*—A tree sometimes small and slender, sometimes robust and 80 to 100 feet in height, the young branches hoary or ferruginous-tomentose ; leaves alternate, pinnate, with about 11 to 21 pinnatifid pinnæ, the secondary lobes or segments entire or again lobed, lanceolate or rarely linear, often above 1 inch long, the margins recurved, glabrous above or sprinkled with appressed hairs and obscurely veined, silky underneath, the whole leaf 6 to 8 inches long and nearly as broad ; flowers pedicellate in pairs in secund racemes, 3 to 4 inches long, solitary or several together on short leafless branches on the old wood ; fruit a follicle, broad, very oblique, 8 or 9 lines long. Habitat, brush forests, Clarence, Richmond, and Tweed Rivers.

Timber highly prized for staves.

221. G. STRIATA.—A small or large tree, the branches tomentose, the foliage pubescent ; leaves alternate, undivided, linear or linear-lanceolate, 6 to 18 inches long, often curved, 2 to 5 lines broad, veined above, striate underneath, with 9 to 13 raised parallel nerves ; flowers small, pedicellate in slender spike-like erect racemes of 2 or 3 inches, pedunculate and usually several together in a leafless panicle, the rhachis tomentose ; fruit a follicle, broad, oblique, and compressed, about ¾ inch long. Habitat, scrub forests and deserts on the Bogan and Darling Rivers.

Qualities of *timber* unknown.

LXXXI. HARPULLIA.

(Natural Order SAPINDACEÆ.)

222. H. ALATA.—A tall tree, the young branches and panicles tomentose, otherwise glabrous ; leaves alternate, pinnate, leaflets 6 to 10, oblong-elliptical or lanceolate, acuminate and toothed, almost lobed, 3 to 6 inches long, or more on barren shoots, rigid, green and veined on both sides ; flowers few, large, on pedicels in short loose panicles ; fruit a capsule, 1 to 1½ inch broad, coriaceous, nearly glabrous inside. Habitat, brush forests, Clarence and Richmond Rivers.

Qualities of *timber* unknown.

223. H. HILLII.—A tree attaining a height of 80 feet, the young branches and inflorescence rusty-tomentose, otherwise glabrous ; leaves alternate, pinnate, leaflets 5 to 11, broadly-oblong or oval-

oblong, obtuse, 3 to 5 inches long, or more on barren shoots, coriaceous and shining; flowers small, on pedicels, in loose panicles little branched; fruit a capsule, $1\frac{1}{2}$ inch broad, tomentose outside, the lobes hirsute inside. Habitat, brush forests, Clarence and Richmond Rivers.

Qualities of *timber* unknown.

224. H. PENDULA.—*Tulipwood.*—A tall tree, glabrous or the young shoots and panicles hoary-tomentose; leaves alternate, pinnate, leaflets 3 to 6 or rarely more, from ovate to elliptical-oblong, obtusely acuminate, 3 to 5 inches long, membraneous; flowers small, on pedicels in loose and slender panicles; fruit a capsule, glabrous or slightly pubescent, 1 to $1\frac{1}{2}$ inch broad, the lobes inflated. Habitat, brush forests, Clarence, Richmond, and Tweed Rivers.

Timber handsome, close-grained, strong, and easily wrought, highly coloured with different shades from black to yellow, and taking a fine polish; well worthy the attention of cabinet-makers.

LXXXII. HEDYCARYA.

(Natural Order MONIMIACEÆ.)

225. H. ANGUSTIFOLIA.—*Native Mulberry.*—A small tree, the young shoots and inflorescence hoary-pubescent, the adult parts glabrous; leaves opposite, petiolate, from ovate-elliptical to oblong-lanceolate, acuminate, acute or rounded at the base, serrate-crenate or entire, 3 to 4 inches long, membraneous, penniveined and reticulate; flowers on pedicels in short axillary raceme-like cymes; drupes 10 to 20, nearly globular, succulent, each 1 to $1\frac{1}{4}$ line in diameter, all closely packed and connate in a globular fruit of 3 or 4 lines diameter. Habitat, brush forests, Blue Mountains, northward to the Hastings, Macleay, and Clarence Rivers and New England; southward to Illawarra and Twofold Bay.

Timber beautiful and soft; suitable for cabinet-making.

LXXXIII. HELICIA.

(Natural Order PROTEACEÆ. Sub-Order *Folliculares.*)

226. H. FERRUGINEA.—A moderate-sized tree, the branches and inflorescence densely villous with ferruginous or fulvous hairs, often persistent on the underside of the leaves; leaves alternate, petiolate, ovate-elliptical or oblong, acuminate, serrate, contracted or rounded at the base, 3 to 4 inches long or twice that size, veined underneath and reticulate; flowers small, in pairs on a common pedicel in rather dense terminal or axillary racemes; fruit hard, globular, indehiscent. Habitat, brush forests, Clarence, Richmond, and Tweed Rivers.

Qualities of *timber* unknown.

227. H. GLABRIFLORA.—A small tree, quite glabrous ; leaves alternate, ovate-elliptical, obtuse or acuminate, entire or rarely toothed, petiolate, 2 to 3 inches long, coriaceous, the veins not conspicuous ; flowers pedicellate in pairs in terminal axillary or lateral racemes, very slender and glabrous, the rhachis almost filiform ; fruit hard, nearly globular, indehiscent.   Habitat, brush forests, Camden Haven and Richmond River.
Qualities of *timber* unknown.

228. H. PRÆALTA.—*Long-leaved Nut Tree.*—A moderate-sized or lofty tree of 100 feet, glabrous except the inflorescence which is tomentose; leaves alternate, lanceolate, narrow, obtuse or acuminate, petiolate, entire, sometimes 3 to 4 sometimes 6 to 10 inches long, coriaceous, shining, penniveined and reticulate ; flowers pedicellate in pairs, in axillary or lateral racemes; fruit smooth and hard, above 1 inch in diameter. Habitat, brush forests, Clarence and Richmond Rivers.
Qualities of *timber* unknown.

LXXXIV. HEMICYCLIA.

(Natural Order EUPHORBIACEÆ.)

229. H. AUSTRALASICA.—A spreading tree, attaining 40 feet, rarely a shrub, the young shoots pubescent, otherwise glabrous, sometimes glaucous ; leaves alternate, petiolate, from broadly ovate to ovate-oblong, obtuse, coriaceous, often shining above, veined underneath, 1½ to 3 inches long ; flowers diœcious, small, pedicellate, solitary or few together in axillary clusters, the males sometimes forming short racemes ; fruit an indehiscent drupe, ovoid-globular, 5 to 6 lines long, smooth, red and succulent, with a bony endocarp.   Habitat, brush forests, Clarence River.
Qualities of *timber* unknown.

LXXXV. HIBISCUS.

(Natural Order MALVACEÆ.)

230. H. HETEROPHYLLUS.—*Kurrajong.*—A small tree of 12 to 20 feet, glabrous except a stellate tomentum on the inflorescence and very young shoots, the branches often bearing small conical prickles ; leaves alternate, entire or deeply 3-lobed, linear, lanceolate or elliptical-oblong, 5 to 6 inches long, serrulate or crenulate, sometimes white underneath ; flowers large, with a white and purple centre, on short pedicels in the upper axils, the calyx often above 1 inch long, densely covered with a stellate tomentum, and the petals nearly 3 inches long ; fruit a capsule, ovoid-globular, acute, densely setose or silky-hairy.   Habitat, brush forests, from Illawarra to the Clarence River.

Timber not used, but the fibre of the bark furnishes the aborigines with material for making nets and fishing lines.

231. H. SPLENDENS.—*Kurrajong.*—A beautiful small tree of 13 to 20 feet, densely clothed with a soft velvety tomentum, the branches and petioles armed with small scattered prickles or bristles ; leaves alternate, petiolate, ovate-cordate or palmately 3- or 5-lobed, 6 or 7 inches long, the lobes oblong-acuminate or lanceolate, often narrowed at the base ; flowers very large, rose-coloured, on peduncles, the calyx at least 1 inch long, tomentose or hispid, the petals 3 inches long or more, glabrous ; fruit a capsule, silky-hairy. Habitat, brush forests, Hastings and Clarence Rivers. *Timber* and bark similar to that of the last species.

LXXXVI. HODGKINSONIA.
(Natural Order RUBIACEÆ.)

232. H. OVATIFLORA.—*Golden Ash.*—A tree attaining a height of 80 feet, with slender branches, glabrous or the young shoots with a few appressed hairs ; leaves opposite or whorled, petiolate, elliptical or ovate, obtuse or acuminate, narrowed at the base, the veins not prominent, $1\frac{1}{2}$ to 3 inches long ; flowers polygamo-diœcious, pedicellate in umbels, 10 to 12 on male plants, 3 to 6 on female plants, on slender axillary peduncles ; fruit a drupe, small, ovoid, or globular, the putamen thick and hard. Habitat, brush forests, Clarence and Richmond Rivers. *Timber* close-grained, of a beautiful yellow colour when fresh ; but little known.

LXXXVII. HYMENOSPORUM.
(Natural Order PITTOSPOREÆ.)

233. H. FLAVUM.—A handsome irregular small tree, glabrous except a loose pubescence on the inflorescence and sometimes on the underside of the leaves ; leaves alternate, ovate-oblong or lanceolate, acuminate, entire, from 3 to 6 inches long, narrowed into a petiole, the upper ones often almost verticillate ; flowers large, yellow, in loose corymbose terminal panicles ; fruit a capsule, stipitate, flattened, about 1 inch long and nearly as broad. Habitat, brush forests, from the Hunter to the Clarence Rivers. *Timber* close-grained, firm, but easily wrought; suitable for wood engraving and carving, but hitherto seldom used.

LXXXVIII. IXORA.
(Natural Order RUBIACEÆ.)

234. I. BECKLERII.—A small tree, quite glabrous ; · leaves opposite or whorled, ovate-elliptical, acuminate, narrowed at the base, 3 to 4 inches long, smooth and shining ; flowers in terminal

rather dense sessile corymbs ; fruit a berry or drupe, 3 to 4 lines in diameter, the endocarp not hard, forming two 1-seeded pyrenes. Habitat, brush forests, Clarence and Richmond Rivers.
Qualities of *timber* unknown.

LXXXIX. JACKSONIA.

(Natural Order LEGUMINOSÆ. Sub-Order *Papilionaceæ.*)

235. J. SCOPARIA.—*Dogwood.*—A small tree with a slender stem, attaining about 20 feet in height, usually entirely leafless, but occasionally the young plants or the base of the branches have a few petiolate oblong or oval-elliptical herbaceous leaves, ¾ to 2 inches long ; branches numerous, erect or pendulous, elongated, angular, glabrous or minutely hoary-pubescent ; flowers rather showy, yellow, pedicellate in one-sided racemes, either terminal or from the upper nodes ; pod flat, oblong, 4 to 6 lines long, tipped by a persistent style. Habitat, open forests, from Port Jackson to the Macleay River and New England, southward to Illawarra; also in the interior.
Timber useless, burning with an offensive odour.
Var. parviflora.—Flowers much smaller. Habitat, Macleay and Clarence Rivers.

XC. KENTIA.

(Natural Order PALMÆ.)

236. K. MONOSTACHYA.— *Walking-stick Palm.*—A small erect palm, 6 to 12 feet high ; leaves in a terminal crown, 1½ to 4 feet long, pinnately divided, the segments irregular and acuminate ; inflorescence a pendulous undivided slender spike of great length (1 to 2 feet); fruit ovoid or nearly globular, about ½ inch long. Habitat, brush forests, from the Hastings to the Tweed Rivers ; also Mount Lindsay and New England.
Stem extensively used for walking-sticks.

XCI. KIBARA.

(Natural Order MONIMIACEÆ.)

237. K. MACROPHYLLA.—A tree of considerable size, perfectly glabrous in all its parts ; leaves opposite, petiolate, oblong or oblong-lanceolate, acuminate, bordered by short teeth or entire, cuneate, rounded or cordate at the base, coriaceous, shining and reticulate ; flowers small, pedicellate in axillary cymes or panicles ; fruit a drupe, sessile, ovoid, smooth, about ½ inch long. Habitat, New England.
Qualities of *timber* unknown.

238. K. PUBESCENS.—A moderate-sized tree, the branches, inflorescence, and young foliage pubescent, the older leaves often glabrous ; leaves opposite, from ovate-elliptical to oblong-lanceolate, obtuse or acuminate, toothed or entire, rounded at the base, at length coriaceous and veined underneath, 2 to 4 inches long, petiolate; flowers in small cymes or clusters, sometimes lengthened into short thyrsoid panicles, sessile or pedunculate ; fruit a drupe, sessile, ovoid, glabrous, 3 to 4 lines long. Habitat, brush forests, Hastings, Clarence, and Richmond Rivers.

Qualities of *timber* unknown.

XCII. LAPORTEA.

(Natural Order URTICEÆ.)

239. L. GIGAS.—*Gigantic Nettle Tree.*—A most remarkable tree, attaining a height of 160 feet and a diameter of 12 feet, the trunk erect, with a soft juicy fibrous wood and smooth ash-coloured bark, supported at the base by prominent angles or almost winglike buttresses ; leaves alternate, cordate-ovate, obtuse or acuminate, sinuate-toothed, often above 1 foot long and nearly as broad, glabrous above or sprinkled with a few stinging hairs, pubescent or villous underneath ; flowers diœcious, clustered along the branches of rather loose axillary panicles ; fruit a nut, much flattened, very oblique, the pedicel and perianth thickened into a curved fleshy mass. Habitat, brush forests, from Illawarra to the Clarence River.

Timber too soft to be of any use as such, but a strong fibre is obtained from the bark by the aborigines.

240. L. PHOTINIPHYLLA.—*Small-leaved Nettle.*—A fine tree of 60 feet, with a straight soft-wooded stem of 30 to 40 feet ; leaves alternate, ovate or almost elliptical, obtuse or acuminate, entire or sinuate-toothed, 3-nerved, nearly glabrous, or sometimes sprinkled with a few stinging hairs ; flowers diœcious, clustered along the branches of loose axillary panicles ; fruit a nut, rather large, the pedicels usually but not always enlarged into an incurved fleshy mass. Habitat, brush forests, from the Hunter to the Clarence River.

Timber soft and spongy, and of no value, but a good description of fibre is obtained from the bark, which is used by the aborigines for various purposes.

XCIII. LEPTOSPERMUM.

(Natural Order MYRTACEÆ.)

241. L. FABRICIA.—*Black Tea-tree.*—A small tree, attaining a height of 50 feet, glabrous and glaucous, the branches often hairy ; leaves alternate, from oblong-lanceolate to almost ovate, ¾ to 1½

inch long, obtuse or mucronate, 3- or 5-nerved; flowers rather large, white, sessile, mostly solitary at the ends of short leafy branchlets; fruit a capsule, prominent above the calyx-rim, the free part about as long as the enclosed portion. Habitat, scrub forests, Illawarra, &c.

Timber hard and dense; formerly used by the aborigines for making their weapons.

242. L. FLAVESCENS.—A small tree, glabrous or the young shoots silky-hoary; leaves alternate, from narrow-oblong or linear-lanceolate to broadly-oblong or even obovate, obtuse or acute, rigid, flat, nerveless or 1- or 3-nerved, from under ½ to ¾ inch long; flowers solitary, terminating the branchlets or axillary and nearly sessile, of variable size; fruit a capsule, prominent above the calyx-tube. Habitat, scrub forests, from Port Jackson to the Blue Mountains, northward to New England, southward to Illawarra; also in the interior.

Timber similar to that of the preceding species.

243. L. LÆVIGATUM.—A small tree, of 20 to 30 feet, glabrous and somewhat glaucous, the young shoots often silky; leaves alternate, from obovate-oblong to oblong-cuneate or narrow oblong, obtuse, ½ to ¾ inch long or more, 3-nerved; flowers axillary, solitary and sessile or nearly so, or rarely two together on a short common peduncle; fruit a capsule, nearly flat, scarcely prominent above the calyx-border. Habitat, scrub forests near the sea, from Twofold Bay to the Hastings River.

Timber similar to that of the last species.

Var. minus.—Branches slender; leaves oblong-cuneate, mucronate-acute; flowers smaller. Habitat, scrub forests on the Darling River.

244. L. LANIGERUM.—A small tree, sometimes low and bushy, the branchlets usually pubescent; leaves alternate, from ovate-oblong to elliptical or narrow-oblong and from less than ½ to ¾ inch long or more, obtuse or mucronate-acute, hoary, silky or hairy underneath or on both sides, sometimes glabrous and 1- to 3- or 5-nerved, but more frequently rigidly coriaceous and the nerves scarcely perceptible; flowers solitary, terminating very short leafy branchlets or rarely sessile on the branches without intervening leaves; fruit a capsule, nearly globular, but depressed at the top, protruding from the calyx-tube, from 3 to 4 lines in diameter. Habitat, scrub forests, from Port Jackson to the Blue Mountains, northward to Mount Mitchell, southward to Illawarra and Twofold Bay; also Cox's River, Macquarie River, and other places in the interior.

Timber similar to that of the preceding species.

XCIV. LITSÆA.

(Natural Order LAURINEÆ.)

245. L. DEALBATA.—A moderate-sized tree, the young shoots softly ferruginous-villous; leaves alternate, petiolate, ovate-elliptical or oblong, acuminate, 3 to 6 inches long, glabrous, glaucous underneath, veined on both sides; flowers pedicellate in sessile clusters, axillary or at the old nodes; fruit globular, 3 to 4 lines in diameter, resting on the enlarged and persistent perianth-tube. Habitat, brush forests, from Illawarra to the Richmond River.

Qualities of *timber* unknown.

XCV. LIVISTONA.

(Natural Order PALMÆ.)

246. L. AUSTRALIS.—*Cabbage-tree Palm.*—A noble erect palm, attaining a height of 120 feet and a diameter of 18 inches; leaves in a dense crown, fan-shaped, 3 to 4 feet in diameter, the lobes or segments acuminate, entire or 2-cleft at the apex, the panicles large, very much branched and glabrous; flowers very small, solitary or clusters along the slender rhachis of the ultimate branches; fruit globular, 6 to 9 lines diameter, the pericarp hard and crustaceous when dry. Habitat, brush forests at Illawarra; also near Kurrajong and Valley of the Grose River.

The leaves of this palm are used in the manufacture of hats, and the seeds are largely exported to Europe.

XCVI. LOMATIA.

(Natural Order PROTEACEÆ.   Sub-Order *Folliculares*.)

247. L. LONGIFOLIA.—*Mountain Beech.*—An erect small tree, glabrous or with a slight ferruginous pubescence on the young shoots and inflorescence; leaves alternate, linear-lanceolate or rarely oblong-lanceolate, acuminate, bordered by distant serratures, tapering into a petiole, 4 to 8 inches long, not prominently veined; flowers pedicellate in pairs in axillary or terminal racemes; fruit a follicle, about 1 inch long. Habitat, brush forests, from Port Jackson to the Blue Mountains, Argyle, and Twofold Bay.

Timber handsome, close-grained, and easily wrought.

Var. arborescens.—20 to 25 feet in height, with large and more terminal racemes, the flowers smaller on shorter pedicels. Habitat, Valley of the Grose River.

XCVII. MACADAMIA.

(Natural Order PROTEACEÆ. Sub-Order *Folliculares.*)

248. M. TERNIFOLIA.—*Nut-tree ; Queensland Nut.*—A small tree, with a very dense foliage, glabrous or the young branches and inflorescence pubescent ; leaves sessile or nearly so, in whorls of 3 or 4, oblong or lanceolate, acute, serrate, glabrous and shining, from a few inches to above 1 foot long ; flowers pedicellate in pairs in terminal or axillary racemes, the pairs often clustered or almost verticillate ; fruit with a 2-valved fleshy exocarp, the putamen globular, smooth and shining, thick and woody, often above 1 inch in diameter. Habitat, brush forests, Clarence, Richmond, and Tweed Rivers.

Qualities of *timber* unknown.

XCVIII. MALLOTUS.

(Natural Order EUPHORBIACEÆ.)

249. M. DISCOLOR.—A tall tree, the branches, inflorescence, and underside of the leaves white with a close tomentum, with longer hairs on the principal veins underneath ; leaves alternate or rarely opposite, petiolate, ovate or ovate-lanceolate, acute or acuminate, thin and smooth, 2 to 3 inches long, rounded or acute and 3-nerved at the base, with flat glands rather prominent; flowers diœcious, pedicellate in racemes in the lower axils of the young shoots, slender, simple, 3 to 4 inches long; fruit a capsule, not seen. Habitat, mountain brushes on the Clarence River.

Qualities of *timber* unknown.

250. M. PHILIPPINENSIS.—A tree often of considerable size, the branches and inflorescence ferruginous-tomentose; leaves alternate or rarely opposite, petiolate, oblong, ovate-lanceolate or ovate, acuminate or obtuse, entire, contracted or rounded and 3-nerved at the base, 3 to 6 inches long, coriaceous, the upper side glabrous, with obscure glands near the base, the under surface pale or ferruginous with a minute tomentum, the principal veins ferruginous-tomentose ; flowers diœcious, in racemes terminal or in the upper axils, the males more branched than the females ; fruit a capsule, tridymous, 3 to 4 lines in diameter, covered with a red stellate tomentum. Habitat, brush forests, Hastings and Clarence Rivers.

Qualities of *timber* unknown.

XCIX. MARLEA.

(Natural Order CORNACEÆ.)

251. M. VITIENSIS.—A tree attaining a considerable height, glabrous or the young branches pubescent or villous ; leaves alternate, ovate, ovate-lanceolate or oblong, acuminate, oblique and unequal

at the base, or rarely equal, 3 to 5 inches long, glabrous or pubescent underneath; flowers petiolate in short axillary cymes
on slender peduncles; fruit a drupe, ovoid, about $\frac{1}{2}$ inch long.
Habitat, brush forests, Clarence and Richmond Rivers.
Qualities of *timber* unknown.

C. MEDICOSMA.

(Natural Order RUTACEÆ.)

252. M. CUNNINGHAMII.—A small tree, glabrous or the young
shoots and inflorescence pubescent; leaves mostly opposite, consisting
of a single leaflet obscurely articulate on a short petiole, oblong-
elliptical or rarely obovate-oblong, obtuse or acuminate, 3 to 6
inches long; flowers large, few, in axillary trichotomous panicles;
fruit separating into coriaceous 2-valved cocci. Habitat, brush
forests, Clarence and Richmond Rivers.
Qualities of *timber* unknown.

CI. MELALEUCA.

(Natural Order MYRTACEÆ.)

253. M. ARMILLARIS.—*Tea-tree.*—A small tree of 20 to 30 feet;
leaves scattered, crowded, narrow-linear, acute and often recurved
at the end, about $\frac{1}{2}$ inch long; flowers almost immersed in the
rhachis of dense or interrupted cylindrical spikes; fruit a capsule,
enclosed in the enlarged and hardened calyx-tube. Habitat, open
forests, from Twofold Bay to the Richmond River.
Timber hard and strong, very durable under ground.

254. M. ERICIFOLIA.—*Tea-tree.*—A tree attaining sometimes a
considerable size, usually glabrous and often glaucous, with virgate
branches; leaves scattered, numerous, often recurved, narrow-
linear, semiterete or convex underneath, obtusely or scarcely
acute, rarely above $\frac{1}{2}$ inch long; flowers yellowish-white or rarely
red, small, (the males?) in ovoid or nearly globular terminal
heads, or the perfect ones in oblong and cylindrical spikes
of $\frac{1}{2}$ to 1 inch, the axils growing into a leafy branch, the rhachis
tomentose; fruiting spikes compact, the calyxes truncate. Habitat,
open forests, from Port Jackson to the Blue Mountains.
Timber similar to that of the last species.

255. M. GENISTIFOLIA.—*Tea-tree.*—A tree attaining 40 feet or
more in height, glabrous or more or less pubescent or hirsute;
leaves scattered, lanceolate or linear-lanceolate, rigid, acute and
often pungent-pointed, flat, about $\frac{1}{2}$ inch long or more, finely
striate, with 7 or more nerves; flowers in loose oblong or cylindrical

spikes, sometimes terminal, but the axils growing out, often interrupted, the rhachis glabrous, pubescent or hirsute; fruiting-calyx not much enlarged, nearly globular.   Habitat, open forests, Port Jackson, Cox's River, and New England.

Timber similar to that of the last species.

256. M. HAKEOIDES.—*Tea-tree.*—A small tree, the young shoots softly silky-pubescent and silvery, the older foliage glabrous; leaves alternate, linear-subulate, terete or slightly compressed, usually sulcate, obtuse or acute, 1 to 2 inches long, the point straight; flowers small, in dense globular or rarely ovoid terminal heads, the rhachis usually villous; fruiting-spikes very dense, globular or ovoid, the calyxes truncate, about 1 line diameter.   Habitat, scrub forests, north-west interior.

Qualities of *timber* unknown.

257. M. LEUCADENDRON.— *White Tea-tree; Swamp Tea-tree.*— A tree often attaining a height of 50 feet and a diameter of 2 feet, with a thick often spongy bark peeling off in layers, the branches slender and often pendulous, but sometimes a shrub with rigid erect branches; leaves alternate, often vertical, elliptical or lanceolate, straight, oblique or falcate, acuminate, acute or obtuse, when broad 2 to 4 inches long, when narrow sometimes 6 to 8 inches long, narrowed into a petiole, 3- to 7-nerved, with anastomosing veins; flowers solitary or 2 or 3 together, in interrupted elongated spikes, from 2 to 6 inches long, at first terminal but growing into a leafy branch after flowering, the rhachis glabrous, pubescent or tomentose; fruiting-calyx about 2 lines in diameter, globular or almost hemispherical.   Habitat, open forests, Port Jackson to the Blue Mountains, Hastings and Clarence Rivers.

Timber hard and close-grained; excellent for fencing-posts in damp situations, being almost imperishable underground.

258. M. LINARIIFOLIA.—*Narrow-leaved Tea-tree.*—A tall tree, with slender branches, the young shoots and inflorescence pubescent, the adult foliage glabrous and often glaucous; leaves mostly opposite, linear or linear-lanceolate, concave or keeled, rigid, acute, ¾ to 1½ inch long; flowers in distinct pairs, in rather dense spikes of 1 to 1½ inch, at first terminal or in the upper axils, but the axis growing into a leafy branch, the rhachis more or less pubescent; fruiting-calyx not much enlarged.   Habitat, open forests, from Port Jackson to the Hastings River.

Timber heavy, hard, and durable.

259. M. NODOSA.—A small tree, sometimes shrubby; leaves alternate, linear or subulate, rigid, pungent-pointed, ½ to nearly 1 inch long; flowers in small dense globular or rarely ovoid axillary or terminal heads, the axis growing out after flowering, the rhachis

tomentose; fruiting-heads very dense, globular, 3 to 4 lines in diameter, the calyxes truncate. Habitat, open forests, from Port Jackson to the Blue Mountains, and Clarence River. Qualities of *timber* unknown.

260. M. PAUCIFLORA.—*Tea-tree.*—A tree of 60 to 80 feet in height and 2 feet in diameter, the young shoots silky-pubescent, the older foliage glabrous; leaves opposite, spreading, from oblong-elliptical and obtuse or mucronate to lanceolate and acute, $\frac{1}{4}$ to $\frac{1}{2}$ inch long, with the margins often recurved and the mid-rib prominent underneath; flowers few, small, in short terminal spikes, the axis growing out, the rhachis pubescent; fruiting-calyx about 1 line diameter. Habitat, open forests, from Illawarra to the Clarence River, westward to the Blue Mountains.

Timber hard, close-grained; very durable underground, but apt to split in drying.

261. M. SQUARROSA.—*Tea-tree.*—A handsome small tree, erect and glabrous, or the young shoots and inflorescence pubescent or villous; leaves mostly opposite or nearly so, from broadly ovate-cordate to ovate-lanceolate, 5- or 7-nerved, rigid, acute, almost pungent, 3 to 4 lines or $\frac{1}{2}$ inch long; flowers yellowish-white, sessile in oblong or cylindrical spikes of 1 to 2 inches, at first terminal, but the axis growing out, or the flowers from the first much below the ends of the branches; fruiting-spikes rather dense, but not compact. Habitat, open forests, Cumberland, Illawarra, and Blue Mountains.

Timber close-grained, hard, and durable.

262. M. STYPHELIOIDES.—*Prickly-leaved Tea-tree.*—A tall tree, sometimes 80 feet in height and 2 feet in diameter, the young shoots and inflorescence silky-pubescent or villous, otherwise glabrous; leaves alternate, ovate or ovate-lanceolate, acuminate, pungent-pointed, about $\frac{1}{2}$ inch long, rigid, finely striate, with numerous nerves; flowers in rather dense oblong or cylindrical spikes, the axis growing out; fruiting-spikes often leafy, the calyxes crowned by the rigid erect lobes. Habitat, open forests, from Illawarra to the Richmond River, westward to the Blue Mountains.

Timber very hard and close-grained; never known to decay underground.

263. M. UNCINATA.—*Common Tea-tree.*—A small tree, attaining sometimes a height of 80 feet, and a diameter of 4 feet, the young shoots more or less silky-pubescent; leaves alternate, linear-subulate, terete or rarely slightly compressed, smooth, sulcate or almost angular, 1 to 2 inches long, with a fine recurved point or rarely obtuse; flowers small, numerous, in very dense terminal ovoid-oblong or almost globular heads, the axis growing out, the rhachis woolly, hirsute or rarely quite glabrous; fruiting-spikes

very dense and compact, rarely above $\frac{1}{2}$ inch long, the calyxes turbinate, truncate, about $1\frac{1}{2}$ line long. Habitat, open forests, Illawarra; also on the Lachlan River and other parts of the interior.

Timber hard, close-grained, and durable.

CII. MELIA.
(Natural Order MELIACEÆ.)

264. M. COMPOSITA.—*White Cedar.*—An elegant tree, attaining a height of 80 feet and a diameter of 3 feet, the young leaves, shoots, and inflorescence sprinkled with a mealy stellate tomentum, disappearing with age; leaves alternate or rarely opposite, twice or rarely thrice pinnate, leaflets petiolulate, opposite, with a terminal odd one, ovate to almost lanceolate, acuminate, 1 to 2 inches long, entire, toothed or sometimes lobed; flowers small, in loose panicles, tomentose; fruit a drupe, ovoid, $\frac{1}{2}$ to $\frac{3}{4}$ inch long. Habitat, brush forests, from the Hastings to the Tweed River.

Timber soft and easily wrought, but deficient in strength and durability; used occasionally for shingles and packing-cases.

CIII. MELICOPE.
(Natural Order RUTACEÆ.)

265. M. AUSTRALASICA.—A handsome tree of 80 feet, glabrous in all its parts; leaves opposite, digitately trifoliate, leaflets oblong-elliptical or rarely ovate-oblong, obtuse or acuminate, 6 to 10 inches long, coriaceous, entire; flowers small, numerous, in axillary trichotomous panicles; cocci erect, distinct, angular, acuminate, under 2 lines long. Habitat, brush forests, Hastings and Clarence Rivers.

Timber light and soft, but little known.

266. M. ERYTHROCOCCA.—A moderate-sized tree, quite glabrous; leaves opposite, trifoliate or rarely unifoliate, leaflets oblong-lanceolate, obtuse, $1\frac{1}{2}$ to 3 inches long, coriaceous, entire or crenulate, on a common petiole of $\frac{3}{4}$ to $1\frac{1}{2}$ inch; flowers rather small, in terminal or axillary panicles; cocci 4 or rarely 5, spreading, ovate, about 2 lines long, wrinkled, of a reddish colour. Habitat, brush forests, Clarence River.

Qualities of *timber* unknown.

267. M. NEUROCOCCA.—A small tree, the young branches, petioles, and peduncles pubescent; leaves opposite, trifoliate, unequal, leaflets ovate-lanceolate or lanceolate, acuminate, 3 to 4 inches long, glabrous above, hairy underneath; flowers rather small, in terminal trichotomous and corymbose panicles; cocci distinct, nearly erect, broad, about 3 lines long, the valves coriaceous and wrinkled. Habitat, brush forests, on the Hastings, Clarence, and Richmond Rivers.

Qualities of *timber* unknown.

G

CIV. MELODORUM.

(Natural Order ANONACEÆ.)

268. M. LEICHHARDTII.—A beautiful tree of about 60 to 80 feet, with flexuose branches, the younger ones rusty-tomentose; leaves alternate, petiolate, oblong, obtuse, or acuminate, about 3 inches long, coriaceous, glabrous and shining, sprinkled with minute stellate hairs underneath, the veins scarcely perceptible; flowers nearly ½ inch in diameter, on peduncles terminal or leaf-opposed, rusty-tomentose; fruit a berry, stipitate, depressed, globose or somewhat oblong, 4 or 5 lines in diameter, or moniliform. Habitat, brush forests, Clarence River.

Qualities of *timber* unknown.

CV. MEMECYLON.

(Natural Order MELASTOMACEÆ.)

269. M. CERASIFORMIS.—*Cherry*; *Red Apple.*—A singularly handsome tree, tall and straight, with a clear bole of 50 to 60 feet and a diameter of 2 or 3 feet, the head rounded; leaves opposite, pinnately veined, coriaceous, the mid-rib prominent; flowers small, in axillary clusters or cymes; fruit a berry, bright red, guava-like, edible, borne in terminal clusters. Habitat, brush forests, near banks of creeks, on the Richmond River.

Qualities of *timber* unknown.

CVI. MILLETTIA.

(Natural Order LEGUMINOSÆ.   Sub-Order *Papilionaceæ.*)

270. M. MEGASPERMA,—A tall evergreen woody climber, sometimes 1 foot in diameter, with a red, resinous and astringent juice, glabrous except a slight hoariness on the young shoots and panicles; leaves alternate or opposite, pinnate, leaflets 7 to 13, obovate or obovate-oblong, shortly acuminate, 1½ to 2 inches long, coriaceous and green on both sides; flowers scattered, purple, in racemes 4 to 6 inches long, several in a terminal almost leafless panicle; pod about 6 inches long, thick, hard, almost woody, densely velvety outside. Habitat, brush forests, Richmond River.

Qualities of *timber* unknown.

CVII. MOLLINEDIA.

(Natural Order MONIMIACEÆ.)

271. M. HUEGELIANA.—A small tree, the young shoots, inflorescence, and underside of the leaves pubescent; leaves opposite, petiolate, ovate-elliptical to oblong-lanceolate, obtuse or acuminate, entire or toothed, rounded or rarely acute at the base, 3 to

4 inches long, coriaceous and shining above and reticulate ; flowers dioecious, pedicellate in little cymes or thyrsoid panicles sessile in the axils, the males on a short common peduncle, the females on a longer peduncle or rhachis, almost forming a few-flowered raceme ; fruit a drupe, sessile, ovoid-globose, $\frac{1}{2}$ inch long, 3 to 4 lines in diameter, pubescent or at length glabrous. Habitat, brush forests, from Illawarra to the Richmond River.

Qualities of *timber* unknown.

CVIII. MONOTOCA.

(Natural Order EPACRIDEÆ.)

272. M. ELLIPTICA. –*Beech.*—A small tree of 20 to 30 feet leaves alternate or very rarely opposite, from elliptical oblong to oblong-linear, mucronate, slightly convex, pale or whitish and veined underneath, from under $\frac{1}{2}$ to 1 inch long ; flowers small, pedicellate, few or many together, forming short racemes, either terminal or axillary, sometimes growing out into leafy branches with a few solitary axillary flowers ; fruit a small drupe, ovoid, with a pulpy mesocarp and a crustaceous endocarp, $1\frac{1}{2}$ to nearly 2 lines long. Habitat, scrub forests, from Twofold Bay to the Tweed River, westward to the Blue Mountains.

Timber very hard and close-grained ; very valuable for handle s of carpenters' tools and turning.

CIX. MUHLENBECKIA.

(Natural Order POLYGONACEÆ.)

273. M. CUNNINGHAMII.—*Lignum Scrub*; *Polygonum.*—A small tree, frequently low and bushy, with numerous terete sulcate or angular branches, the young ones often with a few linear or linear-lanceolate leaves of 1 to 2 inches contracted into a petiole, but most of the branches rigid or rush-like, often clustered and either quite leafless or with a few linear leaves ; flowers dioecious, small, green or whitish, in solitary clusters or in short spikes at the leafless nodes or in the axils of the small leaves forming long terminal interrupted spikes ; fruit a nut, prominently triangled, smooth and shining, enclosed in the persistent thickened perianth, $1\frac{1}{2}$ to 2 lines long. Habitat, Liverpool Plains, Macquarie, Lachlan, Murray, and Darling Rivers, forming sometimes dense impenetrable scrubs.

Timber of no use.

CX. MYOPORUM.

(Natural Order MYOPORINEÆ.)

274. M. ACUMINATUM.—A small tree, exceedingly variable in stature, breadth of leaves, and size of flowers; leaves alternate, from elliptical-oblong to lanceolate or linear, acuminate, contracted towards the base, entire, ½ to 3 inches long, sometimes the broader ones obovate and obtuse, or all smaller, a few of the leaves here and there marked with distant teeth; flowers small, on pedicels, in axillary clusters of 2 to 4 or more, or rarely solitary; fruit a small drupe, nearly globular, 2 to 3 lines in diameter, more or less succulent. Habitat, brush forests, from Illawarra to the Tweed River; also deserts and scrub forests of the interior.

Timber close-grained and firm, but seldom used.

CXI. MYRSINE.

(Natural Order MYRSINEÆ.)

275. M. CRASSIFOLIA.—A small tree, quite glabrous; leaves alternate, petiolate or almost sessile, oblong, lanceolate, elliptical or obovate, obtuse, entire, 3 to 4 inches long or more, coriaceous; flowers small, on pedicels in umbels or clusters, sessile in the axils or at the nodes, usually on the old wood; fruit an indehiscent small globular berry or drupe. Habitat, brush forests, Clarence and Richmond Rivers; also Mount Lindsay.

Timber white and prettily grained.

276. M. VARIABILIS.—A handsome small tree, attaining a height of 40 feet; leaves alternate, ovate-oblong, obtuse or acuminate, entire or bordered by acute teeth, coriaceous, 1½ to 2½ inches long, sometimes nearly twice as large and thinner, narrowed into a petiole; flowers small, often polygamous, pedicellate in umbels or clusters, sessile in the axils or at the nodes, usually on the old wood; fruit an indehiscent berry or drupe, globular, 2 to 3 lines in diameter. Habitat, brush forests, from Twofold Bay to the Tweed River.

Timber white, or sometimes pink, prettily grained.

CXII. MYRTUS.

(Natural Order MYRTACEÆ.)

277. M. ACMENIOIDES.—*Hickory*; *White Myrtle*; *Lignum-vitæ.* —A tree attaining a height of 80 feet and a diameter of 2 feet, quite glabrous, with a smooth reddish bark; leaves opposite, ovate, acuminate, narrowed into a petiole, 1½ to 3 inches long, penniveined, the veins confluent in a fine intramarginal one; flowers pedicellate, usually several together in the axils or at the old nodes, in a cluster or short raceme on a common peduncle;

fruit a berry, about 2 lines diameter, usually crowned by the calyx-lobes. Habitat, brush forests, Clarence, Richmond, and Tweed Rivers.

Timber hard, tough, and durable ; used in coach-building.

278. M. BECKLERII.—*Myrtle.*—A tree attaining a height of 80 feet and a diameter of 2 feet, quite glabrous ; leaves opposite, ovate or ovate-lanceolate, acuminate, cuneate at the base, 1 to 2 inches long, rather thick, penniveined or obscurely triplinerved ; flowers in solitary, filiform, axillary peduncles, rarely above ½ inch long ; fruit a berry, globular, about 2 lines diameter. Habitat, brush forests, Clarence and Richmond Rivers.

Timber of a red colour when fresh, becoming pale on drying ; said to be durable.

279. M. FRAGRANTISSIMA.—A small tree, the young shoots slightly hoary ; leaves opposite, petiolate, broadly ovate, 1 to 2 inches long, glabrous, penniveined ; flowers small, few, in short pedunculate axillary racemes, with the terminal one sessile, or the pedicels solitary and 1-flowered at the base of the shoots ; fruit a berry, but not seen. Habitat, brush forests on the Richmond River.

Qualities of *timber* unknown.

280. M. RHYTISPERMA.—A small tree, with the habit of the common European Myrtle, the young shoots slightly pubescent, the older foliage glabrous ; leaves opposite, oblong-elliptical or oblong-oval, obtuse, ¾ to 1½ inch long, narrowed or rounded at the base, penniveined and green on both sides ; flowers solitary on slender axillary peduncles ; fruit a berry, 4 to 5 lines in diameter. Habitat, brush forests on the Clarence River.

Qualities of *timber* unknown.

CXIII. NELITRIS.

(Natural Order MYRTACEÆ.)

281. N. PANICULATA.—A fine tree, attaining a height of 80 feet and a diameter of 4 feet, the young shoots and inflorescence silky-pubescent ; leaves opposite, ovate-lanceolate, acuminate, narrowed at the base, 1 to 2 inches long, glabrous above, finely veined, silky-pubescent underneath, at length glabrous ; flowers small, pedicellate in short axillary racemes, often forming elegant leafy terminal panicles ; fruit a berry, about 2 lines in diameter. Habitat, brush forests on the Richmond River.

Timber of a red colour when fresh ; very close-grained and hard ; sometimes used in ship-building.

CXIV. NEPHELIUM.

(Natural Order SAPINDACEÆ.)

282. N. BECKLERII.—A tree of considerable size, the young shoots and inflorescence slightly hoary with a minute tomentum, otherwise glabrous; leaves alternate, pinnate, leaflets 3 to 6, ovate-lanceolate or oblong, obtuse or acuminate, 2 to 4 or 6 inches long, entire, narrowed into a petiolule, coriaceous and glabrous; flowers small, numerous, pedicellate in much-branched axillary or terminal panicles; fruit stipitate, 2- or 3-lobed, glabrous, often reduced to a single perfect lobe, with the two others forming tubercles at its base. Habitat, brush forests on the Clarence and Richmond Rivers.

Timber occasionally used in ship-building.

283. N. LEIOCARPUM.—*Wild Quince.* — A tall tree, usually glabrous except a slight pubescence on the young leaves and shoots, and sometimes on the panicles; leaves alternate, pinnate, leaflets 2 to 6, oblong-elliptical, ovate-lanceolate, acuminate or obtuse, 3 to 4 or even 5 inches long, entire, or rarely deeply serrated, narrowed into a petiolule; flowers small, in loose and not much-branched axillary or terminal panicles, usually glabrous; fruit sessile or nearly so, glabrous, distinctly lobed, coriaceous. Habitat, brush forests, from Twofold Bay to the Richmond River.

Qualities of *timber* unknown.

284. N. SUBDENTATUM.—A small tree, the young shoots and inflorescence slightly pubescent; leaves alternate, pinnate, the leaflets 2 to 6, ovate or ovate-lanceolate, obtuse or acute, sinuate-toothed or rarely almost entire, coriaceous, glabrous on both sides and shining above; flowers small, pedicellate in little-branched axillary or terminal panicles; fruit truncate at the top, slightly hoary, usually 2-lobed, hard and indehiscent. Habitat, New England.

Qualities of *timber* unknown.

285. N. TOMENTOSUM.—A fine tree, attaining a height of 80 feet and a diameter of 3 feet, the young branches and petioles clothed with a soft rust-coloured velvety tomentum; leaves alternate, pinnate, the leaflets 4 to 8, from oval-oblong to oblong-lanceolate, acute or rarely obtuse, 2 to 4 inches long, toothed or rarely almost entire, coriaceous, pubescent above or at length glabrous, tomentose-pubescent underneath; flowers small, pedicellate, crowded in short slightly-branched tomentose panicles, sometimes reduced to simple racemes; fruit tomentose-villous, depressed at the top, 2- or rarely 3-lobed, 4 to 5 lines in diameter, hard and indehiscent. Habitat, brush forests on the Clarence and Richmond Rivers.

Timber occasionally used in house-carpentry.

CXV. NOTELÆA.

(Natural Order JASMINEÆ.)

286. N. LONGIFOLIA.—*Axe-breaker.*—A small slender tree, the branches and underside of the leaves or rarely both sides of the leaves pubescent, or the whole plant glabrous ; leaves opposite, ovate-lanceolate or lanceolate, acute or acuminate, tapering into a petiole, coriaceous, reticulate on both sides, 2 to 6 inches long ; flowers small, pedicellate in axillary racemes, rarely 1 inch long ; fruit a drupe, ovoid or globular, about ½ inch in diameter, of a dark bluish colour, with a succulent mesocarp and a hard endocarp. Habitat, brush forests, from Illawarra to the Clarence River.
Timber close-grained, hard, and often finely marked.

287. N. OVATA.—*Native Olive.*—A small tree, frequently of crooked growth, glabrous or pubescent ; leaves opposite, petiolate, ovate or broadly ovate-lanceolate, obtuse or acute, cordate, rounded or contracted at the base, coriaceous and reticulate, 1½ to 2 inches long ; flowers small and few, pedicellate in racemes, usually pedunculate and axillary, but sometimes inserted rather above the axils; fruit a drupe, ovoid or globular, ½ inch in diameter, of a bluish colour, the mesocarp succulent, the endocarp hard. Habitat, brush forests, Illawarra, Cumberland, and Grose River.
Timber close-grained, hard, and firm.

CXVI. OCHROSIA.

(Natural Order APOCYNEÆ.)

288. O. MOOREI.—A slender tree, with a milky juice, quite glabrous ; leaves mostly opposite, narrow-oblong or oblong-lanceolate, acuminate, tapering into a petiole, transversely veined, 3 to 6 inches long ; flowers sessile, in dichotomous pedunculate cymes in the upper axils ; fruit a drupe, scarlet, 1½ to 2 inches long, obtuse and flattened. Habitat, brush forests on the Clarence and Richmond Rivers.
Qualities of *timber* unknown.

CXVII. OLEA.

(Natural Order JASMINEÆ.)

289. O. PANICULATA.—*Marblewood; Ironwood.*—A tree of moderate size, quite glabrous ; leaves opposite, petiolate, ovate-lanceolate or elliptical, acuminate, 2 to 3 or rarely 4 inches long, penniveined underneath and faintly reticulate ; flowers small, pedicellate in loose trichotomous panicles, terminal or in the upper axils ; fruit a drupe, ovoid, resembling that of the common olive. Habitat, brush forests, from the Hunter to the Clarence River.
Timber close-grained, hard, and durable.

CXVIII. OLEARIA.

(Natural Order Compositæ.)

290. O. argophylla.—*Musk-tree.*—A tree attaining 20 to 25 feet, emitting a strong musky smell, the indumentum close and silvery-shining, consisting of centrally-affixed hairs; leaves alternate, petiolate, from ovate-elliptical to oblong-lanceolate, acute at both ends, callous-denticulate or rarely entire, 3 to 5 inches long, reticulate and glabrous above or minutely hairy, silvery-silky underneath; flowers in small heads, numerous, in large terminal corymbs; fruit a nut or *achene*, sparingly hirsute. Habitat, Port Jackson and Mittagong.

Qualities of *timber* unknown.

CXIX. ORITES.

(Natural Order Proteaceæ.. Sub-Order *Folliculares*.)

291. O. excelsa.—A handsome tree of 40 to 60 feet, usually quite glabrous; leaves alternate, on the flowering branches lanceolate, obtuse or acute, tapering into a petiole, entire or toothed, 4 to 6 inches long, flat, reticulate, shining above, glaucous underneath, those of the barren branches often larger, toothed or deeply divided into 3 or 5 lanceolate toothed lobes; flowers small, in interrupted axillary spikes, usually glabrous, the flowers in distant pairs; fruit a follicle, acuminate, about 1 inch long. Habitat, brush forests, from the Hastings to the Tweed River.

Qualities of *timber* unknown.

CXX. OWENIA.

(Natural Order Meliaceæ.)

292. O. acidula.—A small or moderate-sized tree, glabrous, the young shoots glutinous; leaves alternate or rarely opposite, pinnate, crowded at the ends of the often pendulous branches; the leaflets petiolate, from 9 to nearly 30, linear-lanceolate, acute or mucronate, 1 to $1\frac{1}{2}$ inch long, oblique, the mid-rib prominent underneath, otherwise almost nerveless; flowers small, nearly sessile, in clusters or on short branches in axillary panicles; fruit a drupe, $\frac{3}{4}$ to 1 inch diameter or rather more, resembling a russet apple, the epicarp pulpy, of a rich crimson, the putamen hard. Habitat, Gwydir, Castlereagh, and Darling Rivers.

Timber likely to be useful, but unknown.

293. O. venosa.—*Tulipwood; Sour Plum.*—A small tree, quite glabrous, with a milky juice, the young shoots slightly glutinous; leaves alternate or rarely opposite, pinnate, the leaflets 6 to 8, oblong or ovate-lanceolate, 2 to 4 inches long, coriaceous, penniveined, reticulate underneath; flowers small, in narrow

axillary panicles, 3 to 5 inches long; fruit an acid drupe, globular, ¾ to 1 inch diameter, with a woody or strong putamen, eaten by the aborigines. Habitat, brush forests on the Clarence River.

Timber valuable for cabinet work; strong and highly coloured, with different shades from black to yellow, taking a fine polish.

CXXI. PANAX.

(Natural Order ARALIACEÆ.)

294. P. ELEGANS.—*Light Sycamore.*—A large handsome tree, glabrous except the inflorescence; leaves large, simply or doubly pinnate, the rhachis articulate, leaflets petiolate, opposite, ovate, acuminate, entire, coriaceous, shining, often 3 to 4 inches long; flowers singly pedicellate in little racemes, numerous and arranged in a large terminal panicle, the rhachis minutely hoary-pubescent; fruit flattened, about 3 lines broad, the endocarp or pyrenes hard. Habitat, brush forests, from Illawarra to the Richmond River.

Timber soft and perishable.

295. P. MURRAYI—A splendid tree, the trunk simple to the height of 50 or 60 feet, then trichotomously branched; leaves simply pinnate, several feet long, the leaflets lanceolate, from 3 to 10 inches long, quite glabrous; flowers numerous in pedunculate umbels, in racemes or divaricately branched panicles; fruit flattened, about 2 lines broad. Habitat, brush forests, from Twofold Bay to the Hastings River.

Timber similar to that of the last species.

296. P. SAMBUCIFOLIUS—A small tree, quite glabrous; leaves simply or doubly pinnate, leaflets ovate-elliptical or lanceolate, acute, entire, or lobed, 1½ to 3 inches long; flowers numerous in umbels, in a terminal branched corymbose panicle or in a simple raceme; fruit flattened, 2 to 3 lines broad, with a succulent exocarp. Habitat, brush forests, from Twofold Bay to the Clarence River.

Timber similar to that of the two last species.

CXXII. PANDANUS.

(Natural Order PANDANEÆ.)

297. P. PEDUNCULATUS.—*Screw Pine.*—Stem arborescent, emitting stolons at the base; leaves 3 to 5 feet long, broad, tapering into a narrow point, the edges prickly; flowers diœcious, closely packed in dense spikes or heads; fruit drupaceous, densely crowded or more or less connate, in globular ovoid or cylindrical heads. Habitat, brush forests, northern rivers.

Timber of no use.

CXXIII. PENNANTIA.

(Natural Order OLACINEÆ.)

298. P. CUNNINGHAMII.—A moderate-sized glabrous tree; leaves usually alternate, ovate or broadly elliptical, acuminate, 4 to 6 inches long, entire, coriaceous and shining when old, narrowed into a petiole; flowers numerous, in broad rather dense panicles, terminal or in the upper axils; fruit a drupe or berry, ovoid, about ½ inch long, the endocarp scarcely hardened. Habitat, brush forests, from Illawarra to the Clarence.

Qualities of *timber* unknown.

CXXIV. PENTACERAS.

(Natural Order RUTACEÆ.)

299. P. AUSTRALIS.—*Scrub White Cedar.*—A tree sometimes attaining a height of 60 feet, quite glabrous; leaves alternate, pinnate, with a common petiole, of from 4 to 5 inches to nearly 1 foot, the leaflets usually 7 to 11, opposite in pairs, with a terminal odd one, ovate to lanceolate, obtuse or acuminate, 2 to 4 inches long, entire or crenate; flowers numerous, small, pedicellate along the ultimate branches of large terminal spreading and loose panicles; fruit a *samara*, 1 to 1½ inch long, ½ inch to ¾ inch broad. Habitat, scrub forests on the Richmond River.

Qualities of *timber* unknown.

CXXV. PERSOONIA.

(Natural Order PROTEACEÆ.   Sub-Order *Nucamentaceæ*.)

300. P. CORNIFOLIA.—"*Geebung.*"—A small tree, the branches pubescent, the young leaves ciliate on the margins, and sometimes pubescent, the adult foliage glabrous; leaves alternate, from broadly ovate or ovate to elliptical-oblong or even broadly lanceolate, acute when narrow or obtuse when broad, usually mucronate, contracted into a petiole, 1 to 2 inches long, flat, rigid, veined, the mid-rib slightly prominent; flowers yellow or white, on pedicels, solitary in the axils or clustered on a very short axillary branch; fruit a drupe, with a succulent exocarp and a thick very hard endocarp. Habitat, open forests on the northern rivers; also New England.

Qualities of *timber* unknown.

301. P. LANCEOLATA.—"*Geebung.*"—A small tree, the adult foliage glabrous or nearly so; leaves alternate, lanceolate or oblong-lanceolate, mucronate-acute, contracted into a petiole, 1½ to 2½ inches long, flat, the mid-rib prominent, the margins slightly nerve-like, otherwise veinless; flowers yellow or white, on pedicels,

solitary or two together, pubescent ; fruit a drupe, with a succulent exocarp and a thick hard endocarp. Habitat, Port Jackson and New England.

Qualities of *timber* unknown.

Var. lævis.—The whole plant glabrous ; leaves longer and thinner, broad or narrow, the pedicels longer. Habitat, Macleay and Clarence River.

302. P. LINEARIS.—"*Geebung.*"—A small tree of 20 feet, the young branches pubescent or villous, the adult foliage usually glabrous ; leaves alternate, rather crowded, linear, acute or obtuse, contracted at the base, 1 to 2 inches long, ¾ to 1½ line broad, obscurely veined ; flowers yellow or white, in solitary pedicels in the axils ; fruit a drupe, ovoid, with a succulent exocarp and a hard endocarp. Habitat, open forests, from Twofold Bay to the Macleay River ; also Blue Mountains.

Timber of no value.

Var. sericeæ.—Silky-pubescent at time of flowering. Habitat, Shoalhaven.

CXXVI. PETALOSTIGMA.

(Natural Order EUPHORBIACEÆ.)

303. P. QUADRILOCULARE.—*Crab-tree.*—A small or moderate-sized tree, the branches and underside of the leaves silky or tomentose ; leaves alternate, petiolate, ovate or almost orbicular, obtuse or acute, ½ to 1½ inch long, glabrous above when old ; flowers monœcious, rather large, pedicellate in the axils. the males usually clustered but few together, the females solitary in the same or in different axils ; fruit a capsule, globular or almost ovoid, orange-coloured, ½ inch diameter, with a fleshy exocarp and a hard endocarp. Habitat, open forests, on the borders of brush forests, Clarence River.

Qualities of *timber* unknown.

Var. glabrescens—Leaves elliptical-lanceolate, 1½ to 3 inches long, becoming nearly glabrous, the ovary and fruit much less villous. Habitat, Clarence River.

CXXVII. PHEBALIUM.

(Natural Order RUTACEÆ.)

304. P. BILLARDIERI.—A tree attaining a height of 70 feet and a diameter of 2 feet, the branches angular and clothed with small brown scurfy scales ; leaves alternate, oblong, lanceolate or linear, obtuse or acute, from ½ to 3 or even 5 inches long, entire, coriaceous, flat or with recurved margins, glabrous above, silvery-

white underneath, with minute scales ; flowers small, in axillary corymbs, shortly pedunculate, the peduncles and pedicels thick and scaly ; cocci 2-valved, small, broad, with a short beak. Habitat, brush forests, from Illawarra to the Clarence River ; also Blue Mountains.
Qualities of *timber* unknown.

CXXVIII. PHYLLANTHUS.

(Natural Order EUPHORBIACEÆ.)

305. P. FERDINANDI.—A moderately large tree, quite glabrous except the ovary ; leaves alternate, petiolate, elliptical or ovate-lanceolate, acuminate, often obliquely contracted at the base, usually coriaceous and shining above, 2 to 4 inches long ; flowers monœcious, small, on pedicels in the axils, the males frequently clustered but few together, the females solitary in the same or in different axils ; fruit a capsule, orbicular, glabrous or nearly so, much depressed in the centre, about ½ inch diameter. Habitat, brush forests, along the coast.
Qualities of *timber* unknown.

Var. minor.—Leaves smaller, pedicels shorter ; styles longer and more slender. Habitat, New England.

306. P. GUNNII.—A small tree, quite glabrous, with slender branches ; leaves alternate, distichous, ovate or orbicular, rarely obovate-oblong, obtuse or retuse, ½ to ¾ inch long ; flowers monœcious, in axillary clusters of 3 or more males and 1 female, on slender pedicels ; fruit a capsule, about 2 lines diameter, not furrowed. Habitat, Twofold Bay.
Qualities of *timber* unknown.

CXXIX. PISONIA.

(Natural Order NYCTAGINEÆ.)

307. P. BRUNONIANA.—A tree attaining sometimes a great height, quite glabrous or the inflorescence minutely pubescent ; leaves mostly opposite, the upper ones sometimes irregularly alternate or approximate so as to appear verticillate, petiolate, from ovate to obovate-elliptical or oblong, obtuse, 8 inches long or more, sometimes only half that size ; flowers mostly hermaphrodite, pedicellate in small cymes, collected into terminal leafless panicles ; fruit 1-seeded, enclosed in the persistent hardened base of the perianth. Habitat, brush forests, from Illawarra to the Richmond River.
Qualities of *timber* unknown.

CXXX. PITHECOLOBIUM.

(Natural Order LEGUMINOSÆ. Sub-Order *Mimoseæ*.)

308. P. GRANDIFLORUM.—A beautiful tree of 30 feet, glabrous or nearly so; leaves twice pinnate, the pinnæ 1 or 2 pairs, the common petiole and each rhachis 2 to 4 inches long, the leaflets 2 to 6 pairs, ovate, acuminate, 1½ to 2 inches long, penniveined; flowers large, sessile in heads, numerous, on peduncles in terminal panicles; pod not seen. Habitat, brush forests, on the Hastings River.

Qualities of *timber* unknown.

309. P. PRUINOSUM.—A beautiful tree, attaining sometimes a height of 60 feet, the young branches, foliage, and inflorescence rusty with a short pubescence or glaucous; leaves alternate or opposite, twice pinnate, the pinnæ in 1 or 2 pairs, with or without an odd one, the petiole and each rhachis from 1 to 6 inches long, the leaflets usually 3 or 4 pairs, on the terminal pinnæ, but irregular in number, size, and shape, mostly oblong or rhomboidal and acuminate, rarely obtuse, the larger ones often 2 to 3 inches long; flowers numerous, pedicellate in globular umbels on peduncles 2 or 3 together in the upper axils, or shortly racemose; pod several inches long, 7 to 8 lines broad, flat, but much curved and twisted. Habitat, brush forests, from Illawarra to the Richmond River.

Timber hard, close-grained, and of a yellowish colour.

CXXXI. PITTOSPORUM.

(Natural Order PITTOSPOREÆ.)

310. P. BICOLOR.—A tree sometimes attaining a height of 40 feet, sometimes bushy, the young branches hoary or rusty with a close tomentum; leaves alternate, crowded, oblong, lanceolate or linear, obtuse or with a recurved point, 1 to 2 inches long, entire, the margins revolute, nearly sessile or shortly petiolate, thick and coriaceous, glabrous above, silky underneath; flowers purple and yellow, solitary on pedicels, axillary, solitary or clustered, the uppermost sometimes in a terminal cluster; fruit a capsule, rounded, compressed, tomentose, 4 to 5 lines broad. Habitat, brush forests near the coast.

Qualities of *timber* unknown.

311. P. PHILLYRÆOIDES.—A small graceful tree, quite glabrous in all its parts; leaves alternate, usually oblong-or linear-lanceolate, with a small hooked point, 2 to 4 inches long, entire, petiolate, coriaceous and distinctly veined, sometimes short and oblong, sometimes long and narrow; flowers yellow on axillary pedicels, solitary or in sessile or pedunculate clusters or umbels, or the

uppermost forming a terminal cluster ; fruit ovate or round-cordate, compressed, smooth, 4 to 9 lines long. Habitat, scrub forests and deserts in the interior generally.

Qualities of *timber* unknown.

312. P. REVOLUTUM.—A small tree, sometimes shrubby ; the young shoots tomentose ; leaves alternate, ovate-elliptical or elliptical-oblong, acuminate, 2 to 4 inches long, scarcely undulate, petiolate, coriaceous, glabrous above, rusty-tomentose underneath, the upper ones often almost whorled ; flowers large, solitary or in dense ovate or corymbose racemes on terminal peduncles, few or solitary, usually decurved ; fruit a capsule, ½ to ¾ inch long, the valves woody and rough outside. Habitat, brush forests, from Twofold Bay to the Clarence River ; also Blue Mountains.

Qualities of *timber* unknown.

313. P. RHOMBIFOLIUM.—*Diamond-leaved Laurel.*—A tree 60 to 80 feet, glabrous in all its parts ; leaves alternate, rhomboidal-oval or broadly oblong-lanceolate, 3 to 4 inches long, toothed from the middle upwards, petiolate, coriaceous and shining, with pinnate and netted veins on both sides ; flowers white, numerous, rather small, in a dense terminal compressed corymb ; fruit a capsule, more or less pear-shaped or almost globular, about 3 lines long. Habitat, brush forests on the Clarence.

Timber handsome, close-grained but soft.

314. P. UNDULATUM.—*Mock Orange.*—A tree attaining some-times a considerable size, but sometimes small, quite glabrous except a slight pubescence on the young shoots and inflorescence ; leaves alternate, from oval-oblong to lanceolate, 3 to 6 inches long, acuminate, flat, or undulate on the margin, petiolate, coriaceous and shining, with faint veins, the upper ones often almost whorled ; flowers large, white, mostly 3 or 4, in a simple cyme or umbel, forming a pedunculate terminal cluster, one or two often 1-flowered ; fruit a capsule, nearly globular, not more than ½ inch in diameter, smooth, with thick valves and numerous seeds. Habitat, brush forests, from Illawarra to the Tweed River.

Timber very close-grained, but soft and easily wrought ; valuable for turners' work, carving, and wood-engraving.

CXXXII. PODOCARPUS.

(Natural Order CONIFERÆ.)

315. P. ELATA.—*Colonial Deal ; White Pine ; Pencil Cedar.*—A tree attaining a height of 120 feet and a diameter of 3 feet ; leaves alternate or rarely opposite, oblong-linear or linear-lanceolate, very variable in size, in young specimens from 1½ to 2 inches long, in the ordinary form from 3 to 6 inches, straight or slightly falcate,

but in barren specimens sometimes 8 to 10 inches long and much falcate, acute or obtuse, with a prominent mid-rib and a short petiole; amenta axillary, the males sessile in clusters of 2 or 3, the females solitary on peduncles; fruiting receptacle oblong, 4 to 6 lines long. Habitat, brush forests, from Illawarra to the Tweed River.

Timber handsome and valuable, free from knots, soft but close-grained, easily wrought; largely employed for planks, flooring-boards, joiners' and cabinet-makers' work.

316. P. SPINULOSA.—*Native Plum; Damson.*—An erect, much-branched, small tree; leaves alternate, or rarely opposite, linear, rigid, pungent-pointed, 1½ to 2 inches long; amenta axillary, the males sessile in clusters, the females pedunculate; fruiting receptacle 2-lobed. Habitat, brush forests, from Illawarra to the Tweed River.

Timber similar to that of the last species.

CXXXIII. POLYOSMA.

(Natural Order SAXIFRAGEÆ.)

317. P. CUNNINGHAMII.—*Featherwood; Wine-berry.*—A beautiful small tree, quite glabrous, except the inflorescence and flowers; leaves opposite or nearly so, ovate-elliptical, acuminate, acute or obtuse, 3 to 4 inches long, toothed, narrowed into a petiole, coriaceous, penniveined; flowers white or greenish, pedicellate in terminal simple racemes; fruit a berry, ovoid, about ½ inch long. crowned by the persistent calyx-limb. Habitat, brush forests, from Illawarra to the Clarence.

Timber close-grained and soft, but apt to rend in drying.

CXXXIV. POMADERRIS.

(Natural Order RHAMNEÆ.)

318. P. BETULINA.—A slender small tree, with elongated branches, the younger as well as the underside of the leaves often clothed with a rust-coloured tomentum; leaves alternate, oblong or obovate, obtuse, seldom above 1 inch long; flowers nearly sessile, in dense globular heads, solitary or 2 or 3 together, on short axillary or terminal peduncles; fruit a capsule, 3-valved, the endocarp separating into three cocei. Habitat, Pine Ridge, Macquarie River.

Timber handsome and close-grained; should be tried for wood-engraving.

319. P. ELLIPTICA.—A small tree, the young branches rusty
with a very close stellate down ; leaves alternate, petiolate, ovate,
oblong or ovate-lanceolate, obtuse or acute, 2 to 3 inches long, ¾
to 1¼ inch broad, entire or the margins slightly waved, glabrous
above and smooth or scarcely scabrous, white underneath with a
close tomentum, the mid-rib and principal veins often rust-coloured ;
flowers pedicellate in numerous cymes, forming dichotomous
panicles, usually more or less corymbose ; fruit a capsule, about 1½
line in diameter, slightly hairy, 3-valved, the endocarp separating
into cocci. Habitat, brush forests, from Twofold Bay to the
Clarence River ; also New England.

Timber similar to that of the last species.

CXXXV. PSEUDOMORUS.

(Natural Order URTICEÆ.)

320. P. BRUNONIANA.—A small tree of 30 to 40 feet, glabrous
or nearly so, with a milky juice ; leaves alternate, petiolate, elliptical, ovate-lanceolate or lanceolate, acuminate, denticulate, 1½ to 4
inches long, penniveined, sometimes pubescent underneath and
scabrous above ; flowers monœcious, in solitary axillary spikes, the
males dense and cylindrical, the females few and short, almost
reduced to heads ; fruit a small drupe or berry, globular, the size
of a currant. Habitat, brush forests, from Illawarra to the Richmond River ; also New England.

Timber used by the aborigines for making " boomerangs."

CXXXVI. PTYCHOSPERMA.

(Natural Order PALMÆ.)

321. P. CUNNINGHAMII.—*Bangalow.*—A beautiful palm, attaining a height of 80 feet ; the leaves several feet long, in a terminal
crown, pinnately divided, the segments acuminate and entire,
green on both sides ; inflorescence 1 to 1½ foot long and broad,
branching into numerous spikes ; fruit ovoid-globose, about ½ inch
in diameter. Habitat, brush forests, Illawarra.

Timber sometimes split and used for covering rural dwellings ;
the seeds are valuable for export to Europe.

322. P. ELEGANS.—*Bangalow.*—A low or very tall palm ; the
leaves in a terminal crown, several feet long, pinnately divided,
the segments numerous toothed or jagged at the end ; inflorescence the same as in *P. Cunninghamii* ; fruit ovoid-globose, ½ inch
in diameter. Habitat, brush forests on the northern rivers.

Timber similar to that of the last species, and sometimes like-
wise employed ; seeds exported to Europe.

CXXXVII. QUINTINIA.

(Natural Order SAXIFRAGEÆ.)

323. Q. SIEBERI.—A spreading tree of 30 or 40 feet; leaves alternate, oval-elliptical, acuminate, 3 to 4 inches long, entire, narrowed into a petiole, coriaceous, reticulate; flowers small, white, on pedicels in numerous racemes forming a terminal panicle; fruit a capsule, opening at the summit. Habitat, Illawarra, westward to the Blue Mountains.

Qualities of *timber* unknown.

CXXXVIII. RATONIA.

(Natural Order SAPINDACEÆ.)

324. R. ANODONTA.—A tree of considerable size, but flowering as a shrub, quite glabrous, leaves alternate, pinnate, the leaflets 2, 3, or rarely 4, ovate or ovate-lanceolate, obtuse or acuminate, 2 to 4 inches long, coriaceous, reticulate, narrowed into a petiolule; flowers small, in slender terminal or axillary panicles, glabrous and not much branched; fruit a capsule, pear-shaped, triangled, nearly ½ inch broad, the valves woody and densely villous inside. Habitat, brush forests, Clarence and Richmond Rivers.

Qualities of *timber* unknown.

325. R. PYRIFORMIS.—A tree of considerable size, but flowering sometimes as a shrub, glabrous except a minute hoariness on the young shoots and panicles; leaves alternate, pinnate, the leaflets 3 to 6, ovate or ovate-lanceolate, acuminate, 4 to 6 inches long, entire, coriaceous, petiolulate; flowers very small, pedicellate, singly or in little cymes of 2 or 3 along the raceme-like branches of the panicles; fruit a capsule, globular, about 4 lines diameter, glabrous with 3 raised ribs, appearing almost drupaceous and scarcely dehiscent. Habitat, brush forests, Clarence and Richmond Rivers.

Timber close-grained and hard, but little known.

326. R. STIPITATA.—A moderate-sized tree, glabrous except a minute tomentum on the young branches and inflorescence; leaves alternate, pinnate, the leaflets 3 to 6, oblong-lanceolate, acute, 2 to 3 inches long, narrowed into a petiolule, coriaceous, rigid, shining above, the primary veins prominent underneath; flowers small, in axillary and terminal panicles, divaricately branched; fruit a capsule, triangled, depressed at the top, ½ inch broad, the valves coriaceous, almost woody, glabrous and reddish inside. Habitat, brush forests, Clarence River.

Qualities of *timber* unknown.

H

CXXXIX. RHODAMNIA.

(Natural Order MYRTACEÆ.)

327. R. ARGENTEA.—*White Myrtle.*—A tree attaining a height of 100 feet and a diameter of 3 feet, the young shoots, the under-side of the leaves, and the inflorescence silvery-white with a minute tomentum ; leaves opposite, oval or elliptical, obtuse, narrowed at the base, triplinerved, 2 to 3 lines long, smooth and shining above ; flowers small, pedicellate, either 3 together or in trichotomous cymes of 5 to 9, on axillary peduncles, solitary or 2 or 3 together ; fruit a berry, usually globular. Habitat, brush forests, Clarence, Richmond, and Tweed Rivers.

Timber very hard and durable, but seldom used.

328. R. TRINERVIA.—*Three-veined Myrtle ; Black Eye ; Brush Turpentine.*—A moderate-sized tree, the young shoots, the under-side of the leaves, and the inflorescence velvety-pubescent, but not white ; leaves opposite, ovate-oblong or ovate-lanceolate, acu-minate, glabrous and reticulate above, prominently 3-nerved from the base ; flowers small, solitary or rarely 3 together, on slender axillary peduncles, 3 together in a cluster or on a short common peduncle ; fruit a berry, globular, about 3 lines diameter. Habitat, brush forests, from Illawarra to the Tweed River.

Timber close-grained and hard.

CXL. RHODOMYRTUS.

(Natural Order MYRTACEÆ.)

329. R. PSIDIOIDES.—A tree sometimes attaining a great size, the young shoots hoary-pubescent, the older foliage glabrous ; leaves opposite, petiolate, from oval-elliptical to ovate-lanceolate or oblong, acuminate, 3 to 4 inches long, shining above, penniveined and reticu-late on both sides, the margins usually recurved ; flowers pink or white, pedicellate on axillary peduncles, rarely 1-flowered, mostly with 1, 2, or 3 pairs of pedicels besides the terminal one, the lowest often again 3-flowered ; fruit a berry, ovoid-globular. Habitat, brush forests, from Illawarra to the Tweed River.

Timber of a red colour when fresh, close-grained and hard ; used in ship-building.

CXLI. RHUS.

(Natural Order ANACARDIACEÆ.)

330. R. RHODANTHEMA.—*Dark Yellowwood ; Yellow Cedar.*—A tree of 70 to 80 feet, quite glabrous except little tufts of hairs along the mid-rib of the leaflets underneath ; leaves alternate or very rarely opposite, pinnate, the common petiole terete, the leaf-lets usually 7 to 9, oblong, acuminate, 2 to 2½ inches long, entire,

petiolulate, prominently penniveined underneath; flowers diœcious, small, red, pedicellate in dense pyramidal or thyrsoid terminal or axillary panicles; fruit a drupe, globular, shining, $\frac{1}{2}$ inch in diameter, the putamen thick and woody, striate outside. Habitat, brush forests on the Clarence, Richmond, and Tweed Rivers.

Timber close-grained and durable, of a yellow colour and beautifully marked; takes a fine polish, and is very suitable for cabinetmaking.

CXLII. RULINGIA.

(Natural Order STERCULIACEÆ.)

331. R. PANNOSA.—*Black Kurrajong.*—A small tree, softly hirsute with velvety stellate hairs; leaves alternate or irregularly opposite, on the full-grown plant petiolate, ovate-lanceolate or lanceolate, 2 to 3 inches long or more, toothed, rounded or cordate at the base, scabrous-pubescent above, with impressed veins, densely velvety or hirsute underneath, but on younger plants broader and often 3- or 5-lobed; flowers mostly white, small, in leaf-opposed or terminal, rarely axillary pedunculate cymes; fruit a capsule, nearly glabrous, globular, hard and almost indehiscent, beset with rigid subulate bristles. Habitat, brush forests, from Twofold Bay to the Clarence River; also New England.

Timber worthless, but the bark yields a valuable fibre.

CXLIII. SAMBUCUS.

(Natural Order CAPRIFOLIACEÆ.)

332. S. XANTHOCARPA.—*Native Elder.*—A small tree, quite glabrous; leaves opposite, pinnate, the leaflets 3 to 5, petiolulate, the lower pair sometimes again divided into 2 or 3 each, lanceolate or ovate-lanceolate, acuminate, narrowed at the base, serrate or almost entire, 2 to 3 inches long; flowers yellow, rather small, in large terminal corymbs, the primary branches umbellate, the others cymose; fruit a berry-like drupe, yellow, with 3 to 5 seed-like pyrenes. Habitat, brush and open forests, from Illawarra to the Clarence River; also Blue Mountains, Lachlan River, and other places in the interior.

Qualities of *timber* unknown.

CXLIV. SAPINDUS.

(Natural Order SAPINDACEÆ.)

333. S. AUSTRALIS.—A beautiful tree, attaining a height of 80 feet, with a trunk of very irregular growth, and the young branches, petioles, and panicles pale or hoary with a minute tomentum; leaves alternate, pinnate, the leaflets 4 or 6, broadly ovate, obtuse,

3 to 5 inches long, entire, often oblique, narrowed into a petiolule, coriaceous, glabrous, veined, of a pale almost glaucous colour; flowers pedicellate in little loose cymes along the divaricate branches of loose terminal or axillary panicles; fruit fleshy or coriaceous, 2- or 4-lobed, indehiscent. Habitat, brush forests, Illawarra.

Timber close-grained but soft, apt to rend in seasoning.

CXLV. SCHIZOMERIA.

(Natural Order SAXIFRAGEÆ.)

334. S. OVATA.—*Corkwood; Lightwood; Beech.*—A tree attaining a height of 100 feet, with a dense foliage of light green; leaves opposite, ovate or ovate-lanceolate, obtuse or acuminate, 3 to 4 inches long, nearly entire or irregularly serrated, narrowed at the base and continuous with the petiole, coriaceous, penniveined and reticulate; flowers small, in terminal trichotomous cymes; fruit a drupe, ovoid or globular, under ½ inch in diameter, with the calyx-lobes reflexed from its base, the epicarp thick and fleshy, the endocarp bony. Habitat, brush forests, from Illawarra to the Macleay River.

Timber of a white colour, close-grained but light and easily wrought; useful for cabinet work, and also for coach-building.

CXLVI. SCOLOPIA.

(Natural Order BIXINEÆ.)

335. S. BROWNII.—A tree with a fluted stem, attaining a height of 150 feet and a diameter of 3 feet, perfectly glabrous in all its parts; leaves alternate, from ovate to oblong-lanceolate, acuminate, obtuse or acute, rarely rounded at the top, 1½ to 3 inches long, narrowed into a petiole, entire or undulate-toothed, thick and smooth, triplinerved, the veins scarcely conspicuous, with or without 2 or 3 marginal glands underneath; flowers small, on pedicels in short axillary racemes or forming a terminal panicle; fruit a berry, succulent or dry, opening in valves. Habitat, brush forests, from Illawarra to the Clarence River.

Timber hard and close-grained; valuable for many purposes.

CXLVII. SERSALISIA.

(Natural Order SAPOTACEÆ.)

336. S. GALACTOXYLON.—A tall tree, copiously exuding a milky juice, glabrous except the rusty-pubescent young shoots; leaves alternate, petiolate, obovate-oblong or oblong-cuneate, obtuse, coriaceous, penniveined, 3 to 5 inches long; flowers not seen; fruit

a berry or drupe, ovoid, 1 to 1½ inch long, contracted at the ends, the pericarp thin and succulent. Habitat, brush forests on the Richmond and Tweed Rivers.
Qualities of *timber* unknown.

337. S. SERICEA.—A tree of moderate size, sometimes of stunted growth, the young branches and underside of the leaves silky-pubescent, tomentose or villous, rust-coloured or hoary; leaves alternate, petiolate, ovate or obovate, but varying from nearly orbicular and under 2 inches in diameter to broadly elliptical and 2 to 3 inches long, coriaceous and glabrous above; flowers almost sessile, in axillary clusters; fruit a berry, ovoid, under 1 inch long, succulent. Habitat, brush forests, Richmond and Tweed Rivers.
Timber close-grained, but easily wrought; not often used.

CXLVIII. SOPHORA.

(Natural Order LEGUMINOSÆ. Sub-Order *Papilionaceæ.*)

338. S. TOMENTOSA.—A small tree, hoary all over with a minute tomentum; leaves alternate or opposite, unequally pinnate, the leaflets 11 to 17, broadly ovate or orbicular, obtuse or retuse, 1 inch long or more, thick and sometimes silky, rarely becoming glabrous; flowers pale yellow, on pedicels in loose simple terminal racemes; pod indehiscent, moniliform, fleshy, contracted between the seeds. Habitat, brush forests on the Hastings River.
Qualities of *timber* unknown.

CXLIX. STENOCARPUS.

(Natural Order PROTEACEÆ. Sub-Order *Folliculares.*)

339. S. CUNNINGHAMII.—*Silky Oak.*—A small tree, glabrous or the inflorescence slightly pubescent; leaves alternate or scattered, oblong-lanceolate, obtuse or acuminate, 2 to 4 inches long, tapering into a petiole, faintly tripli- or quintupli-nerved, the smaller veins scarcely visible; flowers red or yellow, pedicellate on slender peduncles, terminal or in the upper axils, bearing each a single umbel of 10 to 30 flowers; fruit a follicle, usually narrow and coriaceous. Habitat, brush forests, Richmond and Tweed Rivers.
Qualities of *timber* unknown.

340. S. SALIGNUS.—*Silky Oak; Silvery Oak; Beefwood.*—A tree attaining a height of 80 feet, glabrous or the inflorescence pubescent; leaves alternate or scattered, ovate-lanceolate or elliptical, acute, acuminate or obtuse, tapering into a petiole, 2 to 4 inches long, from penniveined to triplinerved, a few leaves on young trees or barren branches sometimes larger and pinnatifid;

flowers red or yellow, pedicellate on slender peduncles, terminal or in the upper axils, bearing each a single umbel of 10 to 30 flowers; fruit a follicle, usually narrow and coriaceous. Habitat, brush forests, from Illawarra to the Tweed River; also Blue Mountains.

Timber of a red colour, close-grained, hard, and easily split and wrought; valuable for the finer kinds of coopers' work.

Var. Moorei.—Leaves broader and more distinctly nerved, the ovary pubescent. Habitat, Illawarra and Mount Lindsay.

341. S. SINUATUS.—*Yiel Yiel.*—A tree attaining 100 feet in height and a diameter of 2 feet, but sometimes small and slender, glabrous or the inflorescence tomentose; leaves alternate or scattered, petiolate, either undivided, oblong-lanceolate and 6 to 8 inches long, or pinnatifid and above 1 foot long, with 1 to 4 oblong lobes on each side, mostly obtuse, quite glabrous but reddish underneath, penniveined and reticulate; flowers bright red, in umbels of 12 to 20 on pedicels radiating in a single row round the disk-like dilated summit of terminal peduncles, either two or more together in a general umbel, and several at some distance forming a short broad raceme; fruit a follicle, usually narrow and coriaceous. Habitat, brush forests, Richmond and Tweed Rivers.

Timber close-grained, hard, durable, and beautifully marked.

CL. STERCULIA.

(Natural Order STERCULIACEÆ.)

342. S. ACERIFOLIA.—*Flame Tree.*—A beautiful tree attaining a height of 100 feet and a diameter of 3 feet, quite glabrous; leaves large, alternate or irregularly opposite, deeply 5- or 7-lobed, the lobes oblong-lanceolate or almost rhomboid, occasionally deeply sinuate, the whole leaf often 8 or 10 inches in diameter, thin, shining and glabrous on both sides; flowers of a rich red, in loose axillary racemes or small panicles of 2 to 3 inches; follicles large, on stalks, quite glabrous. Habitat, brush forests, from Illawarra to the Clarence River.

Timber soft and spongy, but the bark yields a fibre which is much prized by the aborigines for making nets and fishing-lines.

343. S. DIVERSIFOLIA.—*Black Kurrajong.*—A pretty, small tree, with a stout stem, quite glabrous except the flowers; leaves alternate or irregularly opposite, on long petioles, glabrous and shining, either entire and from ovate to ovate-lanceolate or more or less deeply 3- or 5-lobed, the lobes 2 or 3 inches long, the simple leaves or their lobes always ending in long points; flowers in axillary panicles, rarely exceeding the leaves; follicles nearly

ovoid, $1\frac{1}{2}$ to 3 inches long, thick and glabrous, on stalks of 1 to 2 inches.   Habitat, brush forests, from Illawarra to the Clarence River.

Timber soft and spongy, but the fibre of the bark used by the aborigines for making fishing-nets, &c.

344. S. FŒTIDA.—*Stavewood.*—A tall stout tree, glabrous except the very young leaves ; leaves alternate or irregularly opposite, crowded at the ends of the thick branchlets, deciduous, digitately compound on petioles, the leaflets 5 to 11, elliptical, oblong or lanceolate, 4 to 8 inches long, acuminate, entire, coriaceous, contracted into petiolules ; flowers large, of a dull red, in loose simple or branched racemes; fruit a follicle, large, woody, glabrous outside, fibrous within.   Habitat, brush forests, Hastings and Macleay Rivers.

Timber used for staves.

345. S. LURIDA.—*Sycamore.*—A large tree ; leaves alternate or irregularly opposite on long petioles, deeply 5- or 7-lobed, the lobes sinuate or themselves lobed, the whole leaf 8 to 10 inches in diameter, softly pubescent, especially underneath ; flowers of a livid, variegated colour, in loose axillary racemes or small panicles of 2 to 3 inches ; follicles stipitate, large, tomentose, many-seeded.

Timber of a white colour, soft and perishable, but easily split, and sometimes used for shingles ; the bark yields a strong and valuable fibre.

CLI. SYMPLOCOS.

(Natural Order STYRACACEÆ.)

346. S. SPICATA.—A tree attaining a height of 100 feet and a diameter of 3 feet, quite glabrous ; leaves alternate, oval-elliptical or oblong-elliptical, obtuse or acuminate, entire or toothed, contracted into a petiole, about 4 inches long or more, smooth and often shining; flowers small, sessile or nearly so and often numerous, in axillary spikes, simple or branching into a panicle ; fruit a berry, ovoid, contracted at the top.   Habitat, brush forests on the Richmond River.

Qualities of *timber* unknown.

347. S. THWAITESII.—A tree attaining sometimes a considerable size, quite glabrous, resembling *S. spicata* in habit and characters, but the leaves usually firmer and more shining, and the flowers larger and distinctly pedicellate, forming simple or branched racemes ; fruit a berry, oblong when young, contracted at the top, but not seen ripe.   Habitat, brush forests, from Illawarra to the Richmond River.

Timber close-grained, but little known.

CLII. SYNCARPIA.

(Natural Order MYRTACEÆ.)

348. S. LAURIFOLIA.—*Turpentine Tree.*—A magnificent tree, sometimes attaining a height of 200 feet and a diameter of 6 feet, the young shoots and underside of the leaves hoary-pubescent or glaucous ; leaves opposite, appearing sometimes in whorls of 4 from 2 pairs being close together, from broadly ovate to elliptical-oblong, obtuse or acuminate, glabrous above, 2 to 3 inches long, on petioles ; flowers white, united, 6 to 10 together in globular heads on peduncles at the base of the new shoots ; fruit a capsule, included in and adnate to the calyx-tube, about ½ inch in diameter. Habitat, open forests, from Illawarra to the Hastings River, westward to the Blue Mountains.

Timber valuable for piles and posts of fences, &c., being impervious to the *Teredo navalis* and very durable underground; liable to split in seasoning.

Var. glabra.—Quite glabrous, even the calyx ; flowers rather small. Habitat, Hastings River.

349. S. LEPTOPETALA.—*Turpentine Tree.*—A tree of 50 to 60 feet, the young shoots, underside of the leaves, and inflorescence tomentose or almost scurfy, or at length glabrous, the young branches angular ; leaves opposite, ovate-elliptical or ovate-lanceolate, acuminate, penniveined, glabrous above, 2 to 4 inches long, tapering into petioles ; flowers small and numerous, in dense globular heads, but quite free from each other, on slender common peduncles in terminal clusters or panicles ; fruit a capsule, included in and adnate to the calyx-tube. Habitat, open forests, Brisbane Water, and Hastings River; also in the interior.

Timber exceedingly hard and heavy; useful for turners' work, &c.

CLIII. SYNOUM.

(Natural Order MELIACEÆ.)

350. S. GLANDULOSUM. — *Rosewood ; Bloodwood ; Dogwood.*— A moderate-sized tree, glabrous or the young leaves and shoots slightly silky-tomentose ; leaves alternate or rarely opposite, pinnate, the leaflets 5 to 9, elliptical-lanceolate, acuminate, 2 to 3 inches long, narrowed at the base, coriaceous, the lateral veins few and scarcely prominent ; flowers small, in short dense axillary panicles ; fruit a capsule, depressed-globular, glabrous, about ¾ inch diameter, furrowed opposite the dissepiments, so as to be almost 3-lobed. Habitat, brush forests, from Illawarra to the Hastings River, westward to the Blue Mountains.

Timber fragrant and often coloured ; suitable for cabinet work.

CLIV. TABERNÆMONTANA.

(Natural Order APOCYNEÆ.)

351. T. ORIENTALIS, *var. angustisepala.—Bitterbark.*—A dichotomously branched small tree, with an intensely bitter bark, quite glabrous; leaves opposite, elliptical-oblong, acuminate, narrowed into a petiole, penniveined, 2 to 4 inches long or more; flowers pedicellate in loose pedunculate cymes, two together at the ends or in the forks of the branches or lateral; fruit a follicle, ovoid-falcate, about ½ inch long, generally in pairs. Habitat, brush forests on the northern rivers.

Qualities of *timber* unknown. A decoction of the bark is sometimes sold as bitters.

CLV. TARRIETIA.

(Natural Order STERCULIACEÆ.)

352. T. ARGYRODENDRON.—*Byong; Ironwood.*—A fine tree, attaining a height of 150 feet, glabrous except minute scurfy scales on the young shoots and inflorescence, and often on the underside of the leaves; leaves digitately compound, alternate or irregularly opposite, the leaflets 3 or 5, petiolulate, oblong or lanceolate, obtuse or acuminate, 3 to 4 inches long, coriaceous; flowers numerous, in dichotomous axillary or terminal panicles; fruit-carpels forming distinct *samaras*, about 1 inch long, indehiscent. Habitat, brush forests on the Bellinger, Macleay, Clarence, and Richmond Rivers.

Timber white, close-grained and hard, but seldom used.

CLVI. TETRANTHERA.

(Natural Order LAURINEÆ.)

353. T. FERRUGINEA.—A large tree, the branches and petioles ferruginous-pubescent or villous; leaves alternate or rarely irregularly opposite, from broadly-ovate to elliptical-oblong, acuminate or obtuse, rounded or cuneate at the base, 3 to 5 inches long, firm, glabrous and shining above, ferruginous-pubescent underneath, with raised primary veins and transverse veinlets; flowers dioecious in pedunculate cymes clustered in the axils or at the old nodes; fruit a berry, ovoid, resting on the enlarged cup-shaped truncate perianth-tube, 3 to 4 lines in diameter. Habitat, brush forests on the Clarence and Richmond Rivers.

Timber close-grained and hard, but seldom used.

Var. lanceolata.—Leaves oblong or oblong-lanceolate. Same habitat.

354. T. RETICULATA.—A tree of considerable size, glabrous except the flowers or the young shoots minutely pubescent; leaves alternate or rarely opposite, obovate-oblong or oblong-elliptical, obtuse or acuminate, narrowed into a petiole, 3 to 4 inches long, green on both sides, veined and reticulate; flowers in irregular pedunculate racemes or clusters, on a common rhachis; fruit a berry, ovoid, resting in the enlarged truncate cup-shaped perianth-tube. Habitat, brush forests, Clarence and Richmond Rivers.
Timber similar to that of the last species.

CLVII. TREMA.
(Natural Order URTICEÆ.)

355. T. ASPERA.—*Elm; Rough Fig.*—A moderately large tree, sometimes shrubby, the branches more or less pubescent; leaves alternate, petiolate, obliquely ovate, ovate-oblong or ovate-lanceolate, acuminate, serrate-crenate, rounded or cordate at the base, 3-nerved and penniveined, membraneous, sometimes rigid, green on both sides or pale underneath, scabrous, hirsute on the principal veins underneath, often sprinkled on both sides with short scattered hairs; flowers small, in short cymes, sessile or pedunculate in the axils; fruit a drupe, ovoid, scarcely compressed, about 1½ to 2 lines long. Habitat, brush forests, from Twofold Bay to the Macleay River; also New England.
Timber hard, close-grained, tough, and firm.

CLVIII. TRISTANIA.
(Natural Order MYRTACEÆ.)

356. T. CONFERTA.—*White Box; Bastard Box; Brush Box.*—A fine tree, attaining a height of 150 feet and a diameter of 5 feet, with a smooth brown deciduous bark and dense foliage, the young shoots often clothed with spreading hairs, otherwise glabrous except the inflorescence, the buds of the succeeding year covered with large imbricate coloured scales; leaves alternate, crowded at the ends of the branches so as to appear verticillate, petiolate, ovate or ovate-lanceolate, acuminate or almost obtuse, usually 3 to 6 inches long, penniveined and minutely reticulate underneath; flowers small, yellow or white, in cymes of 3 to 7, usually on the young wood below the cluster of leaves; fruit a capsule, enclosed in and adnate to the persistent calyx-tube, hemispherical or cup-shaped, truncate and smooth, 3 to 4 lines in diameter. Habitat, open and brush forests, from the Hastings to the Tweed River.
Timber valuable, very strong and durable; ribs of vessels made of this material have been found quite sound at the end of thirty years' service.

357. T. LAURINA.—*Water Gum.*—A tree frequently small and of crooked growth in exposed localities, becoming in moist situations sometimes very large, the young shoots more or less glaucous or silky-pubescent, especially the underside of the leaves, the older foliage glabrous ; leaves alternate, lanceolate, elliptical or obovate-lanceolate, acuminate, penniveined, 2 to 4 inches long, narrowed into a petiole ; flowers yellow, pedicellate in short axillary cymes, on a very short common peduncle ; fruit a capsule, obovoid or almost globular, 3 to 5 lines in diameter, adnate at the base, filling the calyx-tube and protruding beyond it. Habitat, open and brush forests, from Twofold Bay to the Clarence River.

Timber singularly close-grained and tough ; used for knees and ribs of boats ; said to be unrivalled for cogs of wheels in machinery.

358. T. NERIIFOLIA.—*Hickory ; Water Gum.*—A tree attaining sometimes a height of 120 feet and a diameter of 3 feet, glabrous or the young shoots and underside of the leaves glaucous-pubescent ; leaves opposite, lanceolate, acute, narrowed into a petiole, nerveless except the mid-rib, $1\frac{1}{2}$ to 3 inches long ; flowers yellow, in opposite axillary cymes, but forming usually a terminal corymb ; fruit a capsule, enclosed in and adnate to the persistent calyx-tube, less than 2 lines long. Habitat, open and brush forests, from Illawarra to the Manning River.

Timber close-grained, tough, and elastic ; used in boat-building ; also for flails, handles of tools, and cogs of machinery.

359. T. SUAVEOLENS.—*Swamp Mahogany ; Bastard Peppermint.*—A tree of considerable size, glaucous or hoary, the young shoots hirsute, rarely quite glabrous ; leaves alternate, petiolate, ovate-elliptical, ovate-lanceolate or elliptical-oblong, obtuse or acuminate, penniveined and reticulate, $1\frac{1}{2}$ to 3 inches long, sometimes even 6 inches ; flowers usually small, in axillary cymes on a common peduncle, more or less flattened ; fruit a capsule, enclosed in and adnate to the persistent calyx-tube, very open, 2 to 4 lines in diameter. Habitat, open and brush forests, Clarence and Richmond Rivers.

Timber strong and durable ; valuable for various purposes.

CLIX. TROCHOCARPA.

(Natural Order EPACRIDEÆ.)

360. T. LAURINA.—*Beech ; Brush Cherry ; Brush Myrtle.*— A tree of 20 to 40 feet, quite glabrous ; leaves usually clustered at the ends of each year's shoots, so as to appear almost verticillate, petiolate, oval or elliptical, acuminate, shining, 5- to 7-nerved on both sides, $1\frac{1}{2}$ to 2 inches long ; flowers small, white, in terminal, solitary or clustered interrupted spikes ; fruit a drupe,

depressed-globular, 3 to 4 lines in diameter, the mesocarp pulpy, the endocarp separating into pyrenes. Habitat, brush forests, from Illawarra to the Tweed River.

Timber close-grained and tough ; used by turners and others.

CLX. VILLARESIA.

(Natural Order OLACINEÆ.)

361. V. MOOREI.—*White Maple; Scrub Silky Oak.*—A lofty handsome tree, glabrous except the inflorescence ; leaves alternate, ovate-lanceolate or oblong, acuminate, 3 to 4 inches long, narrowed into a petiole, coriaceous and shining ; flowers few, almost sessile, in numerous cymes on peduncles along the rhachis of raceme-like panicles, irregularly lateral or axillary ; fruit a drupe, globular, about ½ inch in diameter, rugose outside, the putamen hard. Habitat, brush forests, Illawarra and Clarence River.

Timber white and close-grained ; likely to be valuable, but as yet little known.

CLXI. VITEX.

(Natural Order VERBENACEÆ.)

362. V. LIGNUM-VITÆ.—*Lignum-Vitæ ; White Beech.*—A large handsome tree, attaining a height of 120 feet and a diameter of 6 feet, the young branches, petioles, and inflorescence rusty-tomentose or pubescent ; leaves opposite, simple, oblong or oval-elliptical, acuminate, narrowed at the base, petiolate, 1½ to 4 inches long, coriaceous, shining above, pale underneath, glabrous or the mid-rib pubescent underneath, those of the barren branches sometimes lobed, those of the flowering branches usually entire, but occasionally showing a few angles or short lobes; flowers few, in small, loose, axillary cymes ; fruit a succulent drupe, the putamen separating into 4 hard pyrenes. Habitat, brush forests, from Illawarra to the Clarence River.

Timber very valuable, said never to shrink in drying, and much used for the decks of vessels and verandah floors.

CLXII. WEINMANNIA.

(Natural Order SAXIFRAGEÆ.)

363. W. RUBIFOLIA.—*Marara ; Corkwood.*—A tree attaining a height of 150 feet and a diameter of 3 feet, with a light-grey bark ; leaves opposite, pinnate, the leaflets digitate, ovate-elliptical, acuminate, sharply serrate ; flowers in simple axillary racemes,

several together on a very short peduncle; fruit a capsule, reflexed, 1½ to 2 lines long, narrow, hairy, with 2 or 3 recurved styles. Habitat, brush forests, Clarence River.

Timber close-grained and tough, but easily wrought; highly spoken of by those who have used it.

CLXIII. XYLOMELUM.

(Natural Order Proteaceæ. Sub-Order *Folliculares*.)

364. X. PYRIFORME.—*Wooden Pear ; Native Pear.*—A tree of moderate size, the young shoots ferruginous-villous or tomentose, but soon glabrous, the spikes only remaining densely tomentose-villous ; leaves opposite, on the flowering branches usually entire, lanceolate or ovate-lanceolate, acute, 4 to 6 inches long, tapering into a petiole, on flowerless branches or in younger plants often sinuate and prickly-toothed, about 8 inches long, with short petioles, all at length coriaceous and shining ; flowers sessile in very dense spikes, 2 to 3 inches long, usually clustered, 3 to 6 together and at first appearing terminal, but soon lateral by the growing out of the shoots ; fruit a follicle, 2½ to 3 inches long and above 1 inch diameter, ovoid or tapering above the middle and woody. Habitat, Port Jackson and Illawarra.

Timber of a dark colour and often finely marked, somewhat coarse in the grain.

CLXIV. ZANTHOXYLUM.

(Natural Order Rutaceæ.)

365. Z. BRACHYACANTHUM.—*Satinwood* ; *Thorny Yellowwood ; Moreton Bay Yellowwood.*—A slender glabrous tree, the trunk and branches covered with short conical prickles ; leaves alternate, pinnate, the leaflets usually 9 to 13, opposite in pairs, with or without a terminal odd one, petiolulate, from ovate to oblong-elliptical, acuminate, 2 to 3 or rarely 4 inches long, equal or oblique at the base, coriaceous and shining ; flowers pedicellate in axillary panicles irregularly di- or trichotomous; fruit opening to the middle in 2 valves. Habitat, brush forests on the Clarence, Richmond, and Tweed Rivers.

Timber of a bright yellow when fresh, close-grained but easily wrought ; likely to prove useful for wood-engraving.

CLXV. ZIERIA.

(Natural Order Rutaceæ.)

366. Z. GRANULATA.—*Turmeric.*—A small tree, glabrous or minutely pubescent, densely covered with glandular tubercles, closely resembling *Z. Smithii*, but differing in the narrow-linear

leaflets, 1 to 2 inches long, the margins revolute and whitish underneath, and in the very small flowers, with the petals almost shortly valvate; cocci glabrous. Habitat, brush forests, Illawarra; also near Goulburn.

Timber yellow, close-grained, and strong.

367. Z. SMITHII.—*Turmeric.*—A small tree, glabrous or slightly pubescent, the branches terete or compressed, occasionally covered with tubercles; leaves usually opposite with 3 leaflets, on a common petiole, lanceolate or the large ones oblong-elliptical, acute or obtuse, 1 to 2 inches long, flat or the margins·slightly recurved; flowers small, in axillary di- or trichotomous cymes; cocci about 2 lines long, glabrous and usually tuberculate. Habitat, brush forests, from Twofold Bay to the Hastings River; also the Blue Mountains and Mount Lindsay.

Timber yellow, close-grained, hard and strong; useful for wood-engraving, &c; the bark yields a bright yellow dye.

Var. parviflora.—Leaflets rarely exceeding 1 inch. Habitat, New England.

INDEX.

I

INDEX

Of Local Names applied to the different species, with
Botanical Names and Orders.

Local Name.	Botanical Name.	Page
Borrigan	Eremophila longifolia. Myoporineæ........	57
,, ...	,, oppositifolia. ,,	57
Bimbil	Eucalyptus brachypoda. Myrtaceæ........	59
Bitter bark	Alstonia constricta. Apocyneæ..............	31
,, ...	Tabernæmontana orientalis. Apocyneæ ...	121
Black apple	Achras australis. Sapotaceæ	27
Black ash	Cupania semiglauca. Sapindaceæ	48
Blackbutt...	Eucalyptus obtusiflora. Myrtaceæ	68
,, ...	,, pilularis. ,,	68
Blackeye	Rhodamnia trinervia. Myrtaceæ............	114
Black ironbark	Eucalyptus leucoxylon. Myrtaceæ	65
Black kurrajong	Rulingia pannosa. Sterculiaceæ............	115
,, ...	Sterculia diversifolia. Sterculiaceæ	118
Black myrtle	Cargillia pentamera. Ebenaceæ..............	39
Black oak	Casuarina suberosa. Casuarineæ	42
Black plum	Cargillia australis. Ebenaceæ	39
Black tea-tree	Leptospermum fabricia. Myrtaceæ	90
Black wattle...............	Acacia binervata. Leguminosæ....	20
,, ...	Callicoma serratifolia. Saxifrageæ	37
Blackwood	Acacia melanoxylon. Leguminosæ	24
,, ...	,, penninervis. ,,	25
Bloodwood	Eucalyptus corymbosa. Myrtaceæ	61
,, ...	,, eximia. ,,	62
,, ...	Synoum glandulosum. Meliaceæ	120
Blue ash	Elæodendron australe. Celastrineæ	55
,, ...	Aphanopetalum resinosum. Saxifrageæ ...	33
Blueberry ash	Elæocarpus holopetalus. Tiliaceæ...........	55
Blue fig....................	,, grandis.	55
Blue gum	Eucalyptus globulus. Myrtaceæ	63
,, ...	,, tereticornis. ,,	73
Blue Mountain brush gum.	,, stricta. ,,	72
Blue Mountain pine ...	Frenela Muellerii. Coniferæ	82
Bogum Bogum............	Flindersia Bennettiana. Meliaceæ....	80
Boree...............	Acacia pendula. Leguminosæ	24
Box	Eucalyptus hemiphloia. Myrtaceæ	64
,, ...	,, obtusiflora. ,,	68
Broad-leaved ironbark..	,, melanophloia. ,,	66
Broad-leaved tea-tree...	Callistemon salignus. Myrtaceæ	38
,, ,, ...	,, angustifolia. ,,	38
,, ,, ...	,, Sieberi. ,,	38
Brown kurrajong	Commersonia echinata. Sterculiaceæ	45
,, ...	,, Fraseri. ,,	45
Brush ash	Acronychia Baueri. Rutaceæ	28
Brush bloodwood	Baloghia lucida. Euphorbiaceæ..............	34
Brush box	Tristania conferta. Myrtaceæ	122
Brush cherry	Eugenia myrtifolia. Myrtaceæ	75
,, ,, ...	Trochocarpa laurina. Epacrideæ	123
Brush myrtle	,, laurina. ,,	123
,, turpentine	Rhodamnia trinervia. Myrtaceæ	114
Bulboro....................	Flindersia australis. Meliaceæ	80
Bull oak	Casuarina equisetifolia. Casuarineæ........	41
,, ,, ...	,, glauca. ,,	41
Byong	Tarrietia argyrodendron. Sterculiaceæ ...	121

Local Name.	Botanical Name.	Page.

Local Name.	Botanical Name.	Page.
Tea-tree	Callistemon brachyandrus. Myrtaceæ	37
,,	,, linearis. ,,	38
,,	,, pinifolius. ,,	38
,,	,, rigidus. ,,	38
,,	Melaleuca armillaris. Myrtaceæ	94
,,	,, ericifolia. ,,	94
,,	,, squarrosa. ,,	96
,,	,, genistifolia. ,,	94
,,	,, hakeoides. ,,	95
,,	,, pauciflora. ,,	96
Thorny yellowwood	Xanthoxylon brachyacanthum. Rutaceæ.	125
Three-veined Myrtle	Rhodamnia trinervia. Myrtaceæ	114
Tulipwood	Aphananthe philippinensis. Urticeæ	33
,,	Harpullia pendula. Sapindaceæ	86
,,	Owenia venosa. Meliaceæ	104
Turmeric	Zieria granulata. Rutaceæ	125
,,	,, Smithii. ,,	126
Turnipwood	Dysoxylon Muellerii. Meliaceæ	53
Turpentine gum	Eucalyptus Stuartiana. Myrtaceæ	73
Turpentine tree	Syncarpia laurifolia Myrtaceæ	120
,,	,, ,, var. glabra ,,	120
,,	,, leptopetala ,,	120

U

Union nut	Bosistoa sapindiformis. Rutaceæ	36

V

Valley tree fern	Dicksonia antarctica. Filices	50

W

Walking-stick palm	Kentia monostachya. Palmæ	89
Water gum	Callistemon lanceolatus. Myrtaceæ	37
,,	Tristania laurina. ,,	123
,,	,, neriifolia. ,,	123
White bark	Elæocarpus cyaneus. Tiliaceæ	54
White beech	Gmelina Leichhardtii. Verbenaceæ	84
,,	Vitex lignum-vitæ. Verbenaceæ	124
White boree	Elæocarpus cyaneus. Tiliaceæ	54
White box	Tristania conferta. Myrtaceæ	122
White cedar	Melia composita. Meliaceæ	97
White cypress pine (of the interior).	Frenela robusta, var verrucosa. Coniferæ.	82
White gum	Eucalyptus albens. Myrtaceæ	58
,,	,, coriacea. ,,	60
,,	,, dealbata. ,,	61
,,	,, hæmastoma. ,,	64
,,	,, rostrata. ,,	71

Sydney : Thomas Richards, Government Printer.—1884.